MW00941406

RISE OF THE
FORGOTTEN

THE FORGOTTEN CHRONICLES BOOK TWO

Jason J. Nugent

This is for my son Jackson and
all the readers who have stuck with me.

Thank you for believing.

One

The creature formerly known as Timo stood along the tree line watching his brother Eron pass through the rough stone gate. The Topsider part of Timo's life was now over.

As the youngest boy in the family, Eron's fate dominated Timo's thoughts until he saw him through the Selection. Timo had been near Victory Point before, but its dark gray walls weren't the welcome sight he expected they would be.

The gate slammed shut and locked after Eron passed through. He was the last to arrive, though much to Timo's credit, the Forgotten—or the Truth, as they called themselves—had gained many new recruits. Cape Rouge alone had supplied five new members.

Timo slipped into the brush, avoiding the constant gaze of guards stationed along the top of the wall at Victory Point. Anastasia's red sun would soon sink from the sky, and he wanted to be at the Traveling Tunnel before the first pink glow of the moon settled over the land.

It took nearly an hour for him to find where the Traveling Tunnel was hidden in the forest. A cover of thick, slightly decomposing brush concealed a large pit with steps cut into the side. He slid it over, crawled down, and repositioned the cover. Even in the dark pit, his eyes made out the dirt floor and steps leading down into the catacombs of the Tunnel.

The Truth constructed these tunnels over a span of two hundred years. They crisscrossed Anastasia, connecting large underground cities unknown to the world above. To Timo, it was home. The Topsiders were clueless about their existence...and the extent of the Truth's reach.

Familiar scratching sounds greeted Timo; thousands of tiny feet digging in the red soil, clawing and scraping for food. Dirt grubbers. The Truth used them to create the Traveling Tunnels. The smaller offspring congregated near the planet's surface while the larger parents dug deep within the core.

Timo hesitated and scanned the tunnel, catching the dank earthen scent. He turned left, following the path deeper underground. Toward home. To his family.

Four hours later, guided by glowing marks on the walls, a large bright section of the tunnel revealed the rest station he expected. Lamps lit with dirt grubber blood glowed iridescent green, flooding the tunnel with light as he approached.

"Greetings, Nagi. Welcome back!" the rest station guard said.

Timo—now known as Nagi—nodded. "Greetings, Charl. I request rest for the evening. I come from—" he hesitated. The Truth avoided Victory Point. Recruits weren't likely, and the danger was too great. Armed Anastasian Defense Force guards killed them for sport. But he had to see Eron off. He had to know he made it. Maybe if Eron was the man Nagi thought he was, he'd find a way to end the brutal tradition.

"I come from the Selection, Charl. It's over now."

Charl nodded, the green glow reflected on his black, hairy face, making his eyes appear a deeper onyx. "Come inside. We have a place for you." The two grasped each other's forearms, and Nagi went inside the station.

The rest station had four rooms; two for the guards and two for travelers. At certain times of the year, a selected few of the Truth ventured out toward Anastasia's surface. Most stayed in their cities, living peacefully away from Topsider interaction. Because of the lack of travel, rest stations were necessary, but hardly used points along the dark underground routes. Guards stayed for a month at a time before relinquishing their post to replacements; usually the length of time it took for dirt grubber blood to lose its helpful glow.

"Greetings, Nagi," Jorgan said. The guard sat in a chair against the far side of the entrance, reading a book by the green glowing lamp on the wall. A cage next to him held three dirt grubbers; the half-meter-long insects with twenty legs per side scratching at the bars.

"Greetings, Jorgan," Nagi said. They clasped forearms. "Anyone else here tonight?"

"No, just you. I don't expect anyone else. With the Selection over, I think you might be the last scout. Oh hey, there should be an extra tunic in the back room. You scouts always seem to lose yours!" he chuckled.

Nagi smiled and nodded. "Thanks, and yeah, you're probably right. I don't think I saw another scout out there. Well, I'll leave you to your book. I can take this one?" he said, motioning to a room to the right.

"All yours," Jorgan said.

Nagi thanked him and opened the door. A lamp glowed on a small table next to the bed. He closed the door, slipped on the tunic, and collapsed on the bed. He looked up at the dirt ceiling, the silence soothing him.

He'd been gone from his family for over a month now. Twice a year, he left them to scout the Selection, looking for candidates to bring back to the Truth. They secured at least ten new members. He hadn't heard how they'd fared near Greater Manthus yet. Still, it was lower than expected. They'd been able to gain twenty, sometimes twenty-five new recruits at a time in years past. Rumors spread that Topsiders weren't breeding as much, and the children they did have were weak.

Unlike those of the Truth.

Nagi closed his eyes and passed out.

When he woke, he slipped quietly out of the room, waved goodbye to Jorgan and Charl, and followed the glowing markers leading to his home.

He heard the city before he saw it. Laughter. Children playing. Mothers calling out. The sound of community. The tunnel ahead glowed as bright as their sun. Three dirt grubber farms spaced around the city provided a limitless light source.

He followed a bend in the tunnel and it opened to an enormous cavern. Children ran, dancing and singing. Nagi's eyes glistened. His children were down there somewhere.

The Topsider recruits were in for a surprise. The newest recruits had no idea what their future held once they were part of the Truth. Much like Nagi had been, they'd be scared. Soon enough, they'd come to understand.

The center of the cavern, illuminated by walls lined with dirt grubber glow, was home. A giant metallic structure with windows lining the sides and one open door at the bottom. Along its gray surface, faded blue lines wrapped around the middle and divided the words "USS Freedom."

The city was housed inside the ship. It was the first Earth transport. It crashed on Anastasia.

Two

Eron left victory point with Sarai, escorted by armed Anastasian Defense Force guards. His nose throbbed. His hand felt numb. Deep in a dark pit within him, anger and frustration thrummed.

Sarai held his good hand tight, smiling whenever she caught Eron's eye.

"I'm so excited, Eron! I've been waiting for this moment my entire life."

I wish I could say the same, he thought. Sarai seemed nice enough. He didn't know her at all, but it wasn't his decision. A lesson once learned in school came roaring back to his memory.

The Selection Class 101B: Being Chosen
Surviving members of the Selection are paired according to bio-compatibility, regardless of prior contact or affiliation. Leave your former feelings aside and prepare for a new life.

Since Timo's appearance, Eron's memory of pre-Selection preparation returned bit by bit. His mind began to open, allowing him to see the world anew again. And he hated it.

Too many people had to die. Too many boys perfectly capable of contributing to Anastasian success either lay dead in the forest, or were lost to become

Forgotten. Like Timo.

"Selected, this way please," one of the guards said, breaking his thoughts. He motioned the couple toward a vehicle.

"What is that?" Eron asked. "Is that a transport?" He'd seen them in Rippon, but had never been inside one before. The couple stopped, their mouths hanging open. Before them was a white vehicle with four doors and large knobby wheels.

"Yes. It's prepped to escort you to Beta Prime," the soldier said.

"Beta Prime?" Sarai asked. She looked at Eron with her brows knitted.

"What's a Beta Prime" Eron asked.

"Not what. Where. It's the capitol. Most survivors respond the same way. Soon, you'll understand. Now, this way please." The soldier opened a door on the transport and waved a hand, motioning for them to enter.

"I've never been in a transport before," Eron said. He paused at the door.

"It's safe, I assure you. Please, we're on a schedule," he said. Sarai stepped inside. Eron looked around, then followed. The soldier closed the door behind him and sat in the front of the vehicle. He looked to the driver, nodded, and they were off.

Sarai and Eron glanced at each other, Sarai clutching his arm.

The scenery outside flew by. Eron had never seen anything like it. Not long after they entered the transport, the bumpy ride smoothed out. Eron looked ahead and noticed they were on a smooth surface. "A highway," he said under his breath. He'd read about them. Back in the colony, the streets were packed dirt. This was something more. It looked permanent, like concrete. Where did they get it? He marveled at the way the road continued, flat and even.

"Look," Sarai said pointing out the window. Anthelles streaked the sky. Trees zoomed past. A waterfall to their left sprayed red as it splashed to the pool below.

"Where are we?" Eron asked.

"On the road to Beta Prime," the soldier said. His voice was cold, distant.

"What's it the capitol of, and why are we going there?" Eron asked. His recollection of the five Anastasian colonies had returned, another missing piece of his studies.

"The planet. Queen Anastasia's seat of government. Her counselors, her court...everything that runs this planet is there. You're about to experience a whole new world."

"I don't understand," Sarai said. "I thought the colonies were autonomous. I thought they

governed themselves; that they only cooperated when it came time for the Selection?"

"That's only partially true. It's not my place to divulge more than what I've said. Please, relax. We have a couple hours to go before we're at Beta Prime," the soldier said.

Eron wondered if they should've entered the vehicle to begin with. He didn't know anyone. Was this a trick? How was he supposed to begin a new life when he knew nothing about this Beta Prime or vehicles or roads?

He turned to Sarai. "I'm just as confused as you. I've never heard of Beta Prime, or a queen."

"About a month into the Selection, I was brought from Cape Rouge to Victory Point. Not long before you finished, maybe a couple days, I was introduced to the queen. I didn't believe it at first. But then I realized it was true. It must be, but why have they hidden this from us? Why didn't we know before?"

"You'll find out, I promise," the soldier interjected. "But, please trust me, you need to rest. It's a long way to Beta Prime, and you'll be expected to learn a lot and make important decisions. I advise you to take advantage of this time."

Eron closed his eyes, worrying if death was near. Would Sarai turn on him like Phelan? It had only been a few days since the one he thought was a friend attempted to kill him. Were these soldiers taking them somewhere to kill them? If his life was going to end, he was determined not to make it easy on them. Somehow.

He opened his eyes and looked at Sarai leaning against the window, sleeping. Physically, she didn't seem strong. If he had to, he could fend off her attack and snap her neck. But why? Killing each other served no purpose; he tried telling that to Phelan. But if she did attack, could he do it? He knew how to do it, but would he? He hoped he wouldn't have to find out.

They travelled for about an hour, Eron absently staring at the passing scenery. In the distance, Eron spotted something reaching high into the sky. It looked like a building. His eyes shot wide open. "What?" he said quietly.

Other buildings appeared, most much smaller. Bright lights illuminated the sky.

"Huh?" Sarai said. She rubbed her eyes and looked at Eron. He pointed out the window. She sat up and looked. "What is that?" she said, fully awake and bolting upright.

"That is the Royal Tower. The center of Beta Prime," the soldier said.

The couple stared in disbelief as they approached the city. The city dominated the landscape as the transport neared the outskirts. Soon, they slowed at a heavy metal gate. A tall white wall stretched across the road in both directions as far as they could see. It seemed to wind around the city.

The driver flashed a badge. The gate keeper peered in the back at Eron and Sarai, then waved them through. The gate swung open, then slammed shut after they passed.

Bright lights lined the road. Fields of tall grass separated the walls from the city where buildings sprouted. Gray and glass rose high in the air, illuminated in a dizzying array of colors. Signs flashed. Huge screens showed videos of people playing or working. Movies? Eron thought. On the buildings?

The city looked nothing like anything he'd ever seen. How could they not know about this in Rippon or any of the colonies? Why live in colonies when you could have all this? Why did they scrape by, growing food in the greenhouses and dealing with native dangers, when all of this was available?

When Eron looked at Sarai, he sensed her concern. Maybe she wasn't in on it. Maybe she was as scared and confused as he. Still, he'd not get tricked again.

Three

Nagi scoured the grounds outside Freedom for his children. They should be around somewhere. The laughter and joyous atmosphere of home welcomed him. Unlike the harsh forest above, down here it was tranquil. Most of the time.

"Nagi, is that you?"

Nagi turned to see his wife.

"Balla!" he cried and ran to her, scooping up her slight frame. The hair on her body was a light gold, a stark contrast to his darkness.

"Nagi, I missed you!" she said into his thick hair.

"My dear Balla, I couldn't wait to get home." They embraced for a long time, a small crowd watching them. Returning scouts were afforded a hero's welcome because they often brought back new recruits.

"Where are the children?" he asked.

"Inside at the playground on level three," Balla replied. She snuggled her head into his chest and Nagi held her tight.

"How many did you bring back? The council was anxious for your return."

"And you weren't?" he said with a smile.

"Of course, I was! You're the last to return. You made me worried. I thought..." she said trailing off.

"I know, Balla; it's not easy for you. I'm back. It's okay."

"So how many? The rest of the scouts from Freedom only brought six new converts."

"Six? I thought we had ten. What happened to the rest?"

"I'm sorry, Nagi, but it was only six."

"I didn't bring any back," he said, lowering his head. "I was in a fight. I couldn't save them." Balla gasped. He closed his eyes, thinking about his brother. He hoped his actions were enough to force him to do something to spur a change. It was his only hope of reconciling the Truth with the Topsiders. Kidnapping new converts, either male or female, had always felt wrong to him. It gave him a family, sure, but at what cost? Why couldn't they allow for personal freedom or personal choice? How were they any different than the Topsiders they railed against?

Now was not the time. He made it back. His family needed him as much as he needed them.

"Balla, let's go find the kids."

She smiled. "Of course, my love. This way." They untangled themselves and walked hand in hand up the steps into Freedom.

The air inside was considerably cooler, and the familiar smell of recycled air was comforting to Nagi. When the ship crashed on Kepler 186f three hundred and thirty-seven years ago, it smashed into the planet with such force that it sunk deep into the planet's crust. The dirt and rock caved in and buried the ship. The impeccable construction held firm even after the crash, and the ship withstood the weight of being buried. The internal structures, mainly the power core with a half-life of a million years, still functioned. Most life support systems and electronics worked as well. There were a few holes in the ship's hull, but those rooms were sealed off from the rest, providing an enormous underground self-sustaining structure.

When the ship survived, the follow-up missions intentionally smashed into the planet's surface, knowing their vehicles could withstand the impact. The early reports of the planet's dangerous surface, notably the rain, necessitated the unorthodox landings.

Unlike what Nagi learned as a boy, those first colonists lived well in the ship. They didn't starve or face death. However, no one taught him about the crash and the surviving underground colony until he was captured and became one of the Truth.

The colonists dug out from the crash site, beginning the transformation of what the cavern had become. It took fifty years to do so. It would've been sooner, had they realized the potential of using the dirt grubbers. Once they harnessed the power of those large digging creatures, they finished within five years and established two farms to raise dirt grubbers for a light source. The third was added about a hundred years later with the construction of the large underground traveling tunnels.

Nagi and Balla walked to the elevator, clicked the button and waited for the whoosh sound announcing the car's arrival. They stepped inside, and Balla pushed the button for the third level.

Nagi slumped to the side of the car, closing his eyes.

"My dear, you can have all the rest you want. You've been gone too long up there. I've missed you so much. The children have missed you. I know

Gwenny misses you. She talks all the time about you coming back. Gunther, however, is a little more reserved. He's been quieter than usual. Maybe seeing you will bring him around." Balla hugged him tight.

A ding sounded, and the elevator stopped; the doors opening.

"Come on, Nagi, let's get our kids."

The hall to the right led to one of four play-grounds built within the ship. There was only one when it set off from Earth, and the colonists constructed the others after the crash landing on Kepler 186f. All four play areas were identical.

They turned another corner and a lush, tempting playground came into view. Swing sets, monkey bars, teeter-totters; all the customary Earth-like playground items. There were close to thirty children running around, playing tag, yelling, and laughing.

When Nagi first encountered Freedom, his anger at his kidnappers slowly crumbled the longer he stayed on the ship. It was like a new world forced itself on him, though in truth, he would've opted for it if he'd known about it before.

Topsiders were oblivious to what lay beneath their feet. If they did know, they hid the secrets from themselves. Nagi struggled to understand this when he first converted. His teachers, knowing how volatile the process was for converts, slowly worked him through the mental gymnastics required to make peace with reality. Calling themselves the Truth was not a fact lost on him.

"Father?"

A petite, brown furry child with a dash of blonde

ran to Nagi. He crouched with open arms and scooped her up, hugging Gwenny tight. His heart broke and tears flowed. "Gwenny!" he said, his voice muffled by her hair.

"Father, I've missed you!" Gwenny clutched his shoulders, unable to reach around his body. Nagi closed his eyes and let the comfort of holding his daughter consume him.

"Father? Is that you?" a tiny male voice said. Nagi opened his eyes. His son stood at the edge of the playground.

Nagi nodded. "Gunther! Come here, boy!" Gunther ran to him and Nagi scooped him up. He held his children close, kissing both of them.

"I missed you both so much! It's been too long. Look how big you are!" Gunther grabbed Nagi's thick hair, trying to stay close to his father.

Balla stood to the side, her eyes glistening.

"It's never easy to leave all of you, but it's so rewarding to come back. Come, let's celebrate!"

Nagi bent to let his children down. They wouldn't let go of his hands. Balla led the way to their apartment on the fifth floor, the children beaming at their father as they walked the halls, each holding tightly onto one of his hands. When others approached, Nagi noticed Gunther stood a little taller, and Gwenny's face displayed the pride she felt inside.

They entered the elevator and Nagi relaxed. Eron, I wish I could've taken you back with me. It's not to be. You'll find a new life. I hope it's as good as mine. Nagi closed his eyes for a moment, Eron's scared face before him. Home awaited.

Four

Eron and Sarai sat on a stark white couch. Sarai ran her hand along its smooth surface, the cool synthetic material chilling her hand.

"I still don't believe this. Did you know?" Sarai asked. Eron shook his head.

Their new home—an apartment, they called it, was on the seventh floor of the second tallest building in Beta Prime, significantly smaller than the Royal Tower that loomed large over the city. Their experience through the city with transports and people and buildings was mesmerizing for them both.

***

People of all colors and sizes walked briskly along the sidewalks lining the busy streets. Storefronts advertising fashion and exotic foods called to them.

As they rode, chauffeured by the ADF soldiers, Sarai opened her window to a cacophony of diverse sounds exploding through the silence of the vehicle. The two of them sat in silence, mouths gaping, hoping to make sense of their new surroundings.

The vehicle stopped at the curb beside a building. "This is your new home. It's got all the latest amenities. Kitchen, washing machine and dryer, dish washer, tv, and it's all networked through what you'd call wi-fi."

Eron scrunched up his face. "Excuse me, what did you say?" Suddenly, lessons from history class seemed much more important than he ever realized they would.

"It's not wi-fi as you studied, but it's the closest comparison. Beats calling it Subatomic Network of Nanotechnological Synapses. It's the same principle as wi-fi, but more elaborate. There are many things more complex than you know. We find it easier to relate to them in a shorthand."

Sarai gripped Eron's hand. "What is this?" she whispered. She seemed to be as lost as Eron was. He gave her a sympathetic smile.

"I don't know. It's so confusing."

"Your apartment is on the seventh floor, number 710. I'll walk you in, make sure the doorman knows who you are, and get your key. They'll take you to your room. I realize this is quite overwhelming, but I assure you, once settled, you'll find Beta Prime to be an experience you'll never forget."

"But what do we do? School is out. The Selection is over. We've never lived by ourselves. What are we supposed to do now?" Sarai asked.

"Yeah, what's next?" Eron added.

"I'd suggest a hot shower. Nothing like a good scrub down after what you've been through. You'll find clothes in your sizes in the closet and dressers. The queen spares no expense when it comes to the Victors. We'll be in contact shortly about what comes next. Now, if you don't mind, come this way. We've got a busy schedule to keep." The ADF soldier motioned to a revolving door, where a man dressed in a red velvet uniform and cap waited for them.

"This is Selected Eron and his mate, Sarai. I believe they belong in number 710," the soldier said to the doorman. The man grinned, his perfect teeth sparkling in the red sunlight.

"Of course! So glad to have you, Eron and Sarai! Young couples are always a welcome treat. Please, this way. I'll escort you to the front desk and they'll take it from there."

The soldier stood, waiting for them to enter the moving door, then left. Eron struggled with the door. He'd never used such a thing and Sarai seemed as confused as he. He looked at her and smiled. She certainly didn't seem like Phelan.

"Just push and walk," the doorman said. "The door will turn with you."

The desk clerk greeted them with a smile, his thin mustache turning up at the ends. He called over a boy close to Eron's age and ordered him to take them to their apartment. The boy escorted them to a door that opened with a ding. "This way, please," he motioned to the open door. The couple looked at each other.

"What's in there?" Eron asked.

"Huh? Oh, yeah. You're from the colonies. It's called an elevator. You step inside, press a button, and it takes you to another floor."

"I think I've heard of those," Sarai said. Eron furrowed his brow. The boy acted as though they were ignorant; lacking knowledge. It wasn't their fault they were closed off, was it? How could they expect to understand this new world, when all they knew was the harsh life of the colonies? They didn't even know this place existed until hours ago.

"Please, this way, then," the boy said. He wore the same red velvet uniform as the doorman, though it was a touch too large for him.

They rode in the car for a few moments before the floor indicator lit with the number seven and the door again opened with a ding.

They stepped out of the car into a hallway lined with doors on either side. At the far end of the hall, two ADF soldiers were banging on one of them.

"Come out now! This is not the place or time for this!" one of them yelled. Both held pistols at their sides.

"Oh, let's wait a minute," the boy said to Eron and Sarai. The two looked to each other and back down the hall at the commotion.

"This is your last warning! Open this door before we break it down!"

"No," someone yelled from inside. "Go away! Leave me alone! Why can't I live in peace?"

"This is your life now; get used to it. It's better to understand your new reality. You won't like the alternative. Now, open this door!" the ADF soldier yelled. There was a loud crash inside the room. The soldiers looked at each other, and one nodded. They breached the door, kicking it in.

Gunshots fired, the sound reverberating in the hall. Sarai cupped her ears. Eron winced. Flashbacks of the Selection, of soldiers firing on the boys at the beginning raced through his mind.

One of the soldiers exited the room followed by the second, who dragged a boy by the scruff of his neck. He was roughly Eron's age. Blood trailed behind as the soldiers stalked down the hall toward them. They looked at Eron and Sarai, nodded slightly, and continued to the elevator with the life-less body in tow.

Once the doors closed, Sarai turned to Eron. "What was that? They killed him!"

"Sorry you had to see that, but it happens more than we like. Poor fool couldn't handle the new world. Colonists find it difficult to adjust to Beta Prime. Honestly, I think it would be harder to adjust to colonial living. Anyway, your room is here," he pointed. They avoided the blood trail on the tile floor and crossed the hall to 710. The boy gave them a metal card.

"This is your key. If you need another, please inquire at the front desk. If you turn the television to channel three, you'll find a welcome message explaining what's next. I encourage you to pay attention to the message. It will help you adjust to your new surroundings." He opened the door for them, holding the door until they entered. "Welcome to your new home!" He bowed and left, the door closing slowly behind him.

"Television?" Eron asked. He'd heard of it before.

They looked around the apartment. There was a bathroom, a kitchen, one bedroom, and a living room with a white couch facing a large rectangular screen. Their view was of the heart of the city. Transports moving fast down the streets, people walking, and lights flashing on buildings and signs. Despite all the activity, it was silent in the room. When they finished their inspection, they sat on the white couch, staring at the blank screen in front of them.

·

Five

"Dear, are you sure you don't need any help?" Balla said. Though he'd been gone for over a month, Nagi insisted on preparing the celebratory meal. Balla didn't mind...too much. Nagi wasn't the best cook, but his heart was in it.

"I'm fine, Balla. Relax. Let me finish preparing this meal. It's the least I can do."

Balla smiled. She did miss him. His calm demeanor and his confidence were what had attracted her to him in the beginning. Even though the children weren't his, he stepped right in and became the father they needed. And the husband she wanted.

***

Her first husband, Mabuz, was killed two years ago during Nagi's Selection. He'd attempted to secure five converts by himself near the valley below Victory Point and was overwhelmed by the frightened boys. The memory of his lifeless body carried to the grave-yard just outside of Freedom was something she never forgot.

When Nagi came to the city, she noticed him early on, before he turned completely from Topsider to the Truth. His hair grew thick and dark. His compassion for the other converts astounded her. When one of them grew angry at their captivity, Nagi secured him to the ground without harming anyone else. He held the boy until their instructors could subdue him. It was as though Nagi understood what was going on even before he hadn't yet fully converted and learned the truth.

It was a couple months after Nagi converted and was covered in thick black fur that she noticed him again. Gunther ran out into the cavern surrounding Freedom. She and Gwenny called for him, and soon a small crowd of Truth scoured the area. She grew nervous the longer he was gone. There were dangers out there a small boy wouldn't be strong enough to handle. After nearly four hours of searching, Nagi came strolling back to Freedom with young Gunther at his side. The boy beamed as he looked up at Nagi. Balla ran to them, kneeling and clutching Gunther.

"Where did you go? I was so worried!"

"Momma, I found a secret cave on the other side of Freedom! It was cool! It goes all around the city. I found small—"

"Gunther! What have I told you about running off like that? You scared me to death!"

"But momma, I was exploring! I was—"

"Gunther!" she said.

"Ma'am, he was being curious, as all boys are," Nagi said. "I was outside Freedom and heard a noise. When I discovered the boy, I brought him right back."

Balla felt her cheeks flush. "Thank you, thank you, thank you!" She ruffled Gunther's hair and stood. "I'm Balla," she said, extending a hand. Nagi grasped her forearm.

"My name is Ti—" he paused, "Nagi. Pleased to meet you." He smiled, and Balla melted.

It wasn't long after that they started dating. They met at the theater on level three. They went to dinner at the spacious Starburst Cafe on the sixth floor, and listened to jazz played by holographic images on a stage at the front of the room.

Balla enjoyed her time with Nagi immensely. Within a few months of their courtship, Nagi proposed to her, and soon they were a happy family.

What bothered her the most was when Nagi left to gather converts. He'd be gone for over a month with no contact. The first time he left, she didn't sleep for three days. She worried about him. Dangers above were real. She knew all too well how difficult being a scout could be. She begged him to reconsider for a position within Freedom in hopes she'd keep him close, but he dismissed the idea.

"Balla, I have to do this. Others need to know they're being fed lies. They need to know what we know. I have a brother that will be going through this soon. I must be ready."

Balla cupped his chin with her hand. "Dear Nagi, I know you feel a great responsibility for your brother. I won't stand in your way. But, please see it from my perspective. I've already lost one husband. I don't want to lose you, too. Think of Gwenny and Gunther. They love you. They look up to you. I love you. I don't want to lose you."

Nagi pulled her close into an embrace.

"I know, Balla, I know."

Still he left, telling her it was necessary. She couldn't stand in his way, but that didn't mean she condoned it.

***

"Children, dinner's ready!" Nagi called. They ran into the dining room.

Dinner was...edible. Gunther winced when he bit into the potatoes. Balla saw it and hoped Nagi hadn't. He could be sensitive at times. Right now, all she cared about was that he was home. She wanted to keep him upbeat for as long as possible.

After dinner, the kids went to their room to play. Balla snuggled up to Nagi as they sat on the couch watching a television show on the large screen built into the wall. There were close to sixty stations available to watch. Most aired rerun shows from Earth that were still in constant rotation over the centuries. There were three local stations that broadcast current shows created in the holographic rooms on the fourth floor. The rooms were originally created for the colonists to enjoy an artificial piece of Earth on their long journey across the stars, but they functioned well enough as television studios.

Balla had wanted to ask about Nagi's brother since his return. Now, she decided, was the time.

"Nagi, did you find him?" she asked.

He closed his eyes.

"I don't want to make you upset, but we have to talk about it."

"I tried, Balla. He didn't see who I was until the very end. I saw fear in his eyes. He wasn't made for the Selection."

"None of you are, Nagi. It's wrong. You know this."

"I know, but he was so scared. He almost died. I saved him. I helped him live."

Balla drew herself closer. "What else could you do?"

"More. I could've taken him. He'd learn soon enough I was right. We all do. Most of us."

Nagi turned away, as if in deep thought. Balla wasn't done, but she sensed he was. She let the subject drop. When he was ready, he'd share more with her.

Right now, what mattered was that he was home.

They watched a few hours of television, Balla not paying attention to any of it. She could only think of Nagi and his torment; his desire to save his brother and his failure. She felt sorry for him. Saving Eron drove him from her and the kids, but she understood his need to try. Once converts faced reality and had a moment of mental breakdown, they accepted the Truth with open arms. Maybe there was still time for Eron.

Six

Mina's eyes widened as they approached Beta Prime. Her mother never prepared her for this! Did her mom know about the city? Did she know about the queen? Why didn't she tell Mina about any of it?

"You've been quiet most of the ride. Are you ok?"

Mina turned to the blue boy, the one chosen for her by the queen and cruel science. She wanted nothing to do with him. For years, she'd expected to be with Eron. Her heart was set on them as a couple, having children, growing old, and living a long life together as partners.

This boy irritated her.

"Hmpf," was her reply. The boy, Sar, was from the colony of Greater Manthus. He had an odd way of handling the current situation. He grinned at her constantly and ran his hand through his green hair. A fresh scar on his left cheek distorted his once handsome face. She'd allow that much, but every time he opened his mouth, she loathed him more.

If only he was Eron.

Sar turned back to the window, watching the city grow larger as they entered the gates, Mina ignoring him.

Soon, they arrived at a large tower in the southern part of the city. The ADF soldiers escorted them inside, where they were led to their room on the fifth floor.

Mina absently hung her clothes in a closet, dismissing the apartment's major features.

Sar couldn't stop talking about them.

"Mina, did you see this television? I never thought I'd see one of these! Look! The couch is the brightest shade of white I've ever seen! Look at this view," he said, throwing open the curtains and revealing a spectacular panoramic view of the city before them. Bright lights flashed and buildings rose high in the air; the skyline dominated by a large tower in the city's center.

Mina snapped out of her stupor as she admired the city. She'd come so far from the colony. Dust storms and bullies and craate attacks seemed like childish concerns compared with the bustling city.

"Why didn't we know?" she said quietly.

Sar turned to her. "What do you mean, my love?"

Mina cringed. For all her talk to Eron about not hurting anyone in the Selection, she felt a sudden urge to punch Sar in the nose. She was *not* his love. He certainly wasn't hers! They'd only met hours ago. She thought of Eron and where he was and what he was doing. A touch of jealousy rose up when she thought of him with Sarai. The girl was pretty. But she and Eron were supposed to be together, not she and Sar, and definitely not Eron and Sarai.

"Nothing," Mina replied. She turned from the window and noticed a typed note on the table next to the couch. She picked it up and read it. When she had finished, she dropped into the couch with her eyes closed, clutching the note.

Sar sat next to her and moved to put his arm

around her, which she shrugged off.

"What is it, my dear? What does it say?"

She thrust it in his hand.

"*Welcome to Beta Prime. To acclimate you to your new surroundings and new life as a happy couple, please turn to channel three*," he read aloud. He grinned and fumbled with a long black controller on the table until the television turned on and changed to channel three.

They sat mesmerized by the instructions given to them. The queen herself detailed how they were to reproduce, behave, and think as they started this new life. If they were lucky, the queen said, then they'd get to stay in Beta Prime. However, doing so meant they would no longer return to their respective colonies. They'd be citizens of the greatest city on the planet. Sar could join the ADF, and Mina, if she was willing, could serve in the civilian branch of the ADF.

Mina's face twisted in disgust when the queen spoke on about reproduction. She noticed Sar grinning, his blue face split wide. A sickening feeling grew inside her. She felt it bubble in her belly and percolate upwards. Sar didn't seem to realize her discomfort as he placed a hand on her knee. Her body stiffened, her repulsion of the boy deepening.

This is wrong. I swear; if he touches me, I'll hurt him, she thought as his blue hand rested on her leg.

"I need to use the restroom," she said, jumping up and freeing her leg from his sickening touch.

"Hurry back. There's all kinds of great info here!"

Mina crossed the room to a hallway and closed the bathroom door behind her. She covered her face with her hands, crying softly. If Sar heard her, he'd probably want to "comfort" her, and that wasn't going to happen.

Life in the colony was so easy compared to this. Hope existed there. A dream of a life with Eron brought joy to her there. But now? Things were drastically different. How could her mom let her do this? Why were the adults okay with the boys being slaughtered as if for sport in the Selection and the girls groomed to accept whatever Selected the stupid queen chose for them?

Her heart broke when she thought of Eron with that other girl.

She had to be strong in the moment. The queen directed her to be; not to mention the armed ADF soldiers there to enforce her will. Otherwise, she'd be sent back to the colony as an outcast or worse. Mina followed the instructions, though she knew there was a chance it would upset Eron. She feared for his life while he was gone, and seeing him again, though battered and bruised, brought a feeling of relief over her. She knew going into the tent for the ceremony would hurt her. She knew it was going to be the most difficult thing for her, but at least Eron was alive. Far too many other boys didn't have that luxury.

If she knew exactly what she was in for with Sar, she might have done things differently. This queen who appeared out of nowhere commanded the ADF soldiers around like they were her playthings. It didn't take long for Mina to realize who was in charge.

She had to escape from Sar. She had to leave Beta Prime. She could find Eron and leave; run far away, and never look back. Why, mom, why? You never told me about this place, or a queen, or the possibility I'd end up with a stranger and be expected to act like a good little wife.

She sobbed louder. Sar knocked on the door. "Mina dear, are you all right? What can I do to help? Tell me, love."

Mina dropped her hands, scowling. Her red eyes narrowed as she spoke. "Nothing, Sar. I'm fine. Just overwhelmed."

"Can I get you anything? A cup of kafka, maybe?"

"No! I'm fine." She listened as he walked away. She didn't care if she'd hurt his feelings; she wasn't going to be part of his life. Not for long. The first opportunity she found, she'd be gone. Being by herself was better than playing pretend with someone she didn't want to know.

When she finally came out of the bathroom, Sar approached her with longing in his eyes. "Mina, the queen said—"

"I don't care what she said!" Her chest heaved, and he backed off.

"I'm tired, Sar. We've had a long day. I need to rest. Alone. Please, for tonight?" It disgusted her to act this way, but Sar seemed intent on following the queen's command about procreation. There was no way she'd let that happen.

Sar crossed his arms, glaring at her. "You know I killed six other boys to get here. I expected more."

"Sar, I'm tired. I've been through a lot today. I'll sleep on the couch if you want. I don't care. You can have the bed."

"That's the least you can do for me, after all I've been through," he said.

What you've been through? As if my feelings don't

matter, you selfish jerk!

"Good night, Sar, I really want to lay down."

Sar stalked to the bedroom, slamming the door be-hind him.

Mina let out a deep breath and made herself as comfortable as she could on the sterile white couch.

Seven

A small boy ran through the halls of Freedom, breathing heavy. He had an urgent message for all the scouts. He ran quickly along the gray sterile hallway and stopped at a door on the fifth floor. He pounded hard on the metal door.

"Scout Nagi, please answer," the boy called out. Balla opened the door.

"What is it, young man? You're loud enough to wake the neighbors. Do you know what time it is?"

"I apologize about the noise, but I have an urgent message for Scout Nagi. It's from the Council. Is he here?"

"Yes, he is, but what could they want from him? He's only been back a couple days. It's not time for another Selection."

Nagi heard the noise and quietly appeared behind Balla.

"How can I help you? Quite the racket you're making out here."

Balla flinched when he spoke, unaware he stood behind her.

"Scout Nagi, you must come quick. The Council demands you in their chambers. It's urgent."

Balla looked to the boy, then to Nagi, her face showing worry.

"I'm sure it's nothing, Balla. Let me go find out what

they want, and I'll be right back. Don't worry; I'm not going anywhere. We've got months before I have to go back out." He kissed her forehead and followed the boy out the door.

"Sorry, I've got more scouts to notify. The Council waits, Scout Nagi." The boy ran off to the elevator and disappeared behind closing doors.

What could they possibly want so urgently? They could've used the coms.

The Council rarely interrupted Scouts between Selections. Their sole purpose was to infiltrate the forest and remove as many boys as possible. Topsiders thought the boys killed each other, which did happen, but the Truth rescued many more than the Topsiders realized. Until this last Selection. Far too many boys were senselessly slaughtered in the name of "tradition."

Nagi adjusted his tunic and waited for the next elevator to take him to the Council chambers. It was actually a conference room off the control room of the ship, and it had been used as the Council chambers since the underground city was established. The control room still functioned as such, but instead of maneuvering the ship through space, it was the main hub for all vital activity in Freedom. Engineers and technicians monitored life support systems and addressed issues as they came up. It was an elaborate, yet efficient way of maintaining subterranean life inside the monstrous metal ship.

The doors opened and Nagi entered the elevator, pushing the button for the uppermost deck. When the doors opened again, a chaotic scene greeted him.

Council envoys, like the boy that summoned him, ran to the elevator and almost knocked him over in their haste. Engineers scrambled to control something they pointed to on their screens. One exchange grew so tense, punches were thrown and technicians restrained two of their fellow techs.

"What the—" Nagi said, watching the madness.

"Scout Nagi?" one of the envoys asked. Nagi nodded.

"This way please; there's much to discuss." The boy escorted him to the Council chambers and held the door for him.

Inside, the atmosphere was heated, almost to the level of the control room. He heard arguments and raised voices, half expecting to see another fight.

When he stepped inside, and the door closed behind him, all eyes turned to him.

"Scout Nagi," a deep, cavernous voice rumbled. The chair of the Council, one of the oldest Truth living in Freedom, was a hulking figure. His thick black hair had turned a peppery gray years ago, but his piercing eyes revealed the strength he still held behind his aging coat. He'd been Chair far longer than Nagi had been part of the Truth.

"Chair Thurl. Council. How may I be of assistance?" Nagi asked. He scanned for other scouts, but realized he was the only one.

"As you can see," Thurl began, not offering Nagi a seat, "there's been a great disturbance for our people. The engineers are trying to determine how long we have. The Council is in an uproar, as you've heard, and my anger is close to erupting. Care to tell me why this might be?"

Nagi knitted his brows and twisted his face into an expression of confusion. How could he possibly know what was going on?

"I'm sorry, sir; please forgive me. I just got back from the Selection a few days ago, and—" Someone at the table gasped. Council member Tara covered her mouth with her hand. Others pulled back, as if in disbelief.

"I don't understand," Nagi said.

"You! You brought them!" Council member Seeto said, pointing a thick, furry finger at Nagi.

"What?" Nagi replied. The Council's cryptic accusations made no sense.

"Scout Nagi," Thurl said. The Council members faced him. "Your actions with the Topsiders have brought us great distress. At this moment, the Topsiders are on their way through the Traveling Tunnels, which you have lead them to," he said with a shaky voice, "and they are closing in on Freedom. Never have we ever been in such great danger. This sanctuary of ours; this vessel, which has provided so much knowledge and peace to our people, is in danger. If they discover what is here, we face elimination, and with it, the Truth will be compromised forever."

The Council murmured amongst themselves, voices growing angrier. Nagi still didn't comprehend what he'd heard.

"I did, sir? But how? I followed every protocol I was taught. I covered my tracks. I waited until they were gone. I—"

"Silence!" Thurl growled. "Your carelessness has brought this on us!"

"Your insistence on speaking with that Topsider...the one called Eron, your brother," Tara said. The words dripped like vulbore venom, stinging with every drop. "You exposed yourself, Scout Nagi. Your reckless attitude has brought our destruction, unless we can stop it."

"But, Tara—" Nagi began.

"*Council member* Tara," she corrected.

"Council member Tara, there was no other Topsider present. Not then. Not as I spoke with Eron. I made sure we were alone. And when I left, no one followed."

"That's where you're wrong, Scout," Seeto said. "You were followed. They watched you uncover the entrance to the Traveling Tunnels. They waited and snuck inside, tracking you."

"That can't be!" Nagi protested. "I was careful! It's impossible!"

"Tell Charl and Jorgan. Tell them when you see them in the afterlife," Thurl said.

"What? No!" Nagi said.

"They were murdered. Their bodies were riddled with bullets. Do you know where there may be a gun around here?" Thurl said. He opened his large gray arms wide, inviting Nagi's response.

Nagi dropped his head, closing his eyes.

"I didn't think you'd have an answer. They were discovered by Scout Simeone. He reported to us hours ago, and we've since found our tunnels filled with Topsiders, bringing death with them. This is a horrible situation, Scout Nagi! We're in a dire position."

"But," Nagi began. He looked around the room.

An engineer burst through the door and bent over, panting.

"Council! Chair Thurl...they're here!"

Eight

Three days after settling in to their new life in Beta Prime, Eron and Sarai left their apartment for the first time. They'd watched the television non-stop since their arrival, mesmerized by the video feed, amazed at the entertainment, and worried by the queen's words.

"Sarai, stay close. I don't know what to expect. I'd hate for anything to happen to you," Eron said. They exited the revolving doors in the building's lobby and ventured out into the busy world.

People scurried along the sidewalks; transports clogged the streets, horns blaring. The vast array of buildings filling their view still took their breath away.

"It's so different," Sarai said.

"I know," Eron replied. His eyes widened at the gray world in front of him, so unlike his colony or the world he knew until days ago. Instead of brilliant reds and oranges, tall gray and black buildings illuminated by electric lights, most flashing or blinking or scrawling with words, dominated his view.

The noise was deafening. So many strange and layered voices, horns, vendors calling...an immense wave of sound felt crushing. The couple looked around, adjusting to their new surroundings as best they could.

"Should we go out there?" Sarai asked. She motioned to the commotion.

Eron closed his eyes, then turned to look at Sarai.

"Yeah, we need to see what this is all about. Here," he said holding out his hand to grasp hers, "don't wander from me. Stay by my side." She gripped his hand tight. Sarai wasn't Mina, but Eron had come to enjoy being around her.

After his initial shock at Victory Point, it took a while for him to adjust to his new situation. He knew nothing about Sarai when they met, and didn't care to know more. She was everything he didn't want, because all he wanted was Mina. The look on Mina's face when she left with that blue boy; the detached, uncaring glance she gave Eron hurt him deep. Before he left for the Selection, she promised to be there at the end. *For him.* She was there, but chose that other boy instead. Why? Why did she hurt him like that? Why did Eron have to do so many hurtful things to others, only to face rejection in the end?

The queen's explanation about being "chosen" was weak. Eron didn't buy it. But because of her decree, he ended up with a girl he didn't know and didn't care for...at first.

Since they'd met, Sarai had been nothing but kind to him. She was pretty, but not stunning like Mina. But more than anything, her patience with him, her demeanor, and her ability to hold meaningful conversations won him over. She wasn't Mina, but slowly she was becoming the girl he could see himself with for a long time, and it had only been a matter of days since they'd met.

They strolled along the sidewalk, trying to avoid people who wouldn't move out of the way. Once, a man bumped into Sarai and almost knocked her over.

"Hey, watch it," Eron said. The man grunted, continuing on as if nothing happened. "I swear, Sarai, I'd rather be back at the colony." She nodded, squeezing his hand.

Three blocks from their apartment, Eron noticed they were being followed by a cloaked figure. It felt like one of the Forgotten was stalking him.

"Sarai, I think we're being followed," he said. She looked around, searching for a suspicious person.

"I don't see anyone," she said.

"Behind us, near the white and gray building with the blue flashing sign. By the door. See the person in the white outfit, hood pulled up over their head?"

Sarai turned slowly. "How do you know we're being followed?" she asked. The person looked down, and she couldn't tell if it was a man or woman.

"Every time we stop, they stop. When we move, they move. I thought it was a coincidence at first, but they are keeping our pace."

"Then let's move and see what happens."

They turned the next corner onto a one-way street packed with transports. The crush of people grew denser. At the end of the next block, they stopped. Eron looked behind them and the figure stood next to the building, head bowed.

"We are being followed!" he said. "Whoever it is, they've turned the corner. Look!"

Sarai spotted the person leaning against the building, face still covered by the hood.

"What do we do?" she asked, a nervous hitch to her voice.

"Come on, this way," Eron said, pulling her with him. They darted around another corner, careful to avoid bumping into unaware strangers.

"Oh no," Eron said. They'd made it past a throng of people to find themselves at a dead end. The street continued for a block and ended at a building, the windows reflecting Anastasia's red sun.

When they turned to retreat, the figure was standing in the center of the street, facing them. The hood was pushed back slightly, revealing a female face.

"Eron, come quickly," she called. She looked left and right. "Now! You too, Sarai. Both of you must come with me. It's the only way!"

Eron looked from Sarai to the woman. She shifted her feet and clenched her fists, as if waiting for an attack.

"Eron, this is your last chance. Come with me if you want to see Timo again."

Eron's eyes widened. Sarai put her hands on his arm to calm him.

"How do you know us? How do you know my brother? How can I see him again?" Eron replied.

"Follow me and I'll show you, but we must hurry!"

She turned and ran to the intersection, then glanced back at the couple. "Come on!" she called and darted to the right, disappearing into the crowd.

"Sarai, I have to check this out. Come with me. Let's stay together."

She fidgeted, running her hands up and down her arms. "Are you sure this is safe? What if it's a trap?"

Eron nodded. "I can handle it. I've been through worse." Visions of Phelan attacking him, of Bello trying to kill him, and of Laird murdering his friend Connor flashed in his mind.

"Oh Eron, I trust you. Let's go."

They ran after the woman. Once at the intersection, Sarai spotted her hood two blocks to the right. "That way!" she said.

They ran after her.

She zig-zagged across the city. Eron wanted to stop and rest, to take in the wondrous sights around him, but she kept running, turning back every so often. Sarai had a hard time keeping up, but she didn't complain.

Finally, the woman stopped at a small five-story building. It was run-down; much different than the rest of the city's architecture. The crowds had thinned considerably here. She stood at the entrance to the building. Windows were boarded up, and those that were visible had cracked panes, or no glass at all.

"In here," she said, holding open a weathered wood door, the paint long ago chipped away.

Sarai hesitated. "No way. Tell us why we should trust you."

The woman paused, then pushed back her hood completely.

"Because I'm Samantha, Eron's sister."

Nine

Sirens blared throughout Freedom. The last time they'd been sounded was when the ship crashed in the red Anastasian forest, burying itself deep underground. Now, they warned of impending disaster worse than the crash.

Balla snatched her children and tore from their apartment, rushing out to a sea of Truth running down the hallways. Large, hulking, black-furred figures; pelts of grays and browns; even greens, haphazardly pushed each other to gain access to the elevators. Balla shoved her children close to the walls.

"Stay together! Do not leave me!" she yelled above the noise. Gwenny and Gunther nodded, their eyes wide. Someone pushed into Balla, and she braced herself to prevent from crushing her children.

The sirens screeched incessantly. Red lights flashed along the ceiling. Truth poured from their rooms into the congested halls, shoving their way to safety.

Balla crept against the current, nudging her children to move. She shielded them with her body, a constant beating raining down on her from inadvertent elbows and knees. One caught her in the ribs and she winced, her breath caught within.

"Mom, are you all right?" Gwenny yelled above the sirens. Balla could only nod and continued to move her children toward the emergency stairs at the end of the hall.

Back at the elevator, a fight broke out, and screaming Truth too close to the action were swept up in a frenzied mass of arms and fists.

"Where's Dad?" Gunther asked.

"Not now, Son, move! Keep going!"

Gunther screamed as a small Truth fell to the floor near them and was trampled as others shoved their way to the congested elevators.

A small pocket appeared in front of them, and Balla grabbed her children and ran forward. She dodged a family and turned a corner toward the stairs. They entered the stairwell and joined the light stream of Truth filtering down to the emergency exit at the bottom of Freedom.

When they emptied out into the cavern, they discovered the source of the emergency.

Flooding through the tunnels high up on the ridge surrounding Freedom, the Anastasian Defense Forces soldiers fanned out, training their weapons on the ship. Small armed transports rumbled down the path toward them, followed by marching soldiers.

"No, this can't be!" Balla cried.

Shots were fired into the growing mass of Truth outside Freedom. Neighbors, friends, even young Truth were cut down mercilessly by the ADF soldiers. Bullets screamed past Balla, embedding in the hull of Freedom. Glass shattered as stray bullets struck the ship.

The slaughter continued.

Balla herded her children and ran to the back of Freedom where the small tunnels dug into the earth.

Others had the same idea, and the narrow tunnel was filled with Truth eager to escape the impending death behind them.

Balla thought of Nagi and hoped he was safe. She couldn't do anything for him now. Her children were her priority. She had to escape the madness before she worried about him.

They'd made it about a hundred yards into the tunnel when an enormous explosion behind them shook the ground. A huge blast of heat and flame penetrated their tunnel, knocking them over. Those in the back nearest the cavern were killed immediately. Balla fell on her children and felt the heat along her back. The smell of burnt hair filed the tunnel. When the wave of heat vanished, she rose up on her knees and looked back.

What was left of Freedom burned bright in the cavern. A gaping hole cut through the middle as horrific screams echoed amid small explosions.

"Nagi!" Balla cried. "Our home!"

The remaining Truth in the tunnel screamed and ran away from the blast.

Balla took a step toward Freedom and was pulled back by her children and the mass of confused, scared Truth.

"Nagi!" she called again. Her voice was lost in the growing noise of destruction and screams.

She turned from the inferno and ran with both children in tow. The crowd pushed hard to escape the devastation at their backs. Balla followed, keeping Gwenny and Gunther close at her side.

The tunnel turned left then right, descending to an opening in the Selection grounds near the far east side and to Inventa, the nearest Truth city to Freedom.

Truth poured out of the Traveling Tunnel, dispersing in all directions. Families followed each other; strangers called for their loved ones, hoping to find them in the exodus. Chaos reigned. Balla stood to the side, out of the way as she scanned the rushing mob of Truth for Nagi, her dear sweet husband. He had to be there! Losing another love was just too much to bear. Nagi had to escape the madness.

Screams echoed from inside the tunnel. Gunshots followed. Those around the tunnel's mouth scattered. Balla paused, unsure if she should stay or run. If Nagi came barreling through, she wanted to be there. More gunshots sounded and dying Truth screamed their last breaths. Flames shot out of the tunnel.

Gwenny screamed. Balla whisked her children away in a moment of panic. "Nagi, I'm so sorry," she called to the masses still pouring out of the tunnel, flames and bullets chasing them.

She shoved her children away from the tunnel and they ran. She lost all sense of direction, her only goal to put as much distance as she could between herself and the tunnel. If the ADF kept up their pursuit, they'd need to be as far away as possible.

Gunther struggled to keep the pace. His little legs churned, but were no match for Balla's longer stride. Gwenny was a bit faster than he, but she, too, began to fall behind. Balla picked up Gunther and continued running, slowing a bit. Truth were everywhere, running and crying, unsure where to go or what to do.

They weren't prepared for this. None of them expected the ADF to ever find them. For centuries, the

Truth lived peaceful lives in their subterranean cities, rescuing as many Topsiders as possible through the Selection and careful raids on the colonies. They stayed clear of Beta Prime; the risk was too great, but they were able to grow their numbers through converts and natural reproduction. But the entire time, they stayed hidden; safe from ADF raids and safe from discovery.

As they rushed among the trees seeking safety, the Truth were like the Selected; on the run from hostile enemies in a strange world, a place where death or survival by any means ruled. Maybe they'd find their way to another city like Inventa or Novus.

Balla jumped across a creek, her arms burning with pain.

"Gunther, I have to set you down, just for a moment."

"Mom, no! Don't let them get me!" The boy clung to her, grasping her thick hair and pulling some out, making her wince.

"It's ok, Son, we're fine. I don't think anyone is following us."

Gwenny scanned the area around them, her head darting back and forth. "I think we're ok, Mom. I don't hear anyone. I haven't seen anything move in a while."

Slowly, Balla pried Gunther from her, though he didn't move from her side. She saw the panicked look in his eyes and understood. She rubbed her eyes and held her hands over her face, trying to hold back the flow of tears threatening to burst forth.

Gunther cried softly, his wails muffled by Balla's thick hair as he buried his face against her body. She patted his head, holding him close. Gwenny snuggled into her mother's arm, Balla bringing her close, closing her eyes as she held her children tight.

When she thought of Nagi, tears surged from her eyes. *Please, please be safe, my love,* she thought over and over.

Ten

Thurl shouted; the rest of the council screamed and yelled. Nagi froze, unsure what to do.

"Everyone out, now! Preserve what you can, but I fear it's too late," Chair Thurl said. The council rushed from their seats, nearly knocking Nagi over. He steadied himself against the rush as the sirens screamed to life.

Red lights flashed along the ceilings as Truth ran from their stations in a blind panic. It was a long way down to the exit from where they were, and most had families they needed to collect.

Nagi paused, waiting for the room to clear before following. Unlike the council, he chose the stairs. It was several flights up, but it had to be faster than waiting for an overcrowded and slow elevator.

He burst through the door and started down the stairs.

Out of breath and anxious, he shoved on the door to his floor and pushed hard against the mass of Truth in the hall until he slipped through, the door slamming shut behind him.

When he finally made it to his apartment, the door was open, and his family gone.

They must've left already, he thought.

One last look around the apartment to make sure they weren't hiding anywhere, and he rejoined the panicked crowd in the hall.

Sirens blared, adding to the chaos in the hall. Babies cried, parents screamed, and the constant sound of fear overwhelmed him. The thought of his family in this mess scared him.

"Balla! Gwenny! Gunther!" he called, trying to be heard over the noise in the halls.

"Balla!" he shouted. "Gwenny...Gunther! Where are you?"

If they were there, they didn't reply. Or couldn't hear him.

Something loud slammed against Freedom. Even amid the chaos, Nagi heard it. All attention turned toward the direction of the sound. Another followed, then several more. Screams erupted. Then, a deafening boom followed by a large explosion ripped Freedom open.

About twenty meters to Nagi's left, a giant hole tore through Freedom. Truth that were there suddenly vanished in a bright ball of flame. Others fell into the gaping wound. The rush of Truth to the elevators near the center of Freedom now turned and fled the flaming center. Mothers screamed, trying to save their children before falling themselves into the destruction.

Freedom vibrated, shook, and then began listing to the side. Nagi fell to the floor and crawled near the wall to avoid being trampled. The mass of Truth pushed against him, making it difficult to stand again.

The stairwell at the end of the hall was his only way out, but it was crammed with Truth trying to escape the fiery destruction in the center of Freedom.

An apartment door stood open, and Nagi fell inside, tumbling into a table and cracking his head on the corner. "Ouch!" he said, rubbing the spot, pulling his hand back to reveal blood.

He ran to the back of the apartment to the thick glass overlooking the cavern where Freedom had crashed. There was another explosion and Freedom listed again, violently, causing the furniture in the apartment to slide against the wall. A blast of flame burst through the hall, illuminating the apartment in bright red and orange. Screams filled the hall.

Nagi scanned the window for an emergency latch. All the windows on the ship had been retro-fitted with them once Freedom found its final resting spot deep underground.

He found it and pulled, but it wouldn't open. Nagi yanked harder, his hands aching and his arms burning as he pulled and fought with the latch. The ship shifted again, and he fell, slamming against the wall.

He stood on shaky legs and kicked at the latch. Finally, after the third kick, it loosened, and he pushed hard until the window opened. It flew out and landed in the dirt below.

Nagi poked through the small window and looked for a way to climb down before Freedom shifted again.

He saw an emergency ladder on the side of the hull at the floor just below his.

There was no easy way to get to it. He looked around for a rope or anything to use to lower himself. Another explosion, and the ship listed again, knocking him over. Time was running out.

He climbed out the window, dangling from the ledge. The metal rungs built into the hull were less than a meter from his foot. Freedom vibrated, making his hands tingle. His muscles ached. He had one chance to make the rungs. If the ship shifted when he let go, he'd miss and plunge to his death.

Nagi hesitated, waiting for a sign. He closed his eyes. *Balla. Gwenny. Gunther...Eron.* He inhaled deep.

One.

Two.

Three.

Nagi let go of the window ledge. The rungs flew past as he slipped down. He reached for the first one and his hand slipped. He slid and grasped blindly at the hull, looking for anything to stop his fall. His hand clutched a thin metal bar. He clung to the metal, kicking his feet until they found something to push against.

He'd made the ladder! Adrenaline coursed through him. He looked up and realized he'd missed the top rung of the ladder by a good ten meters and had slid sideways away from it. He'd grabbed hold of another ladder at the last moment. Had he slid any farther, he'd have missed it entirely.

When he recomposed himself, Nagi climbed down. All around him, screams and weapon fire echoed in the cavern. Freedom shook violently from an unseen explosion on the other side. Truth fled from every exit, some finding their escape from windows like he did, but far too many fell to their death below.

Why? Why are they doing this? Did I cause this? How can this be my fault? Nagi cursed himself for bringing destruction to his people.

The screams filling his ears, accused him of his crime. They were like thousands of judges handing down sentence on him. He'd caused this! He'd made this happen! Death was on his hands!

He hoped his family had escaped the burning inferno. He hoped they'd made it out alive. He hoped to one day see them again.

An immense explosion boomed within the cavern, creating a blinding light. Freedom exploded from the middle, separating and falling into two pieces. A giant burst of fire like an underground sun pushed the hulls apart and sent streaks of flame in every direction. Nagi fell the last fifteen meters and landed on the hard ground. Flames shot out from Freedom, singeing his hair. He felt hot wind force its way into his lungs. Another burst, and the entire cavern went white from the heat.

Dying Truth screamed as the flames engulfed them. A sickening stench of burnt hair and charred meat mingled with the scent of fuel burning. Another fiery burst, and Nagi's world turned black.

.

Eleven

Mina successfully dodged Sar's advances for over two weeks. She sensed his anger and disappointment, but what did it matter to her? The moment she found the opportunity, she was leaving. This jerk wasn't for her. No way was she going to let anything happen between them. She'd find Eron. Somehow.

Sar's incessant nagging drained her. Even if she did like him, he would have worn her out with his constant chatter and badgering. She could care less what the stupid queen commanded; she was not going to "further the Anastasian people" with Sar. Nope. Not gonna happen.

After the customary five-day waiting period, Sar enrolled in the ADF officer's training program. As a victor of the Selection, he had a choice of several different careers. Mina urged him to try the ADF, mostly because it meant he'd be gone a lot. It also meant she could never go home again. ADF soldiers and their families were forbidden to return to their colonies. Violation of the queen's command meant death.

Mina enjoyed most days without Sar. She explored Beta Prime. Its enormity enthralled her. Every day, she learned something new; something different from the simple life she lived in Rippon. Sar was in his second week away at boot camp when Mina went out to explore the city.

She still hadn't adjusted to the cramped living conditions and massive amount of people. When she walked along the sidewalk, dwarfed by tall buildings and screeching, honking transports, she felt small and insignificant. It made her feel worthless and unnecessary, no matter what the queen said.

The first time she heard the queen speak on television, Mina was in awe. She'd never seen such a device, and when Sar turned it on, it took her a few moments to realize it wasn't someone in a box on their wall. But then, she grew disillusioned by the queen's words.

"Be prepared to take charge in the home," the queen said. "When your Selected chooses his profession, you'll be expected to tend to the home and meet his needs. It's a necessary requirement for the advancement of our people. Be courteous, be kind, make sure to compliment—" Mina shut off the message. She recoiled inside at the queen's commands. Who was she anyway?

When she was preparing to leave for Victory Point, she first learned about the queen. A couple of ADF soldiers arrived at her door two weeks into the Selection. She'd been pouting and deep in thought, hoping and praying that Eron would make it safely through the Selection. Her mother told her the chances of him escaping death were extremely slim, forcing her dark mood. When the soldiers arrived and announced she'd be going to Victory Point, her hope was once again renewed.

"You mean, I get to see Eron?" she asked. The soldiers stood quietly, waiting for her to pack a bag.

"Dear," her mother said. "Please don't get too attached. There may be other plans for you. The queen might—"

"The what?" Mina replied. She froze, a pair of pants in one hand; the other, holding open her bag. "What did you say? Who's the queen?"

"Never mind, dear. I'm sorry. I don't mean to—"

"Mean to what?"

"Ma'am, you'll need to excuse us," one of the soldiers said to Mina's mom. She nodded and silently walked out of the room.

"Mina, please hurry, we've got a schedule to keep. You must be at Victory Point in..." he paused, looking at his watch, "fourteen days. It's a long way from here."

"I'm not going! Forget it. This is stupid."

The ADF soldier sighed. "Are you sure you want to do this? I don't recommend—"

"I don't care what you recommend! I'm not going!"

"Have it your way. Boys, come in here!"

The other two ADF soldiers entered and shoved Mina's clothes in her bag. Then, one of them slipped a pair of metal bindings on her wrists.

"What the—what are you doing?" she cried.

"Mina, it's time to go," the lead soldier said. The other two pushed her through the doorway, kicking and screaming. Her mother tried to calm her, but her efforts were no use.

"Mom! Why are you letting them do this to me? What's going on? Mom!"

Her mom sobbed. "I'm so sorry, dear. It's the queen's command. I cannot stop her."

"The queen? Mom!" she said as she was forced from

the home and into a transport vehicle.

She screamed at the soldiers for nearly an hour before her voice gave out. When she was finally quiet, the soldiers informed her about the queen and what Mina's role would be in the Selection. That's when she found out that she could never be with Eron. He wasn't "biologically compatible" with her, whatever that meant. The queen monitored the Selection closely, and there were five boys left that Mina was compatible with. The odds of one of them surviving to Victory Point was great enough, so she was taken there.

She sat in stunned silence as the soldier dictated how she was supposed to live the rest of her life. The shock of it all consumed her, especially since her mother knew. She knew!

The boys were given Selection classes. How to find edible plants, how to fend off a craate attack, what to do when it rains. But the girls? Nothing of the sort! They weren't given any special instruction at all.

***

Mina was shaken from her thoughts by a loud screech. She looked up. On every screen in the city, the queen's pretty, yet stoic face appeared. Traffic seemed to slow.

Those walking on the sidewalks stopped, all glued to the nearest screen.

"My dear citizens of Beta Prime...greetings!" The queen's voice echoed. It was as if she stood a thousand meters tall and loomed over them. "Today, I come to you with information about our latest ADF measures. Through careful intelligence, we've been able to infiltrate and annihilate a hidden sanctuary of the

Forgotten, those vile creatures who remain a constant threat to us."

The queen's image cut away to a scene of a giant wrecked ship in a cavern, flames belching from its midsection. Dead Forgotten lay strewn on the ground. Mina heard gasps around her. She held a hand to her mouth in disbelief.

"We are in the process of eliminating these threats. As your queen, it is my obligation to keep you safe. Your Anastasian Defense Forces are working hard to ensure you have the lives you deserve. Be safe, and be well." The queen's image lingered a few moments more before the screens returned to normal, once again flashing advertisements and television shows.

Mina heard grumbling from those around her. "'Bout time they did something," one man said. "I don't know why we didn't do this sooner," a woman replied.

Mina shook her head. She'd never met a Forgotten. She knew about them, but didn't consider them a threat. To her, they seemed like any other animal— fine if left alone, but when you messed with them, they'd fight.

She understood that mentality; admired it, really. She wouldn't be forgotten, but maybe if she was careful, she'd be gone, away from Sar and closer to Eron. Anywhere but there.

Twelve

Eron couldn't sit. He hadn't seen his sister in years. He thought for sure he'd never see her again, but there she was, standing before him and Sarai, though thinner than he remembered.

"Eron, this is real. The queen is evil. She's wrong. Everything about the Selection, Beta Prime, the ADF—it's wrong. The Forgotten? They're so much more than you know."

Eron closed his eyes. "But what about your family? Your husband and son? I know I'm an uncle. I think..."

Samantha paused, shuffling her feet. "My husband is one of them," she said, stressing the word as if it tasted disgusting. "Do you know what the ADF is really for?"

"No, I don't. I'm still trying to figure everything out. It's not like we're schooled in this stuff in Rippon. I didn't even know this place existed!" he said, waving his arms.

"I know; I wish I could've said something to you and Timo. Have you seen him? Do you know where he is?" she asked. Her eyes brightened when she mentioned their brother.

"Sort of. I thought he was dead. When he went into the Selection..." he hesitated, the screams once again flooding his memory, "he was shot. He tried to escape. I guess he did. He became a Forgotten. He found me in the Selection and —"

"He's a Forgotten? Are you sure?" she asked, grasping his shoulders and staring deep into his eyes.

"Ouch. Yeah, why?"

"That's bad, Eron. Really bad. We've got to do something."

"What are you talking about?"

"Our people think the queen is moving to eliminate all the Forgotten who live on Anastasia. She claims they threaten her power. I don't see how, but she's doing something."

Just then, they heard a loud screech outside. The three of them ran to a nearby window as the monitors outside came alive with the queen's face. She started talking. "My dear citizens of Beta Prime...greetings!" She continued her message before the video cut away to a burning ship with dead Forgotten on the ground.

"No, no!" Eron cried. "Timo! Please don't be there! Please be somewhere else!"

"This is awful," Sarai said. She put her hand on Eron's arm, gentle and comforting. He turned to her and nodded, grasping her hand.

"She's moving quicker than we thought. We've got to do something. It might be too late, but we have to try," Samantha said.

After the queen's brief message, the screens returned to normal.

"But wait, what about your son? And your husband? What are you up to, Samantha?" Eron asked.

They moved away from the window and Samantha waved a hand at the decaying couch, gesturing for them to sit.

"My husband Colere is one of them. He's an ADF soldier; a sergeant. He leads a highly skilled team in pursuit of the Forgotten. During the Selection, he acts as a guard in Cape Rouge. You know those blind followers that ensure you go to your death? He's one of them. I've learned a lot from him, though he didn't know I was using his information to inform the CDL about his actions."

She paused, looking at her boots. "At first, I thought I loved him. He was kind, caring...all I ever wanted in a partner. When they brainwashed him into their sick military, I began to see a change. I was scared for myself and Mychael. I happened to find out about the CDL from Colere. I investigated further—I was home with Mychael a lot—and realized the messed-up situation we're all in. Colere took our son and left. I've been trying to get Mychael back since. That was two years ago. He's seven now. I miss him so much." She wiped at her eyes with the back of her hands. Her voice shook. "I will not give up until I find him. I won't stop until I end this."

Eron leaned back on the couch, a small cloud of dust puffing into the air.

"Why would being in the ADF scare you? What's the CDL? I don't follow, Samantha. I thought everything was fine. We never heard from you, so I guessed it was going well."

Samantha shook her head. "No, it wasn't going good for me. I wasn't allowed to contact you. Or Mom. Or Dad."

Eron bolted upright. "Dad! Do you know where he is?"

"I wish, but the last I heard, he was ADF, too. A

commander, or something like that. I've not seen him since I've been here. Colere talked about him, but he'd never met him; just what he heard from other soldiers."

Eron's mind reeled. There were so many things he wanted to know.

"So, Dad's ADF...Colere is ADF...why are they the bad guys?"

"Eron, did you ever know about Beta Prime before coming here? What about you..."

"Sarai," Eron said.

"What about you, Sarai? Did you know about Beta Prime?"

She shook her head.

"It's because the ADF keeps it silent. The queen commands them. They listen, they obey. There's this huge city with every amenity known, yet we were all raised in colonies that barely survived. Why is that? Why keep five colonies in the dark, struggling to live? What's so valuable about the colonies that they'd not allow their people to leave for this city? Why go after the Forgotten? If you've met Timo, you know they aren't brute savages. They're intelligent. Did you know they call themselves the Truth?"

"The what? Truth? No. I didn't even know they existed until just before the Selection," Eron said.

"You mentioned the CDL, the group you're with. Who are they?" Sarai asked.

Samantha nodded. "The Combatant de Libertie is, let's just say, opposed to ADF policies. We...do things to make a difference. We fight for the truth. That's why I need you, Eron," she said, looking at him. "I think you might be the key to unravel all of this. You've seen the destruction they're bringing on the Forgotten! Our brother could be there!"

Eron closed his eyes, a picture of Timo's black hairy face staring at him, so calm and free of fear.

"How can I do anything? I'm new here. I don't know anything. I barely know my way around the few blocks near our building. I don't know anything about the ADF or CDL, or whatever else might be out there."

Sarai placed her hand on his arm, gently squeezing.

"Eron, in a few days, you'll be instructed via the in-home monitor to choose to join the ADF or return to your colony. They make the ADF look so attractive that hardly anyone returns home. Besides, if you do go back, they'll wipe any memory of this place from your mind. Their ruthless control knows no bounds."

"Ok, so they offer me a career choice. So, what? How does that help?"

"You choose the ADF."

"But why would I do that? You just said they were evil!"

"You can help us from the inside. We've lost our latest contact. You can do this! Think of Timo. Think of all the lives you can save. You can help end this...all of it. The Selection, the queen, the forced colonies. You, Eron."

He closed his eyes. What Samantha was telling him felt wrong. How could so many people be in on such a ruse?

"How do I know the CDL isn't the evil group? How do I know you aren't secretly trying to use me for something bad?"

Samantha jumped to her feet and placed her hands

on her hips. "Are you serious? Eron, I'm your sister! I would never do anything to harm you! I've got my son to find and a brother to save, if he's still alive. The ADF is wrong, Eron; so very wrong. When the time comes, you'll make the right decision."

She paced the room before speaking again. "Please choose wisely, Eron. We need you." She walked to the window, peering through the blinds, then turned back to Eron and Sarai. "I have to go. So do you. It's not safe out here anymore. Soon, ADF patrols will be by, and they can't find us together like this. I'm already known to them. You can't be seen with me, or it screws up everything. Goodbye, Eron. I hope you'll do the right thing. We'll be watching. We'll contact you when the time is right." She nodded to Sarai, then slipped through the front door.

"But Samantha—" Eron said as he watched his sister run off into the street and vanish.

"Eron, you should at least consider her plan. She might be right," Sarai said.

Eron nodded. "Yeah, I'll think about it."

Thirteen

For three days, Balla and the children searched for the Traveling Tunnels.

"They have to be around here somewhere," Balla said. The last Truth they saw was a small group the day before. They were shaken and not too friendly, so Balla continued on with her children, unsure if the group would hold them back or not.

She thought of her husband often, hoping he'd made it out alive. The children didn't talk much, but eventually, they'd have to deal with the situation. At the moment, they were too engrossed in this unfamiliar new world.

The bright red and orange forest mesmerized the children.

"Look at that!" Gunther said, pointing to a small group of gracers soaring overhead. The small purple creatures jumped from tree to tree, gliding in the air until they landed on a branch. Their noisy chittering filled the air.

"Those are gracers," Balla said, relishing the opportunity to think about something other than the horror back at Freedom.

"Gracers? Oh yeah, I've heard of them!" Gunther replied.

"I'd hope so, or I'd think you weren't paying attention in school."

Gunther smiled at Balla. Her heart melted. He was much more confident than he had been only a few days ago. He seemed to be adjusting to their temporary situation better than Gwenny. The poor girl moped and barely said a word. She lacked the enthusiasm Gunther had for their new surroundings.

"How much farther?" Gwenny said. She lagged behind her mother and brother, moving slow as if to stall them.

"I don't know. I'm not familiar with this area," Balla said. She looked back at Gwenny, and her heart leapt in her chest.

"Gwenny! Run, now!"

Several brightly colored craates were creeping behind her daughter. They'd fanned out on either side of Gwenny, closing in on her.

"Huh? What?" Gwenny said, not looking up.

"Craates! Gwenny, hurry!" Balla cried.

Gunther screamed when he saw a craate emerge from the brush. It snarled, baring its long fangs. It moved closer to Gwenny, who had finally noticed the pack closing in on her.

"Mom!"

Gwenny ran from the craates, which bolted after her. The lead craate suddenly let out a fierce, pained howl. It tumbled forward from its momentum.

A giant blue slithering creature with fins along its back quickly circled the craate, flicking its long tongue. It opened its mouth to reveal two rows of sharp teeth, and clamped down hard on the craate's leg. It bellowed as the wurmel's fangs cut into its flesh. The craate thrashed its leg to free itself, but the wurmel's jaws were fixed tight. Bone crunched as the wurmel bit down harder, and the craate kicked with its other legs. It snapped at the wurmel, but couldn't reach it.

The other craates stopped dead in their tracks. Slowly, they began to back up, whining. The wurmel continued to attack the craate, crunching on its leg, until eventually the craate gave up the fight.

Balla gathered her children and ran. "Come on, we've got to go! The wurmel might turn on us!"

Gunther cried. "Mom, please make them go away! Please, Mom...please!"

Gwenny wiped tears from her eyes.

Balla ran, staying close to her children.

After escaping the beasts and gaining some distance from them, Balla slowed. She was winded, and Gunther had yet to stop crying out.

"Son, please be quiet. You don't want to attract more of them, do you?"

He whimpered. "But Mom, they'll try to kill us!"

"I know, Son. That's why I need you to be quiet. Please. For your sister and me."

Gunther covered his mouth, trying to stifle the cries.

"That's it, Son, calm yourself down."

"Why'd they try to do that?" Gwenny said.

"They're animals, dear, looking for an easy meal. We need to be more vigilant out here. It's not like home. It's much more dangerous."

"I miss Father," Gwenny said.

"So do I, Dear; so do I." Balla sat on a log, exhausted and hungry. They hadn't had a decent meal since they'd fled Freedom.

They hadn't found anything but a few haynuts and

berries.

Gunther clung to Balla's legs, squeezing tight as if she might leave them.

"Son, it's okay now. We're safe. Those craates and the wurmel are far away from us."

"I wanna go home," Gunther said.

Balla closed her eyes. She did, too. They'd never be able to go back. She hoped there was room for them in Inventa or Novus.

"We can't go back, Son. Home is gone now. But we'll find a new one, I promise." She stroked his thick fur, patting his head.

"But, my friends! What about them? Where are they?" he asked.

Balla hugged him tight. "I don't know, Son. All I know is I've got you two. That's all that matters now."

"And Father? What about him?" Gwenny asked. "Is he safe?"

Balla considered the questions, not wanting to upset her children.

"If I know your father, he's safe somewhere, looking for us. He's resourceful and strong. Don't worry about your father," she lied. "I'm sure he'll be back with us soon."

Her words seemed to have calmed the children...enough for now, anyway.

"We need to find shelter before night falls, then we'll find the Traveling Tunnels and decide what new home you two want to explore. I've been to Inventa; maybe we can try Novus?"

Gunther smiled. "Novus? I hear they've got a huge library! And a swimming pool. Three of them! Can we go there, Mom? Can we?" She rubbed the soft fur on his head.

"Sure, Son; we can try it."

About forty minutes later, they'd made shelter under a grantham tree, the overhanging branches with large red leaves like a roof. It was barely large enough to cover the three of them, but they made it work. Gunther nuzzled next to his mom. Gwenny lay with her back to them.

Anastasia's pink moon soon hung high in the sky as night settled, its pink glow washing the dark forest in an eerie light. In the distance, craates howled.

Soft rustling in the leaves around them made it difficult to sleep. Balla wouldn't let her eyes close for long, fearful for her children. She hadn't spent much time in the forest. She was born in Freedom, never having been part of the world of the Topsiders.

Gunther fell sound asleep in his mother's arms. Gwenny tossed and turned all night. At some point, Balla dozed, though for how long, she didn't know.

When the red sun rose above the horizon and rays of light poked through the leaves, a growing cacophony surrounded them. Waking animals chattered, running and jumping and leaping across the forest.

Gwenny sat up straight, watching her mother and brother as they slept. When Balla woke, Gunther still slept soundly at her side.

"Can we go now, Mom? I want to leave," Gwenny said. Balla nodded.

"Yeah, we should probably get going."

Fourteen

Nagi wasn't out for long. When he opened his eyes, the cavern was filled with fire and smoke. Freedom was in ruins. Men shouted, Truth screamed. A constant ringing in his ears reminded him of the explosion he barely survived.

He scrambled to his feet, swaying on shaky legs. He caught his balance and carefully stepped forward and fell to the ground. He crawled away from Freedom toward the small tunnel at the back of the cavern that was meant to be used for emergencies only.

Nagi crawled to a nearby rock, pulling himself to his feet. A dull pain rose up his legs, but he tried to ignore it. If he succumbed to the pain, he'd never get far.

When he felt steady enough, he started for the tunnel. Though wobbly, he stumbled to the back of the cavern, the tunnel in sight. There were only a few Truth exiting the disaster through it. The one-person-wide tunnel felt cramped when he entered. He tried not to think about how easily he could get stuck in the tight space. If a stampede forced its way in, they'd soon crush everyone inside and block their escape.

Several hundred meters from the cavern, the tunnel opened to one of the larger Traveling Tunnels. Injured and crying Truth lined the tunnel in both directions. Nagi took a quick look among the injured, hoping to find his family.

"Have you seen my family?" he asked a female Truth sitting with her back against the wall, her head gashed open and blood trailing down her face. She didn't reply. He asked another female who scowled back at him.

"I don't know your family. Look around you. The Topsiders have ruined everything! Our home, our lives, our families...gone!" she said, turning away from him and tending to a young male holding his arm and crying.

Everywhere he looked, the sad faces of destruction peered back at him. He felt their accusations. It was as though they all knew he was the careless one who had led the Topsiders to Freedom. Gaining their help to find his family would be impossible. He saw judgment in the faces of the injured that stared back at him, the weight of his actions too much to bear.

One last quick look around and not finding his family, Nagi left the mob of Truth in the Tunnel and went to Inventa. A small stream of Truth followed the same path, the glowing light of dirt grubbers illuminating their way.

At the next intersection, Nagi considered leaving the tunnel to travel in the forest above, but the more he thought about it, the more he was sure his family wouldn't be up there. Balla had very little experience outside the subterranean world where they live. She wouldn't expose their children to something so foreign to her. Instead of leaving the tunnels, he continued to Inventa. He'd find rest once he got there, and hopefully his family was waiting on him.

Nagi followed the small stream of Truth pushing their way forward. It took two days on foot to make it to their sister city.

The tunnel opened on a ledge overlooking a giant red and blue ship. Near the entrance at the bottom in glowing letters was the name of the ship, Inventa. The long line of Truth from the tunnels to the ship was met by a small group who directed them where to go. Nagi wasn't sure what they were doing, but the promise of rest and finding his family over-rode his curiosity.

He followed the line down a twisting path until he was ushered to the left, following a path around the ship to where another group of Truth entered names in a data pad. When it was Nagi's turn, he asked them about his family.

"Have you seen my family? Balla, my wife, and our two children, Gwenny and Gunther?"

The Truth entering names scanned his list. "No, I'm sorry, I don't see anything here, but that doesn't mean they haven't made it. Could be on the other side of Inventa. Once we get you settled, you can search for them. There will be a list of all refugees on the network that you can access in your room. I'm afraid you'll have to share, but it's the best we can do. Room 321 is where you're headed. Next, please!" he called, dismissing Nagi.

"But, my family!" he said.

"Sorry, we've got a lot to do here. Next!" the Truth called. Nagi followed those in front of him inside the ship.

He was ushered down the corridor to an elevator where he was directed to the third floor. Nagi followed the directions and opened the door to a room with three other male Truth inside.

"Umm...sorry; I must have the wrong room," Nagi said. One of the Truth, taller than Nagi with blue fur tinged with gray, shook his head.

"Nope, you're in the right place. We gotta share the rooms. They weren't quite ready for such a large crowd," he said, smiling. "Welcome home!"

The other two Truth looked to still be in shock, barely registering Nagi's presence.

"Don't worry about them much; they're lost in thought or scared...or hell, I don't know. Been like that ever since I got here. Hope you ain't like them. Could use some good conversation."

Nagi wiped his face with his hands, hoping the gesture would remove all the horrors he'd seen the past few days.

"No, I'm not like them. Hey, look, you seem like a good guy, but I can't stay here long. I gotta find my family. They should be here somewhere. I need to look for them."

"Family, huh? Shoot, I can help with that. I ain't got none myself. It'd be nice to get out of this room for a bit. Mind if I come along? Four eyes are better than two."

Nagi stood frozen for a moment, unsure he wanted help.

"Listen, I ain't gonna get in the way. I was a scout once, long ago. Don't go out much anymore. I can help find your family. At least it'll take my mind off this," he said, waving his arms around the apartment.

"A scout?" Nagi replied. The Truth nodded.

"Years ago," he said. "My name's Garwyn. Most call

me Gar, though."

Nagi considered his proposal for a moment. "Okay, Gar; sure, you can help. It would be nice to have another scout helping me look for them."

"Another? You a scout, too?"

"Yeah, just got back from the last Selection a few weeks ago. It was a tough one."

"I'll be! Glad to meet ya—" he paused with his hand out to shake Nagi's arm.

"Oh, Nagi," he said extending his hand, shaking Gar's arm.

The other two Truth in the room sat on the couch staring straight ahead, as if Nagi and Gar weren't there. Gar motioned to them with his head.

"Never could get a name outta either one o' them. Must've had some serious loss back in Freedom. Damn Topsiders."

I can't save them all, Nagi thought. Finding his family was his only concern now.

"Come on, let's see if we can't find a list of refugees somewhere," Nagi said.

The two left the room, scanning the incoming Truth for Balla and the children.

"My wife's name is Balla, and I have a daughter named Gwenny and son named Gunther. He's six and Gwenny is eight. Both kids are medium brown, and Balla is golden. She should be easy to spot; not too many of us are that color."

"Got it. If they're here, we'll find 'em; don't worry." Gar placed a hand on Nagi's shoulder and gave a gentle squeeze.

I hope you're right. They mean everything to me.

Fifteen

Days after meeting up with his sister, Eron and Sarai were alerted to an incoming message on the video screen in their apartment. It was still something Eron marveled at.

The screen lit up and the face of the queen appeared. She looked older than when Eron last saw her only weeks ago.

"Greetings, Selected! I trust you've enjoyed your stay in Beta Prime. This magnificent city has much to offer, and I hope you explore your surroundings.

"You are faced with an extraordinary decision; one that can change the course of your life. No doubt, you're overwhelmed with the magnitude of your new reality. Most Selected are. It's not every day that you find out the colony you've lived in is not the most highly advanced settlement on our planet. Anastasia has many secrets, Beta Prime being the crown jewel of our species.

"Today begins the five-day decision. You must choose to either serve in the Anastasian Defense Force or return to your home. Lest you think either decision is the easy one, there are consequences of both, most of which will be described in detail over the next couple days. Then, you'll have a day of reflection, where you'll be in isolation to contemplate your decision.

Your service to your queen in either case is a privilege only a few get to choose, so do not make a rash decision. I urge you, Selected, choose wisely. Much depends on it."

With that, the screen went blank and a dense silence filled the room. Sarai moved closer to Eron, putting an arm around him.

"What are you gonna do?" she asked.

Eron shrugged. "I don't know. I guess it depends on what info I get about the decisions."

"What about Samantha? Do you think she's right? Is the ADF evil, and the queen the evilest of them all?"

"Maybe. I don't really know. How can I? I have no information about any of this, except from what Samantha told us. Maybe she's been brainwashed, too."

"Your sister? You really think she'd want you to get hurt?"

"Didn't stop my mom, did it? Who lets their son go through an event where the likelihood of death is almost certain? The Selection is crazy! So many boys wanted to kill me, and why? So they could live. Afraid that I might be the one to kill them. That's not me. But the Selection forces us to act on our most animalistic instincts. It was awful. And my mom let them take me. She raised me to accept it. Why wouldn't my sister follow suit? Maybe she's trying to dupe me as well; make me think her cause is just and put myself on the line for what? Because it's how it is?"

He stood and went to the window overlooking the brightly lit city.

"You just said your reasons, Eron," Sarai said.

"What do you mean?" He couldn't turn to look at

her, afraid of the seriousness of her tone.

"You said the Selection was wrong; that all the schooling and teaching you had led you to an evil event. Even your mom following suit in sending you to it. You said it was wrong. The Selection is part of the queen's plans. She's the one in charge, right? If the Selection is wrong and the queen commands it, maybe she's the one that needs to be removed. I don't know why your mom did what she did. I'm sure there's a reason for it. But Samantha might be right. Maybe the ADF needs to go. You saw what they're capable of. You can be better than that. You are better than that."

Eron turned and leaned against the window, regarding Sarai as if for the first time.

"Did you know I fought the entire Selection so I could be with Mina?"

"Who's that?"

"She was at the ceremony with you. She chose the blue boy."

"We don't get to choose. Not really. When we get there, if only one of the boys we're paired with is alive, then the choice is not ours. I'm sorry to disappoint you."

She scowled, turned, and folded her arms on her chest.

"No, no; please don't take this wrong. What I'm getting at is that I'm glad you were paired with me. You've got this wonderful caring side to you. It's like you truly want the best," Eron said.

"Why wouldn't I? We're in this together. We have to be, right? I had a boy in mind when I was first brought to the Selection, but soon found out no matter if he made it or not, we weren't compatible. Something about biology. I don't really know; my heart was broken, and I didn't listen to the explanation. What I do know is we're supposed to be together, you and me. It's destiny, I guess. You're a lot nicer than I expected when I first saw you. Your face was slightly mangled, and I wasn't sure who you might turn out to be. I got lucky. We both did."

Eron regarded her, admiring her soft features.

"Timo told me I could make a difference. He swore that somehow, I could change all this. After what I've been through, the Selection and Phelan's betrayal, maybe he's right. Maybe I can do something. Samantha wants me to infiltrate the ADF and pass along information so we can find a way to end the madness. I can do that. Someone needs to end this. I'm not a bloodthirsty killer. I have no desire to see more boys die for the queen. The entire process is absurd. Then when we're done, we're forced to pair with someone we don't even know, only because we're more biologically compatible than the person we really wanted to be with? What happened to natural selection? What happened to freedom of choice?"

Eron paused, watching the expression on Sarai's face turn sour.

"I'm sorry. I don't mean to say there's anything wrong with you. You're right. We were lucky. Somehow, I feel I couldn't have been paired with a more perfect person. It's true that I wanted Mina, just like you wanted someone else, but here we are, rationally talking about working together to take down the queen and the ADF. Kinda crazy, huh?"

Sarai looked up, her eyes glistening, and smiled.

"Yeah, it is. Think we can do it? Think we can change everything?"

"If not, we're sure gonna give it one heck of a try! Are you okay with this? I mean, you are part of it now, whether you wanted to be or not."

Sarai nodded. "Yes, Eron, I am. We are in this. Together."

He stepped toward her and extended his hand. She took it, rising from her seat.

"Thanks, Sarai, that means a lot to me. I don't have many friends left in this world. There aren't too many people who believe in me anymore. Having you with me will help me get through."

He wrapped his arms around her, holding her tight. She returned the gesture, and they stood, embracing each other for quite some time.

Sixteen

Balla used what she remembered of Novus to try to lead her children to safety. Inventa was closer, but keeping her distance from the ADF was the deciding factor. Hopefully Nagi did the same; if not, they'd contact Inventa from Novus and alert him that they were there.

Not exploring much above ground in the past, Balla found navigating to be difficult. Everything was strange and worrisome. So far, her experience wasn't the most pleasant.

"I think it's this way," she said as they pushed through the forest.

"Are you sure, Mom?" Gwenny said. Her voice was cold and icy. She'd grown increasingly bitter toward Balla since they left, as if Balla was the cause of their current situation.

"No, I'm not, but it's the best I can do," Balla said with an edge to her voice that she hadn't intended.

"Sorry, Gwenny. I don't mean to be angry. It's not your fault. I'm not angry with you."

Gwenny huffed, rolling her eyes.

At about midday, they approached the edge of the forest where it opened to a large body of water.

"Wow," Gunther said. "I've never seen anything like it!"

He ran to the water's edge, soft waves gently rippling and splashing on the shore.

"Careful. You know how the water can be," Balla called out.

"Mom, that's only the rain," Gwenny said. She shot her mom a look of disgust, but Balla ignored it.

"Look at it! It's huge!" Gunther said. He stalked back and forth on the orange sand. He pulled off his sandals and pushed his toes in the sand. "Feels funny!" he said. His face lit up like a lantern. He ran and splashed his feet in the red water.

"It feels awesome!"

"Be careful! You don't know what's in—" Balla called when Gwenny's scream cut her off. Gwenny pointed to the water.

"Look out! Gunther, get out now!" Gwenny cried.

"Huh? What?" he said, looking back at Gwenny. He turned to where she pointed and screamed.

"Come on, get out of there," Balla cried. Gunther ran from the water, stumbling across the sand.

Balla and Gwenny ran to him, meeting him half-way.

"What is that?" he said, clutching his mom.

The three of them stood watching the water in awe of the giant black fin trailing behind a long, spear-like object. Then it breached the red surface, spouting water into the air. The spear-shaped object protruded from a black forehead in front of the dorsal fin. It crashed back into the water again.

"I, I don't know," Balla said.

"I think it's a mobiathan," Gwenny said, "but I thought they didn't exist. I thought they were a myth."

The mobiathan circled in the water about fifty meters away, breaching the water and splashing down again.

"Will it hurt me?" Gunther asked.

"I don't know, but I don't wanna find out," Balla said. "We'll need to find a way around this."

Gwenny watched the mobiathan as they walked along the shore several meters from the water's edge.

"Are you sure Novus is this way, Mom?" she asked.

Balla nodded. "Yeah, I think so."

"You think? You mean, you don't know?" Gwenny said, her tone accusatory.

"Dear, I've not spent much time on the surface. I don't exactly know the lay of the land. My world has been Freedom and the Traveling Tunnels. I never had a reason to be up here. Besides, the ADF has a better chance of catching us when we're above ground. Why would I have spent time up here?"

"I can't believe you have no idea where we're going! What if we never find it? What if we get caught by the ADF?"

Balla turned and grabbed Gwenny by the shoulders, leaning down to face her. "Listen, I'm doing my best. It's not like I expected to be forced from our home, seeking a new place to live. I never wanted any of this for you two, but it's what we have to deal with. I'd have hoped you'd understand our situation better and quit blaming me for it."

"Dad would know where to go. He knows things," she replied.

Balla's heart broke. She let go of Gwenny and stood.

"I miss Dad," Gunther said.

"I know dear; I do too. We'll find him."

"I doubt it," Gwenny muttered. Balla fought back the urge to yell. Screaming at Gwenny wouldn't help, but the desire to let her have it was strong.

"Let's go; we've got a long way yet," Balla said and led them along the water.

The mobiathan followed them, its long spear and black fin poking through the red surface. Occasionally, it dove down and disappeared for long stretches of time before breaking the surface and startling them.

"Why's it doing that?" Gunther asked after it had come up for air again.

"I don't know. How could it possibly know where we are?" Balla said.

Gwenny shook her head. "They've got some kind of sonar or something. I don't remember the name of it. It tracks its prey with it. It's probably waiting for us to get close to the water to snatch us and eat us."

Gunther clung to Balla. "Don't let it eat me, Mom, please!"

"Gwenny, stop scaring your brother! Gunther, it's ok, dear. It can't get us. We're out here and it's in the water. We're safe."

"Are you sure about that?" a strange voice behind them said. Balla screamed. Gunther and Gwenny jumped.

About ten meters behind them stood a man dressed in a gray uniform. An ADF uniform. An evil smile was splashed across his face.

"Safe? You animals don't deserve to be safe," the man snarled. He was alone, his hand on a gun strapped to his leg.

"Where did you come from?" Balla asked. Gwenny

and Gunther cowered behind her, Gunther's hands clinging to Balla's legs.

"Doesn't really matter, does it? I'm here, and you animals shouldn't be. You belong in the ground, and I don't mean in that decrepit transport you call a home." The soldier unholstered his gun and raised it toward them. He swung it from Gwenny to Gunther to Balla, aiming at each one.

Balla raised a hand as a shield. "There's no reason to shoot any of us." Behind her, Gunther whimpered, his fingers digging deeper into her leg.

"My orders are to eliminate any roaming Forgotten. You're not allowed to live. You savage creatures are a threat to her Highness and her resources. The queen doesn't need that kind of aggravation. Weak animals such as yourselves deserve what you get. Be stronger or die."

He pointed his gun at Balla's head.

"No, wait!" Gwenny cried. She stepped out from behind Balla.

"Please, we aren't savages. We aren't evil. I don't know what you're told about us, but it's not true. We're alive and human just like you."

"Human? Are you kidding me? Look at you! You're covered in fur! No human looks like that. Maybe if your men had been stronger you wouldn't be in this situation, but they weren't. They were weak, and because of that, you've all become animals. Whatever you are, it's not human. You may have been once, but your weakness has made you into animals, and animals have no rule in this world. We do."

Gwenny stepped closer to him.

"Don't move, or I will kill you!" he said, turning his

gun on her. Gwenny stopped, her arms raised in surrender.

"No, please, don't shoot her!" Balla cried. She moved to her daughter, wrapping Gwenny in her arms.

"Stop moving, or I'll shoot all of you right now!"

Balla sobbed as she clung to her daughter. Gunther wailed, holding tight to Balla.

"Shut that one up before I do!" the soldier said.

Balla tried to calm him as best she could. She looked up at the soldier. "Just do it," she said in a low voice. "If you won't see reason, just shoot all of us. If we're gonna die, we can at least be together when we do. As a family."

The children cried. The man raised his gun. "As you wish."

Seventeen

Mina enjoyed her time alone while Sar was training. She explored Beta Prime, even finding a museum that explained so much of Anastasia's history she hadn't known before.

Like how the planet was named for a brave colonist on the first transport. How every queen's lineage was traced to this colonist. How the planet itself affected reproduction in humans; specifically, how it caused more boys to be born than girls, leading to the necessity of the Selection. It was a way of culling the ranks and ensuring there was no population imbalance.

There was an entire wing dedicated to the Selection. A map on the wall showed the five colonies surrounding the vast Selected grounds; the treacherous, forbidden area of the planet only accessible during the brutal event.

At the far southern tip of the Selected grounds, a large mountain labeled "Victory Point" marked the end. Mina traced the long, winding road from the mountain to Beta Prime, which looked like it was on the other side of the planet. No wonder they'd not known about it back in the colony. But how did they manage to keep it a secret for so long from so many?

She stood pondering the enormous effort needed to suppress such a secret. Why keep it a secret at all? Wouldn't it make sense to let everyone know about it?

Resources couldn't have been that scarce, could they? Nothing she'd seen here in the city indicated any such thing. On the contrary, there was so much of everything in the city that it seemed gluttonous. Her colony seemed like a forgotten outpost compared to Beta Prime.

"First time here?" a female voice said, startling Mina.

"Oh! Yeah, it is. How could you tell?"

"You're not the first girl I've seen spend an obscene amount of time in this part of the museum." The woman was much older than she with long gray hair braided and fixed with a gold clip. She was lean and barely able to walk, though when she did, her long flowing robe gracefully floated behind her.

"Sorry," Mina said, "but there's so much I didn't know before. This is overwhelming."

"Always is. As it should be I guess. The queen takes great pride in her little secret. My name's Annabelle. I'm the curator of the museum. And you are?" she asked, extending her hand. Mina shook it.

"Mina, from Rippon. There," she said pointing to the colony on the map.

"Is that so? My husband was from there. Been dead for a while now. I never did get a chance to visit. I hear it was kinda dirty, as all the colonies are."

"He was? I'm sorry. This is just so much to understand."

"No apologies needed, my dear. I've been here long enough to know how the system works."

"Yeah, I guess you must," Mina replied. She wanted to ask so much more, but who was Annabelle? Mina was wary to trust.

"So, what did your Selected choose as his vocation? Are you to return to the colonies, or did he choose the nobler path of the ADF?"

Annabelle sat on a dark gray bench situated across from where the map hung, to allow visitors to ponder the Selection. She motioned for Mina to sit, but she declined.

"Sar chose the ADF. He intends on being on officer and leading squads after the Forgotten. He claims they're an abomination and must be eliminated."

"Fully committed to the queen, huh? I'll give him a pass on that. There's something to be said for loyalty, I suppose."

Mina furrowed her brows. "Yeah, he's committed, all right. Intends on doing everything she demands." Her voice was low; dark. She recalled the look in Sar's eyes when the queen spoke about reproduction. A deep anger simmered within. She wasn't going to allow her body to be used for that purpose. It was wrong. She was a person, not a means to an end.

"The queen demands many things, as is her right. Though..." Annabelle trailed off, waving her hand in the air, "she doesn't seem to grasp the truth around her. If she did, I'd imagine she would change her tactics. Brutality only inspires so much confidence."

"What do you mean by that?"

"Let me ask you something...Mina, right?"

"Yes, ma'am."

"Do you agree with the queen? Is she right? Do the Forgotten deserve to die? Should you bear children for the sake of Anastasia's future?"

Mina considered her words carefully. She didn't

know Annabelle at all. How did she know if the old woman would turn her in for treason if she spoke out of line?

"I believe whatever the queen demands must be right. She's the queen."

"Pah! That's an answer I'd expect from one of those slobbering boys who thinks just because he was lucky enough to live through the Selection, his opinion carries more weight. Mina, tell me what you think."

Mina turned, unsure if she should give her opinion. Finally, she replied, "I don't agree. It seems like a waste of resources and endangers the lives of too many people. I've not met any Forgotten, but if they were once human, how could they be all that bad? And as for procreating..." she paused, "well, I don't agree with that, either."

A chill ran through her, sure she was going to face confinement or some sort of punishment for her words. Surely, the old woman would alert the authorities and she'd be in a bunch of trouble.

"Now, that's more like it. I'll take your honesty any day over spouting words you think are expected of you. Did you know the Forgotten live in massive underground cities?"

Mina's eyes went wide. "Wait, maybe. I thought something was broadcast all over Beta Prime about a ship and some ADF attack on the Forgotten."

Annabelle dropped her head. "Yes, that's correct. Poor things had no idea an invasion was coming. They had no idea the queen ordered such an attack. Do you know how many died? Nearly all of them. There must've been a couple thousand of them in that ship.

Men, women...children. All murdered by the queen's command. Because she feels that the Forgotten are 'wrong,' or some such nonsense." Annabelle rubbed her temple, her eyes closed in deep thought.

"Do you know what they call themselves?"

"Who?" Mina replied.

"The Forgotten. They don't use that term." Annabelle's voice dropped to a whisper. "They call themselves the Truth. They claim to grasp more of our Earthly ancestors' ways and thoughts than we do, and they see the truth of our world. Gotta say they might be right."

"The Truth?" Mina said.

"Careful, girl, not too loud. That term is never to be uttered aloud where it can cause you trouble." She looked around the museum to make sure they were alone.

"I don't understand," Mina said. Annabelle nodded.

"You will in time. I've said too much. I don't suppose you're gonna tell any ADF about our little conversation, are you?"

Mina shook her head.

"No? Good. I didn't think so. I get the sense that you might be a candidate for us. Come back soon and talk sometime, all right? Just...be careful who you trust. You never know who's on your side and who isn't." She rose and glided away. Mina felt like she'd been struck on the head with a rock.

What an odd, odd woman, she thought.

Eighteen

Nagi and Gar scoured the second floor of Inventa looking for Balla and the children. Hours passed, and they'd gotten no closer to finding them than when they started.

"Have you seen my wife?" Nagi asked complete strangers. He accosted an older Truth, her hair mostly gray with streaks of black. "Please, have you seen Balla?" The woman turned away from him without a word and slipped into a room, slamming the door behind her.

"My wife! Has anyone seen my wife? Or my children?" Nagi yelled over the din of Truth trying to adjust to their new city and finding their temporary homes. Nagi recognized a few faces from Freedom.

"Have you seen my children?" he asked a male Truth.

"No. I don't even know who you are!" he replied. "I've got my own family to find." He stalked down the corridor, disappearing into the crowd.

"Nagi, I know ya want to find 'em, but stay sane. Ain't no one gonna help a raving lunatic."

"Gar, I can't lose them!"

"I know, I know. If they're here, they'll be safe. Be patient, that's all I'm sayin'."

"Patient? How's that been working out for us?" Nagi growled.

When they reached the end of the corridor, Nagi found a member of the Inventa Council near the stairwell directing refugees.

"Please, you've got to help me find my family," he said to the council member. "Are there lists somewhere of incoming Truth from Freedom?"

"Somewhere, but I don't have time to find them for you. I'm kinda busy here." He waved the line of Truth on, a look of disgust on his face. "Over this way, please," he called out. "There's more room on the floors above. Keep moving! We've got a lot of you moving in. No time to mill about. Hurry, get moving now," he said, ignoring Nagi.

Gar grasped Nagi's shoulder, turning him away from the council member. "Come on Nagi, let's try another floor." Nagi nodded and followed Gar's lead up the stairs to the third floor.

Unlike their floor, the center was wide open. Lush green fields and tall green trees sprouted from the bowels of the ship. A gently flowing brook bisected the fields with clear water. Children played while parents, wary of the mass of incoming strangers, lined the outer edge of the field to keep vigil over the innocence inside.

Nagi paused to watch the children. Blackness grew inside him like an open wound, faint at first. It felt sore and full of regret; a deeply disconnected pain. "I gotta find them," he muttered.

"Come on, this way," Gar said, pulling Nagi away from the strange fields to the living quarters ahead.

They entered every open door and knocked on the closed ones. Nagi found Tara, one of the council members of Freedom, though she remained silent.

"Council Member Tara, please; you've got to help me! Have you seen my family?" Tara sat deep in a low chair, and Nagi crouched to her eye level. "Tara, please, have you seen Balla and the children?"

Tara scowled. "I have not. This is your fault! All of this! Our home is gone because of you! You did this!" she yelled pointing at him. "This is all because of you, Scout Nagi! We'd be safe if it weren't for you!"

Gar pulled Nagi away. "Come on, she ain't gonna be much help."

Nagi stood firm. "No, she knows! She has to know!"

"All I know is you led the Topsiders to us! You exposed our home, and now many of our people are dead because of you!"

Gar forced Nagi out of the room. "We'll have better luck searching the rest of the rooms," Gar said.

Nagi reluctantly allowed Gar to direct him down the corridor.

Several hours passed, and yet they found no trace of Balla and the children.

"Gar, where are they?" Nagi asked in a weak voice. He hadn't eaten in days. Hope faded from his voice.

"We'll find 'em, I promise ya that. We scouts know how to find what seems to be hidden, and I'm positive your family don't wanna be hidden. They're out there looking for you as much as you've been looking for them. Eventually, they'll show up."

"How do you know? How can you be so sure they're alive? We lost a lot of Truth in Freedom. The dead were everywhere. What if Council Member Tara was right? What if I brought this on all of us, and by doing so, brought death to my family?" Nagi slumped to the floor, leaning against the smooth metal wall. Truth rushed through the corridor, the chaos of newcomers slowly fading from the earlier high tide of refugees.

Gar sat next to him. "Ya can't think like that. You gotta believe. Don't give up hope. Never do that, ya hear? If the Truth had done that in the beginning, we wouldn't have our cities. We wouldn't have the truth of our people. The principles we fight for, the principles we live for would mean nothing. We fight the Topsiders and recruit new members because we never gave up. You need to do the same. Keep fighting. Keep searching. Keep hope alive in ya. It's what'll get you through the day. And the next one after that."

"Yeah, sure. Hope is what drives us to the point of death. Hope makes us do things we never would otherwise." It's what made me let Eron go so we could reconcile with the Topsiders.

"That's the spirit, Nagi! Come on, maybe if we find food, we'd be in better shape than what we are now." Gar stood, extended his furry hand, and helped Nagi to his feet. The two of them found their way to a cafeteria where guards from Inventa were handing out ration tickets to those who had come from Freedom.

"Here, you're gonna need these to get anything to eat," the guard said, shoving a small booklet in the hands of Gar and Nagi. "Names, please?" he asked.

"Gar and Nagi, both from Freedom," Gar replied. The guard tapped on a small electronic pad. "Got you both here. You'll be eligible for another ration pack in five days. I suggest you keep them secured. It's not likely someone will steal them, but you never know.

Better safe than sorry." He waved them into the cafeteria and repeated his instructions to the next Truth behind them.

Gar and Nagi followed the long, winding line to the counter where they ordered their food—Gar ordering for Nagi, who seemed lost in his thoughts—and then found seats at a table in the far corner of the room.

"Nagi, come on, snap out of this. How do ya expect to find your family if all ya do is mope around? Go back to your training. Remember your lessons. Push the thought of loss behind you, and focus on your task. You are a scout, and scouts find people. It's your job. It was mine once, too. Together we ought to find them soon enough. Eat your food; build up your strength. Your family's gonna need it. They're gonna need you."

Nagi pushed his food around on his plate. "Yeah, sure, Gar. I can't shake the feeling that this is all my fault, though. Freedom. The dead. My family missing. It's because of me."

Gar opened his mouth to counter, but stopped. "Eat, Nagi. We'll search for them when we're done."

Nineteen

When the five days were up, Eron's decision was made.

Three ADF soldiers at his door looked menacingly at him as they stood behind an envoy of the queen. "So, have you decided, young Selected?" the frail old man asked.

Eron nodded. "I have. I wish to join the ADF and serve the queen, may she live and thrive." He shuddered inside at the mention of the queen, but it was protocol, and the video had been explicit about how to answer this question.

"Excellent," the old man said. "Tomorrow morning, a squad of ADF will arrive to take you to your training. You will be gone for two weeks. Miss," he said to Sarai, "you will be taken care of. You will be visited by another envoy tomorrow afternoon with options for your service, as well."

Sarai nodded. They knew what to expect from the five days of video messages leading up to this point. They'd already talked about what she would do. She would serve in the ADF medical staff.

"I trust all is well, then. You've made the right decision. The queen has need of strong soldiers like yourself. Lots of work to do. Lots of work." He turned and shuffled down the hallway, the soldiers falling close behind.

"That's that," Eron said, closing the door. "Seems we're now on our path. For good or bad."

"For good or bad," Sarai replied.

Later that day, they decided to explore more of Beta Prime to distract themselves from what was about to come, but also to get a better feel for the city. They'd been out a few times since their arrival, never going far.

"Let's see how far the city goes," Sarai said once they were on street level.

"Sure, why not!" Eron replied.

They held hands as they ventured west, going several blocks along the crowded streets. Buildings loomed overhead. Vendors on street corners sold drinks and snacks, calling out their wares.

"Goibing berry juice"

"Haynut bars! Get yer haynut bars!"

They walked past the noisy vendors and constant traffic, heading toward a part of the city where they'd never been. Buildings were smaller, trees more abundant. Gone was the constant gray and glass of the city, replaced with brighter reds and oranges.

"This feels more like home," Eron said. Despite the large houses and living quarters, the colors and plant life were closest to what was familiar.

They turned a corner and were about halfway down the block, when three scrubby-looking boys appeared from out of an alley.

"What're ya doin' out here? This is our turf. We run this," one of the boys said. He was tall and lean, and dressed in tattered clothes. The missing teeth in his mouth made him look more menacing than his voice sounded.

The other two boys, one blue, and the other minus an eye, stood on either side of him, scowling.

"I'm sorry, we didn't mean to intrude. We were just exploring, that's all," Eron said. He stepped in front of Sarai, shielding her.

"Exploring? Don't matter. You don't belong here," the tall boy said.

"We've not been here long. We aren't here to cause trouble. We'll be on our way," Eron said.

"From the Selection, huh? I bet yer gonna be one o' them high and mighty Defense Soldiers, aren't ya? Never did like those jerks. Maybe we ought to teach ya a lesson before ya decide you're too good for folks like us."

Eron shuddered. It had been weeks since he'd had to face anger like this. It felt like being in the Selection all over again.

"I don't want any trouble," Eron said, "I'd just like to leave with my girl and be on our way."

Sarai clutched his arm. Eron sensed her fear through her shaking hands.

"Your girl might need to know what a real man is like," the blue boy said. He leered at Sarai, a sick grin creeping across his face. The one-eyed boy cracked his knuckles.

Eron's anger swelled, fueling his reaction.

"You touch her," he said through gritted teeth, "and that will be the last thing you do."

"Got some balls on ya, eh?" the tall boy said. The other two chuckled.

"Don't think about it, any of you. We want to be on our way, that's all. No need for violence." Eron's knuckles turned white as he held his fists at his side. His breathing was deep and calm.

"What do ya think yer gonna do to the three of us? You can't win. You're too weak. I can see it all over your face. You ain't made for this." The tall boy looked to Eron then to Sarai. "She sure is a pretty thing. Too good for you. Boys!" he yelled, and his two companions lunged at Eron.

Eron pushed Sarai back. A little too hard, he realized, after she fell to the ground. At least she was out of the way.

Eron dodged the blue boy, but the one-eyed boy punched him in the stomach, doubling him over. Eron stumbled, trying to regain his footing. The blue boy kneed him in the face. Blood sprayed from his mouth, and a tooth went flying. Sarai screamed.

"Ha ha ha ha! What are ya gonna do now, boy? My friends already made ya lose a tooth!" the tall boy said. Eron's vision blurred. No! They can't win. They can't have their way.

Eron rushed the nearest blurry figure, slamming him to the ground. He kicked and punched at the body beneath him. The boy cried out in pain, then one of the others kicked Eron's leg, buckling it and dropping him to the ground, writhing in agony.

"Get off him! Let him go!" Sarai cried.

"He's gotta learn his lesson," the blue boy said.

Eron twisted on the ground, rolling away from his attacker. The tall boy blocked his escape. "Where do ya think you're going? We ain't done yet." He kicked at Eron, who dodged the blow, then rolled into the boy's plant leg, crushing it.

The boy screamed in pain. Eron heard a crunch as he pushed harder, hoping to end the madness.

One-Eye punched Eron in the back, the loud thud of his immense fist connecting accompanied by the sharp pain radiating from the blow. He punched Eron several times, aiming for his kidneys and forcing him to relent his attack on the tall boy.

Sarai screamed louder. Eron turned, and Blue Boy held her by the throat. "If you want to save her, you better back off!"

Eron's anger burned. He'd not let these idiots hurt Sarai. She was innocent. She did nothing to deserve this. He stood on shaky legs.

"Let her go. This is between us!"

Suddenly, a transport screeched around the corner. It was an ADF patrol vehicle.

"Damn, get out of here!" Blue Boy said. He tossed Sarai to the ground and ran. One-Eye followed.

They weren't fast enough. The ADF patrol cut them off. Soldiers leapt out of the vehicle, weapons trained on the boys.

"Halt! You know the penalty for assault!" one of the soldiers called out. The boys ran.

"Fire!" the soldier said, and his two companions let loose a volley of gunfire that dropped both boys to the ground, dead.

Two of the soldiers checked on the boys while the lead soldier approached Eron and Sarai.

"Are you two all right? Did they hurt you?"

Eron smiled, his bloody mouth exposing the missing tooth.

"Not too bad," Eron said, "but I might need to get this fixed."

"Don't worry, we've got you. My team can take you back for med care. You gotta be careful out here. We'll need you healthy if you're gonna serve in the ADF."

"How'd you know—" Eron started, and the soldier raised a hand.

"We look after our own. Always have. Here, let me get you outta here." He extended a hand and lifted Eron off the ground. He helped Sarai up and attended to the tall boy, still writhing in pain on the ground.

"As for you," he said to the boy, "you're gonna spend a nice long time in a cell. Heck, we might even let you join those dirty Forgotten! I hear they're always looking for recruits." He kicked the boy in the side before securing his hands with restraints.

Twenty

The ADF soldier stood, gun drawn, ready to shoot the family. Balla closed her eyes. Nagi, I'm so sorry. This isn't your fault. None of this is. Please know that.

Gunther bolted from Balla's grasp, Gwenny following. "No!" Balla cried.

The soldier pointed first at Gunther, then at Gwenny, but they were too fast, and each grabbed a leg, forcing his shot in the air. Balla rushed him and the three of them wrestled him to the ground. He struggled, Balla feeling his strength as he began to push upwards.

"Come on, keep him down. Don't let him shoot!" Balla cried. Gwenny beat on the soldier's hand, trying to pry the weapon from his grasp. Balla pushed down with all her weight, but it wasn't enough. He rose higher off the ground, Balla perched on top. Gwenny's punches did nothing, so she bit his arm just below the wrist.

"Ouch! Get off me, you freaks!" the soldier cried.

He dropped his gun.

"Don't move, or I'll shoot you," Gunther said. He stood to the side, grasping the gun with both hands and aiming at the soldier's face. When he noticed the boy, the soldier ceased his struggle.

"Come on now, kid, put the gun down. No need to shoot me. We're all friends here, right? Just having a little fun, that's all."

"No! You were gonna kill my mom! And my sister. And probably, me. You killed my friends. You burned our home!" Gunther's little body trembled.

"I was only following orders, kid. It's what soldiers do. If the queen commands it, we obey. No questions asked. Do you under—" A blast from the gun silenced the soldier. Gunther's aim was true. The bullet went through the soldier's eye and out the back of his head. Blood pooled beneath him.

Balla cried out. "Gunther! What did you do? You killed him!"

Gwenny screamed. "I can't believe you did that!" she scolded.

Gunther let the gun drop to the ground. "He was gonna kill us, Mom," he said in a quiet voice. "He already killed our friends, and maybe Father. The ADF is bad, Mom. They hurt others."

Balla moved away from the corpse and hugged Gunther. "Oh, Son, this is terrible. Everything we're going through. I'm so sorry it's come to this." Gunther clung to her, sobbing. Gwenny curled into a ball, rocking back and forth, her arms covering her head.

"We can't be like them. We're better than the Topsiders. They kill, but we need to be stronger than that. They don't know our truth. They don't understand who we are. We're better. We're not animals. We're more human than they are."

In between sobs, Gunther asked Balla, "Am I bad person, Mother? For killing him?"

"It isn't the Truth way. It was done in anger. You are not a bad person, Son; just an angry one. Unfortunately, we lost a life today. All life is precious."

"They didn't think that when they invaded our home and killed the Truth!" Gwenny cried out from within her cocoon.

"I know, Gwenny, but we have to hold onto our humanity, or we lose it, like they have. Maybe this is the start of something new. Maybe we can try and collaborate with the Topsiders if they can see things from our perspective. Their queens have led them down a dark path for far too long."

The children went quiet. Balla sighed. Too much death and too much ignorance. It had to stop. She had to get her family to safety. Maybe the Truth could figure out a way to change things. There had to be a way. Killing each other was not the answer.

Balla rose and collected rocks of various sizes and placed them around the soldier's body. Soon her children followed her lead, gathering rocks and covering the body. It took several hours, but they found enough rocks to cover the soldier.

Balla stood at his feet, looking down on the red mounds beneath her. "We don't know his name, we don't know his family, and we don't know his thoughts, but we do know he was a loyal soldier. He was tenacious in his pursuit and never gave up the search. Though he was the enemy, may we learn from his spirit, and may his death not be in vain." Balla closed her eyes for a moment, then turned from the body. "Let's go, children, we still have a long way to go."

Gunther reached for the gun. "No, Son," Balla said. Balla tucked it into the cinch around her tunic and they left.

Within a few hours, the red sun began dipping toward the horizon. "We need to find shelter for the night," Balla said, breaking the silence that hung over them. The children were unusually quiet.

They continued to follow the large lake, keeping it to their left as they followed the shoreline. Most of the inland areas were large, grassy plains with red and orange tufts waving in the breeze.

"How about there?" Balla said, pointing. In the distance, it looked like a stand of trees, if not the edge of a forest. The children didn't reply. "Sounds good. We'll go there," Balla said, more to herself than the children.

It took half an hour to reach the trees. As they grew closer, Balla noted it was indeed the beginning of a forest. Trees in shades of orange and red with a little yellow splashed in stretched as far as she could see. "This ought to do. Let's stay close to the water and hide in the trees. It should give us good shelter for the night."

She found a large garnia tree with oversized leaves that protruded from the massive trunk. "There," she said pointing to the tree. "That will do just fine, don't you think?"

"Yeah, sure, whatever," Gwenny said.

"Oh, she speaks! You do have a voice!"

Gunther stifled a giggle.

"And the boy, too! There is life in there, after all!" Balla said, smiling. She hoped her chiding would break the tension and bring back her children. The seriousness brought on by their situation was too much to handle. They were children! They shouldn't have to deal with something like this.

They gathered large sticks to build a wall against the evening winds. The tree's large fronds made an excellent roof. If it rained, they should stay dry.

Not long after completing their structure, they lay down to rest. Gunther's stomached grumbled.

"Mother, I'm hungry," he said.

"I know, Son. We'll find something in the morning. We'll need our strength to continue. Now, close your eyes and try to sleep."

The sound of the lake lapping at the shore was calming. It pushed all the horrible events of the past few days out of Balla's mind as she focused on the insular sound, that soothing rhythm of waves on the shore.

Twenty-One

Mina continued to visit Annabelle at the museum, each time both shared a little bit more about themselves.

On her third visit, Mina decided to test the old woman's honesty.

"Annabelle," she started. They sat on the familiar gray bench in front of the map of the Selected grounds. "Why did you choose to speak to me? Do you talk with every young girl that stops in here? If so, you're taking a huge risk. How do you know I won't turn you in?"

Annabelle grinned. "You...turn me in? Not likely, my dear. I know things...many things about many people. Do you know who Samantha is?"

Mina shook her head. "No, I don't think so."

"Come on, girl, think. Do you remember anyone named Samantha?"

Mina sat quietly, the sound of footsteps echoing in the museum's halls.

"Well, maybe. I think a good friend of mine had a sister named Samantha, but that's all."

"A good friend? Mina, if we're gonna be friends, you can't lie to me. I know your love for Eron, and that his feelings for you are just as strong."

"How did—"

"I told you, girl, I know many things and many people. His sister's name is Samantha, and she's who

I'm referring to."

"I thought she was married with children and living on some outpost on the far side of Anastasia? At least that's what Eron always said." Mina cocked her head to the side, regarding Annabelle. She still didn't know if she should trust the old woman or fear for her life. She'd already said too much to Annabelle; enough to get her in deep trouble with the queen and the ADF. The queen, that manipulative...

"Yes and no. She did get married to a Selected, much like you're to do. However, things are a bit different for her. She's part of—"

Footsteps grew louder. It sounded like several people were approaching.

"Annabelle?" a male voice called out. Mina and Annabelle turned, and behind them stood four ADF soldiers, their sidearms holstered on their thighs.

"Yes, can I help you? There's an ADF display in the south wing. If you turn down that corridor and take a left, you'll find it—"

"We're not here for your false histories. What are you doing with this girl?" one of the soldiers said. The gold ropes looping around his arm indicated his status above the others.

"Young Mina and I were just chatting about the Selection and admiring the wisdom of the queen. Is that against the law?" She crossed her arms and stared intently at the squad leader.

"We've had reports of insurgent ideas coming from you to the newcomers. What do you have to say to that?"

"I don't know what you're talking about. I'm a loyalist. I side with the queen; may she rule in peace and grace."

The soldiers echoed her words, saying, "Rule in peace and grace."

"I don't buy it, old woman," the squad leader said. He paused, narrowing his eyes as if to bore a hole through her skull. Mina looked down, uncomfortable with their exchange.

"What evidence do you have to accuse me like this?" Annabelle said. Her voice grew stronger, heated. Mina saw anger in her eyes. It was as if her own mother was scolding her for forgetting to clean her room. She felt bad for the soldiers, but not bad enough to contradict Annabelle.

The squad leader grinned. "We will have our evidence soon enough. When we do, I'll arrest you myself. It'll be a pleasure to remove an insurgent like yourself."

"I told you already, I'm loyal."

"Lies only make it worse. You, girl," he said to Mina. Her head shot up. "Be wary of what this woman tells you. She'll fill your head with lies, and then you'll be in as much trouble as she's about to be in." Mina said nothing. Her voice was caught in her throat. *In trouble?* She didn't want the ADF coming for her. She wanted free of Sar, but openly opposing the queen and the ADF? That wasn't her desire. Eron was. She had to get back to him, but would Annabelle's connection to his sister help?

"You've been warned," the squad leader said. He snapped his fingers and the rest of the soldiers followed him out of the museum, the echo of their boots stomping on the hard floor reverberating throughout.

Annabelle waved a hand, dismissing them. "Idiots. All of them. They're so blinded by the queen, they don't know the truth from a hole in the ground."

"I-I've got to go," Mina said.

"What's the hurry?"

"I need to get back home. I've got things to do. Sorry, I can't stay much longer. You've been so helpful."

Annabelle grinned. "You gonna let those fools scare you off? I'd be more cautious if I were you. That boy of yours...Sar, is it? He'll turn on you in a heartbeat. He'll choose the ADF over you every time. It's demanded of them."

Mina didn't reply. She scurried out of the museum into the fresh air. She leaned against the building, clutching her chest and heaving. What did that old woman try to do to her? Who did she think she was? Why couldn't she find Eron and get back to him? Why was she stuck with that idiot Sar? She shook her head. *Doesn't matter. It's not my decision anyway.*

She left the museum, half paying attention to the people around her.

When Mina entered the door to her apartment building, she was more confused than ever. What did those soldiers intend to do to Annabelle? Because she was talking to the old woman, was she implicated in something as well? Would the ADF come looking for her? What kind of trouble was she in? What about Eron? Where was he? How could she be free of Sar, no matter what the queen demanded, and be with her true love? Or was she destined for something else?

She wanted answers, but only had more questions. Her head hurt.

"Good evening, Miss," the bellboy said, nodding and pushing the elevator button for her.

She smiled. "Thank you."

As she stepped inside, the bellboy reached in, pushed the fifth-floor button and whispered, "The ADF came looking for you. I think you're okay. Be careful. We can help."

Mina looked at him with shock. His stoic face revealed nothing.

"Excuse me? What did you say?" she asked.

He smiled. "Welcome back, Miss, I hope all is well." The doors closed, and she was more confused than before.

"What was that? Am I hearing things?" she said aloud.

Nothing seemed right anymore. It was as if she were in the middle of a game, yet had no idea what it was or how to play. Her cloudy mind couldn't piece anything together.

She entered her apartment and plopped down on the white couch. Her head pounded. She couldn't make sense of Annabelle, and now...the bellboy? What next, the queen? She'd need to figure out her next moves before they were decided for her. It felt too much like others were trying to direct her fate.

Twenty-Two

Long into the evening, Nagi and Gar searched all the decks of Inventa, but found no sign of Balla and the children anywhere. Nagi grew quieter as the search dragged on. Gar continued to engage him, though Nagi refused to bite at the distraction. He was too worried, too concerned; too scared it was all his fault. If his family was dead, he'd never forgive himself.

"Let's call off the search for the night," Gar said.

"No! I've got to find them! If you want to leave, fine. I'm not stopping. I can't stop!" Nagi replied.

"Sorry, Nagi. I don't mean to sound like I'm giving up. I'm not. Here, hold on." Gar approached a nearby Inventa guard.

"My friend here has lost his family from Freedom. The names are Balla, Gwenny, and..." he paused, looking to Nagi.

"Gunther. My son's name is Gunther," he said in a weak voice.

"Balla, Gwenny, and Gunther. Have they checked in yet?"

The guard tapped his small electronic pad. "No, not yet. Refugees keep pouring in. I'm sure they're here somewhere. If not, they'll be here soon."

"Can you alert us when they do? We're in room 321. They'll be looking for my friend Nagi, here. I'd sure appreciate any help," Gar said.

"I understand. I'll put the request in. There's a lot of them, so please be patient as we try to sort through this mess. I fear this might be the beginning of something bad."

"Thank you fer your kindness and opening yer home to us," Gar said. He smiled at the guard, and nodded slightly as he walked away, pulling Nagi with him.

"See? They'll alert us when they check in."

Nagi grunted and let Gar lead him back to their room. Their door was open, and the other two Truth from earlier were gone.

"Can't say I'm gonna miss those two. The weird silent types always git under my skin," Gar said. He searched the apartment, but there was no sign of either Truth. "Looks like we got some space all to ourselves. Not bad! Why don't you rest, and we'll resume in the morning? Besides, if they show, we'll know it when they call our room."

Nagi followed Gar's lead to one of the bedrooms and plopped down on the bed. His thoughts fell to his family and what he'd done to put them all at risk. It took some time, but eventually he fell asleep.

The sound of a screeching alarm startled Nagi awake. He jumped from the bed, almost falling as he ran to the living room area where Gar met him.

"What's that?" Nagi said. Gar pointed to the communications panel on the wall.

"Maybe they found something?" Gar said.

Nagi pushed the small red button. "Hello?" he said, his heart racing.

"Scout Nagi from Freedom?" a harsh female voice

called back.

"Yes, that's me."

"This is Council Member Thera from Inventa. You're needed in the Council chambers immediately."

Nagi closed his eyes and placed a hand on the wall. "Have you found my family?" Being called to the Council chambers was never in his favor. This had to be bad news.

"To the chambers immediately. Council Chair Deelia requests your presence. It's an urgent matter." The speaker in the panel went silent.

Gar grasped his shoulder. "Gotta be good news, right?"

"Not in my experience." Nagi's heart dropped. His family must be dead. Why else would they call him to the Council chambers?

Nagi and Gar rode the cramped elevator to the top floor where the Council chambers were housed; Inventa's former control room. The outer area was a flurry of activity as engineers addressed the needs of a swelling population.

"Scout Nagi?" a short reddish-colored female Truth asked when the elevator doors closed.

"Yes?" Nagi said.

"Follow me, please." She turned and walked quickly away. Nagi had to catch up before she turned a corner. Gar followed.

The red Truth stopped just outside a set of heavy double doors. "In here, please. Alone," she said, nodding toward Gar.

"I'll be right here, Nagi. I'm not leaving without ya."

Nagi paused, then opened the doors to the Council chambers.

The interior was much like Freedom. Truth of assorted colors sat around a large table in the center of the room. At the far end was a frail looking female Truth. Her fur was mostly gray with streaks of deep brown. Next to her was Council Member Tara from Freedom. Her face was stoic, and she stared straight ahead, ignoring Nagi.

"Scout Nagi," the frail female Truth at the end of the table said. "I'm Chair Deelia. It has come to my attention that you might know something about the cause of this commotion."

Nagi scowled.

She continued. "We are beyond capacity. Our life support will not be able to handle this population for very long. We've kept this ship functional for well over two hundred years, as have the Councils on Novus and your former home, Freedom. We've been careful about how many Truth we house in our cities for good reason. We can't out-strip our resources, or we're forced to Anastasia's surface. This catastrophe has indeed pushed us to the limits. I fear it is only a matter of time before we, too, must face certain extreme measures."

A murmur grew from the assembled Council. The members leaned toward one another, whispering and pointing at Nagi.

"Silence!" Deelia said. The Council hushed at her command.

"What can you tell us about this mess?" she asked Nagi. He took a deep breath, composing himself.

"I inadvertently led the Topsiders to Freedom after the last Selection." His words echoed in the room.

Several Council members gasped. Tara nodded her agreement.

"I wasn't careful on my return. I focused too much on my brother to realize the mistakes I had made when I left the Selected grounds. The Topsiders must have followed me through the Traveling Tunnels without my knowledge, and brought their forces to us in Freedom."

One of the council members slammed his large fist on the table. "If you brought them to Freedom through the Tunnels, what's to stop them from finding us? This is a disaster! The Topsiders will surely come after us, too!" Other council members voiced their agreement.

"He's right! We're doomed!" a taller brown female Truth said.

"We must prepare for evacuation!" a small male Truth said.

"Silence!" Deelia said to her Council, scanning the table.

"What you've done is a terrible problem for all," Deelia said. "We're now faced with an unprecedented situation. For centuries, we've lived apart from the Topsiders, preserving the knowledge of our people, of the humans that bravely left Earth to colonize this planet. If we're wiped out, our history is gone with us, something the reigning queen has been planning for some time. She's determined to eradicate us. We represent the only counter to her power and the only force able to undermine her hold on the planet. I fear your actions have forced our hand at last."

Nagi cocked his head to the side, unsure of Chair Deelia's meaning.

"But, Chair, we will be exposing ourselves to the

Topsiders. We'll give them everything they want and every opportunity to destroy us like the queen wants!" Council Member Tara said. "He's the cause of this problem! He should be banished!" she said, pointing at Nagi. He hung his head, knowing she was right.

"What happened to Freedom was inevitable, unless we could have done something sooner. The Councils have dragged their feet for far too long. Scout Nagi was not the reason we're in this mess; we are. We should have acted sooner."

"No! This is wrong! He should be banished for this! He's the problem!" Tara screamed. She jumped from her seat, slamming her fists on the table. "He did this!" she screamed, pointing at Nagi. "He's at fault for Freedom's destruction!"

"Sit down, or leave my Council!" Deelia said. Though her frame was small and weak, her voice carried unmistakable authority. Tara looked around at the seated Council members, then sat.

"Scout Nagi, though the Topsiders followed you to Freedom, it was bound to happen. We can't keep our heads down any longer and hope to get by. Conflict with the Topsiders was inevitable. I find no fault in your actions. You are not the reason we're in this mess."

Tara fidgeted in her seat. Deelia glared at her.

"Regardless of what others may charge you with, I find you innocent in this matter. It is the Truth as a people who are guilty; guilty of inaction, which led to this disaster. I fear conflict with the Topsiders has just begun."

Deelia rose from her seat, the rest of the Council

rising with her in respect. She exited through a door at the back of the room with the aid of a Truth on each arm. The Council dispersed, Tara scowling at Nagi as she left.

Nagi stood at the end of the table in the empty room, trying to process what he'd just heard.

Had war just begun?

Twenty-Three

The morning after Eron and Sarai were assaulted, a squad of three ADF soldiers arrived at their apartment.

Sarai hugged Eron before he left, holding tight for longer than Eron was expecting. She wasn't Mina, but she seemed to genuinely care for him.

"Be safe, Eron. I'll miss you," she said. He broke the embrace and looked into her wonderful eyes, glistening with tears.

"Hey, it'll be okay, I promise. I'll be back. We'll be together again. I swear. It's part of my job now." He hesitated, then kissed her on the forehead. Her skin was warm beneath his lips.

"We need to get moving, Recruit; we've got to get your tooth fixed before training begins," one of the soldiers said. Eron gave Sarai one last hug and left, leaving her in silence.

The soldiers escorted him to their transport parked in the street. Siren blaring, they cruised along, forcing other vehicles out of the way. Eron watched the city fly by, buildings growing smaller as they left the city center.

He'd never imagined himself as a soldier. His dream was to be an engineer; to build things, to create wonderful buildings and monuments. For a moment, he wondered if the ADF had such a career path, and if so, how he'd be able to enter it. Then, it dawned on him.

He wasn't there for a career. He was traveling a path toward danger, much worse than the Selection. At least in the Selection, he knew who his enemies were...well, except for Phelan. He never expected that. But here, with the ADF and CDL both vying for his assistance, it was difficult to know who to trust. He chose to side with Samantha and the CDL, mostly because she was his sister and they both felt the Selection was wrong. So very wrong. How many boys were killed for the queen? It was too much to consider. He was now able to do something. He'd promised Timo he would. He understood it at Victory Point. He could change things; he just didn't know how. He would soon find out what he was capable of.

The transport stopped at a barricaded gate. A short white rock wall stretched right and left, a tall fence with razor-sharp barbed wire along the top behind it. Inside the fence, a large compound of white buildings spread out before him. Soldiers in gray athletic uniforms jogged along the fence, their drill sergeant riding on a small two-wheeled transport and yelling at them. A cloud of red dust followed.

Out here, far from the city, the landscape was barren. There were very few trees, mostly military buildings, and lots and lots of dust. It felt very much like home to Eron. The buildings resembled those in the colony.

They entered, the transport taking a hard left past the guard station.

"Gotta get you to Med before we drop you off with your DS," the driver called over his shoulder.

The hard-packed streets were laid out in the same familiar grid pattern as Rippon. A few blocks down from the guard station, the transport came to a stop. "We're here. Smitty's gonna take you in. Shouldn't be long."

The soldier in the back turned to Eron. "Come on, this way."

When he entered the Med station, a nurse escorted him to the back. "Doctor will be in shortly," he said, then left Eron and the soldier.

Soon after, a blue-skinned woman wearing a long white lab coat entered the room. "Hello. I'm Doctor Lithe Sharine. I hear you've got a tooth missing?" She extended her hand, Eron shaking it.

"Yep, right here," he said, pointing to his mouth.

"It's *yes, ma'am*," the soldier said, striking Eron on the head.

"Ouch! What the heck!" he said, rubbing the spot.

"You're ADF now. You say *yes, sir; no, sir;* or *yes, ma'am; no, ma'am.* Got it? You aren't civilian anymore. Whatever they taught you in Rippon means little here."

Eron glared at him.

Doctor Sharine broke the tension. "So, how'd this happen? Fall down?"

"No. I mean...No, ma'am," he said as the ADF soldier raised a hand. "I was in a fight. Three boys attacked me."

"I see. Well, you'd better pay better attention during your training. I've seen way worse injuries come from that."

"Yes, ma'am, will do."

She smiled at him. "Quick learner. That'll go far. I'll

be right back."

It didn't take long for her to return. She carried a tray of dental instruments and a porcelain tooth inside a sealed plastic bag. It took over an hour, but she repaired the missing tooth.

"That should do it. Be careful eating anything tough for a while. If you've got any further complications, come back and see me. I wish you the best." She shook his hand again and left.

"Come on, Recruit, you've got somewhere to be," Smitty said. He opened the door and gestured to Eron.

A few minutes later, the transport stopped at a large building with a curved roof. "This is your stop, kid. Time to get to work," the driver said. Smitty exited and held the door for Eron.

"This way. Your life is about to change."

Inside the cavernous room, there were two rows of bunks separated by a center aisle. "Your new home," Smitty said.

There was a man at the far end of the empty room. "You better get yourself in line, boy, now!" the man called. Eron looked at Smitty.

"I'd do as he says, kid; he's your instructor. Don't wanna end up scrubbing toilets, or something worse."

"This is where I'm supposed to be?" Eron asked. He wasn't quite sure what to expect.

The man at the far end called out again. "I said, git yourself down here now!" His angry tone caught Eron's attention. Smitty nodded.

As Eron started toward him, Smitty called out, "I'd run if I were you. He doesn't like to be kept waiting."

Eron looked back to Smitty, then to the man at the

end of the room. He jogged, slow at first. "Damn, boy, can't you go any faster than that? Looks like you've got some learning to do," the man bellowed. Eron ran faster, wincing. His tooth throbbed. For a moment, he wondered if it would fall out, though something told him he'd just have to deal with it if it did. This man obviously wouldn't care.

When Eron approached the man, he was stunned by his appearance. His short gray hair spoke of years of experience. Older men were hardly known in the colonies. There were only a few, which made them a rarity.

Eron's eyes grew large.

"What? Haven't you seen an old man before?" he asked. Eron shook his head.

"Not many," he said.

"Not many...what?" he replied.

"Not many old men," Eron said.

"No, Recruit, that's not what I mean. Not many, sir," he said, drawing out the last word.

Eron winced. He'd already been cuffed once for not recognizing his superiors.

"Not many, sir," Eron said, a weak attempt at following protocol.

"Better. Damn recruits get more disrespectful every time. My name's Sergeant Ahimo. I'm the one charged with making you an effective ADF soldier. From the looks of it, I've got a lot of work to do."

Eron stepped back. "Sergeant...Ahimo?" he said, almost afraid to say the words.

"Dad?"

Twenty-Four

The next morning as Anastasia's sun rose bright red and warm, Balla and the children left their camp, walking along the shoreline of the lake. The forest ran thick to their right, animal sounds echoing through the trees.

"You hear that? Sounds like a vulbore," Gunther said. "And that one? That's gotta be a braythin. It's gotta be!"

Balla smiled. At least her son had found excitement in their ordeal. If only Gwenny could do the same, the trip wouldn't be as bad. She understood why her daughter was upset; why she'd be angry, but it didn't help Balla cope with her any better.

"Gwenny, can you pick out which sound belongs to which animal?" Balla asked.

"I bet ya can't! I know better than you!" Gunther said. He grinned, mischievous.

"No, and I don't care," Gwenny said. "Can you just stop? Please. It's stupid. We're stuck roaming around like animals. I want my home back. I want my room back."

Balla sighed. "I know, dear. We all do, but it's not going to happen. We must adapt. It's what we Truth do best. How else have we have been able to survive underground for centuries?"

"I hate this. I hate that we had to leave. If Dad was

here, he'd get us out of this. He'd know what to do!"

Balla had no answer. Gwenny was right. Nagi would have probably known exactly where to go and what to do. It was his job to know those things. Scouts spent much of their time among the Topsiders, studying and observing. They knew the lay of the land better than anyone.

Gwenny stalked ahead of them.

"Don't go too far ahead, dear," Balla called out. Gwenny turned and raised her hands as if to ask, What? and kept going.

"She'll be okay, Mother," Gunther said.

"Yeah, she will. So, what other sounds can you hear?"

Gunther rattled off names that Balla didn't know. She wasn't one for the outdoors, though she was trying her best to enjoy their situation. Constant vigilance took its toll on her mind, as well as her worry about Nagi.

Would she ever see him again? She hoped so, but she began to mentally prepare for the opposite. It's not like she hadn't had the practice.

For weeks after Mabuz's funeral, she'd find herself talking to him, only to be met with silence. Each quiet moment without him gnawed at her. It was like picking at a wound as it began to scab over, exposing herself to the pain once again. In time, and with Nagi's company, she grew to accept his loss. Sort of. She still felt it at times, but the once-sharp pain was now a dull remembrance. In time, if Nagi suffered a similar fate, she'd learn to dull the loss again.

"Mom, look!" Gunther said, pointing ahead and

breaking Balla from her thoughts.

Gwenny stood at the shore, hands on her hips, staring at the red water.

The lake filled the horizon to their left as far as they could see. Directly in front of them, a river emptied into the lake, winding off to the right until it curved and disappeared into the forest.

"I don't know how we can cross," Gwenny said, staring at the river. It moved swiftly into the lake, swirling and cascading down the rocks.

"I mean, we could try, but it's fast and pretty wide. I don't know how deep it gets, either," Gwenny said.

Balla often forgot her daughter was only eight. She acted so much older; she had been through a lot for her young age.

"Do you see any rocks we can step on?" Balla asked. She and Gunther approached Gwenny and scanned the river. Balla looked into the river. There was nowhere to cross; no fallen trees no rocks to jump to.

"I guess we go that way," Balla said pointing to the river's edge. "There's gotta be a way to cross down there, right?"

Gwenny shook her head. "I don't like this at all," she muttered.

"Come on, children, this way. Let's cover some distance before it gets dark."

They continued on and saw the river widen at the bend where it disappeared into the forest.

"No way we're gonna find a place to cross. There's no end!" Gwenny said.

Balla wanted to scold her for being negative, but she was thinking the same thing herself.

"I think you might be right, Gwenny. So, now

what?" she asked, more to herself than to the children.

"Cross it!" Gunther said, his enthusiastic spirit crushing the dark mood.

Balla stepped closer to the river's edge. "Actually, Gunther, you might be onto something. It doesn't look too deep...maybe waist high? I think we might have a chance."

"I'm not going in there," Gwenny said, her hands on her hips. "I'm not gonna get soaked."

"Yes, dear, you are. It's our only way across. We can dry off on the other side."

"I don't like this. Not one bit," Gwenny said.

"Come on, let's go." Balla shooed them into the water, Gwenny moving slow. Gunther was already ankle deep before Balla could stop him.

"Hey, hold on there. Stay close to me. I don't want you drifting away!" She grabbed his hand and reached for Gwenny with the other. Gwenny refused to grab hold. "Gwenny, hold my hand. Stop sulking. No one wanted this, but we must deal with it the best we can. Now..." she wiggled her fingers, inviting Gwenny to take her hand, which she eventually did, but not without rolling her eyes and huffing several times.

Balla led them slowly into the river, carefully finding her footing.

"Watch out. It's slick over here," she said as she caught herself after slipping on a rock.

"Hey, what's that?" Gunther asked. "Something touched me!"

"Probably some shrimp, seeing if you're something tasty. They won't eat you. Well, not too much of you,"

Balla said, winking at him.

"What?" he cried out.

"I'm kidding, Son; they're harmless. Now, come on. Focus. We're almost halfway there."

Balla fought the current. Several times she paused, trying to find a sturdy rock to step on so the rushing river didn't drag her and the children under.

"Whoa," Gwenny said, slipping. Balla held her hand tight, pulling her up until she found her footing. Balla's arm ached from the exertion.

"You okay?" she asked Gwenny. Her daughter nodded and squeezed Balla's hand.

They made it another five meters when the river bed turned from a rocky bottom to a muddy one. Balla stepped down first, her foot getting caught.

"Wait! Hold on a minute," she said, "my foot's stuck. There aren't any more rocks."

She wiggled her foot, trying to pull it out of the river bed. She yanked her foot free but was unable to see it in the mucky bottom. "There we go. Free!" she smiled.

"Ok let's go this—" her words were cut off as a large, black eight-legged creature with bright green eyes on thin stalks rose to the surface of the river. It was just a bit smaller than a craate, but its two large front claws were about half the size of its entire body.

"Mother, look out!" Gunther said. "That's a barcca. They'll tear you up!" He backed away, Gwenny at his side.

Balla's eyes widened. "What do I do?"

"Come here. Come this way," Gwenny said, tugging on her mother's hand to lead her away from the barcca.

Gunther cried out. Balla turned. Four other barccas had appeared.

"Look out!" Balla said. Barccas surrounded them, snapping their claws. The sound grew louder. Gwenny and Gunther clung to Balla, the three of them clustered together in the center of a circle of barccas.

"The gun, Mother! Use the gun!" Gwenny said.

Balla forgot she was carrying the thing. She pulled it from her waistband and aimed at the nearest barcca. She pulled the trigger and a deafening shot rang out, striking the barcca in the chest, knocking it backwards. The bullet ripped a gaping hole through its body.

The other barccas snapped their claws, unaware.

Gwenny and Gunther covered their ears. Balla spun and shot the barcca nearest to Gwenny, severing its eyestalk and punching through the shell on its back. Its claws stopped moving and it drifted away in the current.

She shot at another and missed, the bullet splashing in the water. She pulled the trigger again and nearly shot Gunther in the arm. Gunther screamed, but her shot was true and the barcca was thrown back, struggling to right itself before being forced downstream by the river's current.

The remaining two barccas continued their attack.

"Ow!" Gwenny screamed. One of them had clamped down on her arm and tried to pull her under the water.

"Gwenny!" Balla cried. Her daughter disappeared below the red river's surface.

Gunther screamed, drawing Balla's attention. The last barcca had sliced his arm and blood gushed from the wound.

"No!" Balla screamed and shot at it, striking the barcca through its thick shell and killing it. Gunther cried and held his arm. Knowing he was safe, Balla frantically searched the water for Gwenny.

"Gwenny! Gwenny! Where are you?" she called out. She pointed the gun at any movement in the water.

Then, about five meters to their left, Gwenny popped out of the water, gasping and flailing her arms.

"Gwenny!" Balla cried and tried to run to her, though the thick mud underfoot stunted her progress. She took two steps toward her daughter and Gwenny went under again. "No!" Balla screamed.

Behind her, she heard Gunther crying. "No, Mother! Don't let them get Gwenny!"

He screamed. "Something touched me! It's back! No!" he cried. He let go of his bloody arm and reached for Balla. When he was close enough, she pulled him to her. He clung to her leg.

Water splashed to their right and Gwenny rose above the water, her arms waving frantically. Balla aimed, but didn't shoot. The barcca was too close to Gwenny. She didn't want to risk hitting her daughter.

"Gwenny! I need a clear shot! Move," Balla called. Gwenny screamed and punched at the barcca's claws. She nudged the nearest one away. Balla shot, the bullet piercing the barcca's shell. Its claws opened and closed, but it seemed weaker now. Gwenny pushed herself away from it and the barcca didn't pursue. Balla fired another shot, and finally the bullet punched through the barcca. Its claws stopped snapping and it drifted with the current, away from them.

Twenty-Five

Mina pulled her cloak tight around her head. The wind had picked up, as if a storm was approaching. She'd decided to trust Annabelle, if for no other reason than to find a way to get closer to Eron. She didn't completely trust the old woman, but after the visit from the ADF and avoiding trouble, she gave the old woman some credit.

The bellboy hadn't said a word to her about the ADF in the days since his shocking revelation. He acted as though everything were back to normal, but she knew better. There were forces outside her realm of understanding that were watching out for her for some reason. She could exploit that for now. If things went bad, she'd always have Sar and the ADF to bail her out; not that she wanted anything from him, but it was an out if needed, nonetheless.

The streets in Beta Prime were unusually less chaotic. The odd sense of dread she felt when the wind first kicked up became more intense as she walked farther.

"Go to the shopping district on the south side," Annabelle told her. "There, you'll find Brooklyn Avenue. Take it to the end until it intersects with Malden Street. Go left, and at the end of the street about five blocks down, you'll find an old office building. It looks deserted, but it isn't. Knock three times and wait."

The whole thing sounded stupid to Mina, but avoiding ADF scrutiny was more important than critiquing the methods to avoid them. If Annabelle was going to betray her, it would happen in an old part of the city where she shouldn't be. The Selected and their mates weren't supposed to get themselves into compromising situations.

Mina found the building. It stood three stories high, taller than anything in her colony. The windows were boarded shut and the fading gray exterior was stained a reddish color from Anastasian dust and dirt.

She stood in the quiet road, contemplating if she should follow through. Her stomach fluttered. The old woman could be setting her up; a test, maybe. Something to see if she was loyal to the queen or sided with the insurgents. She felt foolish standing there, considering knocking on a door to wait for some shady character to open, and then what?

Annabelle never told her. All she said was, "If you want to be rid of that awful Sar and do something worthwhile with your time, go to the building. You'll meet someone who can help; someone that might even be able to reunite you with that Eron boy." That was the part that convinced Mina to go. The chance...the slimmest hope she'd find Eron again and make things right.

The look on his face when she took Sar's hand; the anger and disappointment he couldn't hide bothered her. By the time Eron arrived at Victory Point, she already knew she couldn't be with him. She'd learned about her heartbreak on the trip to Victory Point. She'd cried and cried and screamed and slammed her fists against the seat of the ADF transport. When they'd arrived and she met the queen, she was broken. "Are you all right, my dear?" the queen asked. False concern dripped from her voice. Mina grew angry as she spoke.

"No, I'm not," Mina replied. One of the queen's personal guards spoke up.

"It's No, my queen. You best learn your place."

Mina scowled. "No. My queen," she said a bit sharply. The queen raised an eyebrow.

"I'll let you off. For now. You colonists are never well mannered. That's the worst part of keeping you here. You'll learn proper etiquette soon. They all do."

Mina shifted from one foot to the other, looking down at the ground. Anger simmered inside. Who'd this woman think she was anyway? Queen? She still didn't believe what the ADF soldiers told her, even with the queen in front of her.

"So, what's bothering you, child?" the queen asked.

Child? She's not much older than I am! Who does she think she is?

"The queen asked you a question," the soldier said, nudging Mina's shoulder. "You best answer her."

Mina glared at him. If he touched her one more time...

"Growing up, I always thought I'd be free to decide my future. What I wanted to study in school. The vocation I wanted. Who I'd get to be with. It was all fake, wasn't it? I mean, we have no choice, do we? The boys are thrown into a brutal game, having to decide if they live or not. If they do live, what then? If they're killed, no one blinks an eye. It's like it's the most natural thing ever, and no one cares. How many boys have been killed over the years? Why are we led to believe we're free when we're not?"

"Watch your tone, girl," the soldier said. He stepped closer, his hand on his firearm.

The queen held up a hand, making him back down.

"We do what we do because it is what it is."

Mina's face twisted in confusion.

"Child, we all have roles to play in this world. We all must follow the path laid out before us. We cannot escape it; we cannot change it. The future of our people depends on those roles being fulfilled. Like it or not, it's what you were born for. We all were. Do not try to discover some greater meaning than this: we're all born for a purpose, and if we fail to live up to those expectations, the consequences are dire. We do what we do because it is what it is. No more, no less."

In that moment, the instant the queen scolded her, Mina knew life was more complicated than she'd ever imagined. She was led by lies her entire life, all leading up to this point. If she tried to deny her circumstance, she'd never find a way out of her situation. If she played along, she could at least try to find a way to free herself from the life already planned for her.

She looked the queen in the eye, the queen a few inches shorter than her. "I understand, my queen."

From that point forward, Mina played their game. She spoke when appropriate, smiled when it seemed right, and gave the queen all the deference she demanded. It sickened Mina inside, but she was willing to play the game if it meant at some point she'd be free of this snare.

Mina's thoughts returned to the office building in

front of her. This was the step she needed to take to free herself from the queen. Her mind was made up.

Each step from the street to the building felt heavy. Her heart raced with anticipation. By the time she reached the doors with the wood slats across them, her hands were clammy.

She took a deep breath and knocked three times, the sound echoing through the streets.

Her heart beat faster as the silent response worried her. Finally, she heard footsteps inside. The door creaked open just a crack.

"Are you alone?" the female voice whispered.

Mina looked around, then back to the dark slit in the door. "Yes, I am."

The door opened wide and a woman a few years older than herself stood there. She looked familiar.

"Welcome, Mina," the woman smiled. "I'm Samantha, Eron's sister."

Twenty-Six

After Nagi was called to the Council chambers, a massive effort was set in motion by Chair Deelia's command. It seemed the entire city of Inventa knew their roles and poured everything they had into them.

Gar and Nagi watched the commotion, unsure of what they could or should do.

"Deelia did this, huh?" Gar said.

"Yeah. I think she's organized a counter to the ADF. I know the Topsiders haven't breached Inventa, but she's determined to not let that happen. This is all my fault."

Gar put his arm around Nagi's shoulder. "No, it's not. You know that. Deep down, you know that. Deelia cleared ya, too. Don't keep up with this nonsense. I ain't gonna put up with it." He grinned at Nagi. "Come on, she's right. It was bound to happen."

"But what about my family? How am I going to find them now?"

"We will, Nagi. I promise ya that. We Scouts know how to find things. Remember your training and rely on your instincts. You know this. Come on, let's get moving before we're caught up in this mess. We've got some folks to find."

Nagi wiped a tear from his furry cheek. Gar didn't need to help. He had no stake in helping to find Nagi's family. Gar's strength would have to be enough to carry them both for a while. The growing sense of loss inside was dulled slightly by Gar's insistence. Nagi clung to that hope. It was all he had left.

They decided against taking the crowded elevator and raced down the stairs to the exit at the bottom of the ship. Truth of assorted colors and sizes scrambled up and down the stairs, gathering arms, screaming obscenities at the Topsiders, and calming nervous youth. The erratic scene stung Nagi.

This has to be all my fault. I don't care what they say. If it wasn't for me, none of this would have happened. Stop thinking like that! Deelia and Gar are right. You didn't cause this. The Truth did. Nagi wrestled with his thoughts, trying to grasp his innocence while accepting fault. No matter what they said, he couldn't shake the guilt. Maybe he'd get past it in time, but now, it weighed heavy on him.

Near the bottom of the stairs, the number of Truth grew immense. There was hardly any room to move. Screaming, crying young Truth who were unable to assist in the war effort were dragged out of Inventa by their mothers.

"I want to stay here!"

"Why do we have to leave?"

"Is Darlona coming with us?"

All those voices calling and trying to be heard over the crushing chaos of Truth pushing and shoving overwhelmed Nagi. He paused, slowing enough that Gar pushed into him.

"You all right? Come on, Nagi, we're almost out." Gar fought his way ahead of Nagi and cleared a path for them.

They spilled out of Inventa, landing on the soil, and were nearly trampled by Truth fleeing for their lives.

"Get up, Nagi, now!" Gar yelled. It was hard for Nagi to hear him over the commotion. He felt someone yank on his arm, and soon he was on his feet, pushed out of the way. "Snap out of it! I want to help, but unless you help yourself, I can't do a damn thing for you! Now, get yourself together; you're better than this!" Gar screamed at him. Nagi bowed his head slightly. Gar was right. Self-loathing did no good. Continually blaming himself for what happened to Freedom was getting him nowhere. If he was going to find Balla and the children, his mind needed to be in the right place.

"Okay, Gar, I get it now. I'm sorry. It's just so much to worry about."

Gar grabbed him by the shoulders. "Worrying won't do a dang thing. You know this. No more, Nagi; got it? No more worrying. No more blaming yourself. I swear, you do that again, I might leave ya to the Topsiders. Got it?" Gar's face was inches from his. His eyes were full of fury and his grip on Nagi's shoulders strong.

"Yes, yes, I get it. I know. No more. I promise."

Gar looked deep into his eyes, making Nagi feel uncomfortable. "Good. I don't wanna lose ya, kid." He ruffled the fur on Nagi's head, much like Nagi'd done to his own children.

Gar led them away from Inventa to the Traveling Tunnels. Nagi followed with a renewed determination. Something inside him snapped. Something in Gar's tone brought him out of his stupor. He was alert. It was as though he'd drank an entire pot of kafka and then some. As they raced from Inventa, he envisioned his family, and his longing to find them intensified. His mind focused on the positive while forcing out the nagging feeling they were dead. He'd not think like that. Not anymore. They were alive. He was going to find them. Nothing was going to get in his way.

The cavern curved to the left and a steady stream of Truth, mostly elderly and the very young, were already following the Tunnels, most likely heading to the remains of the city left untouched by the Topsiders.

"Gar, we're gonna need to go up top. I fear they may have gone out of the Tunnels."

They fell in line with the other Truth and marched through the glowing tunnels, dirt grubber blood lighting the way.

"Why do you say that? I wouldn't go up there if I didn't have to."

Nagi thought about it. "I don't know. Maybe they didn't, but I think we might have to at least consider it."

"As a last resort for sure," Gar replied, "because I don't think they'd leave the safety of the Tunnels and other Truth. It's dangerous up there. Any of those ADF soldiers spot 'em, they're gonna shoot. I can't imagine your wife leading your children to such dangers."

Ahead of them, a small family huddled around a Truth lying on the ground in the tunnel.

"Please, help us. Someone help us!" a young male Truth called out to those passing as they ignored him. Gar and Nagi also passed by, but the more he called out, the more Nagi's heart broke. What if it were his children?

"We've got to help them, Gar," he said. Gar looked at him.

"But what about your family?"

Nagi closed his eyes, the young Truth's voice echoing inside his head. "We have to stop. No one else is helping them. We've got to." He paused, watching the Truth stream down the tunnel. "It's the right thing."

Gar slapped him on the back. "Darn right it is. Come on, then; let's get to it."

They approached the small family, one boy and one girl, and an older female Truth with gray-tinged fur. She was lying on the floor, her eyes swimming in her head.

"What's wrong?" Nagi asked.

"Our grandma. She's hurt. I don't know what happened to her." the young male Truth said.

"We can try to help. My name's Nagi, and this is Gar." Gar waved, though his face had a look of concern.

"I'm Trober, and this is my sister, Callia. We were leaving for Novus when we heard a rattling sound, and a creature bit her," he said, pointing to his grandma. "I didn't get a good look at it, but soon after she was too dizzy to walk."

Nagi leaned down and peered into her eyes, though it didn't seem to register he was there.

Gar nudged him on his shoulder and pulled him to the side. In a whisper he said, "She's been bitten by a veenam. You know what that means, right?"

Nagi nodded. "Yeah, she's gonna die. No way she'll survive."

"And it also means there's more of 'em. They don't

ever come out alone. Ever. If there's one, it means this entire tunnel is infested with 'em."

Nagi looked at the children. They were a few years older than his own. "What about them? Who will tend to them when she dies?"

"Maybe we can find a kind family to take them in, but we better hurry. We're gonna need to get out of here fast."

The children were frantic. "Hurry, I think something's wrong!" Callia said. The gray-haired Truth's body thrashed on the ground, foam spilling from her mouth. Nagi and Gar rushed to her side, Gar holding her head to keep her from smacking it against the tunnel's wall.

"What's happening?" Trober asked. "Can you help her?"

Her body shook violently, her arms thrashing; then with a great heave of her chest, she exhaled and fell silent.

"Grandma!" Callia cried. She pushed Nagi aside and clutched the older Truth. "Grandma, what's wrong?" She looked up at Nagi, then to Gar, both of them unable to speak.

"What's wrong? Why'd she stop?" Trober asked. Both children were trying to wake her, but it was too late. The bite had taken its toll.

"I'm sorry," Nagi finally said. "I fear she's been bitten by a—" his words were cut off by a scream. Then another. Screams were coming from all sides in the dark tunnel. Underneath the Truth voices, Nagi heard it.

"Oh no," he said.

"I hear 'em, too. We gotta go," Gar said.

"What? Why do we have to leave? What about Grandma?" Trober said.

Gar sighed, raising his hands as if to ask Nagi a question.

"Come with us. We can't do anything else for your grandma. I'm sorry, but if you don't hurry, you'll be in the same situation. Please, come with us," Nagi said.

"We can't leave her!" Callia said.

"Little girl, you're gonna have to make a choice. And soon!" Gar said.

Trober stood. More Truth were screaming. The rattle of the horns on the veenams' heads cut through the screams. There must have been hundreds slithering in the tunnel, seeking prey.

"Come on, Callia, maybe they can help us. Grandma is...she's dead. We gotta go." He pulled on his sister's arm.

"No! We can't leave her!"

"Callia, come on! Don't you hear that sound? That's what we heard right before grandma got sick! I don't want that happening to us!"

Sobbing, she let him pull her away from her grandma.

"This way! We'll get you out of here," Nagi said. He followed Gar's lead as the rattling grew louder and the screams more desperate. The veenams had found easy prey, and the Truth were paying the price.

Twenty-Seven

"What are you sayin' to me, boy?" Sergeant Ahimo said. He stood with hands on his hips staring at Eron, his face betraying the confusion inside.

"Dad," Eron said in a low voice. "My dad's name was Ahimo. I've not seen him since—"

"Wait a minute, kid. You mean to say that..." his eyes went large and the gruff exterior faded. "Eron? Son?" Eron could see Timo in his father's eyes. It had to be him!

Ahimo stumbled a bit before composing himself. He waved Smitty away, and soon they were alone in the barracks.

"I need a seat," Ahimo said. His shaky legs barely made it to the nearest bunk. "Eron. I never expected to see you again."

"Me, too. I mean, I wanted to. So much has happened since you left. Mom, Samantha, Timo." He said the last name slowly and with reverence. His brother, now a Forgotten, still lived. He'd make it back to him some day.

"What about them? Are they all right?"

"Mom's fine, I guess. Samantha is in...she's around. Her husband is ADF, too. And Timo...Timo didn't make it through the Selection."

Ahimo gasped. "No. Please tell me that's not true."

Eron hesitated. He wanted to tell his father everything; yet, something held him back. How much could he trust a man that had left his family to fend for themselves and never returned? He was ADF, after all. But still, he was Eron's father. His dad!

"He didn't make it. I saw it myself. Just after the start, he was shot."

Ahimo closed his eyes and nodded. "As is the way of our people. He should've known better." His father's reaction confused Eron. Shouldn't he be upset that his own son was killed? Not that he actually had been killed, but his father didn't know that. He should still be angry, but he didn't seem that way at all.

"So, you made it through, and from the looks of it, mostly intact. Good for you!" He stood and clapped Eron on the shoulder. "I can't tell you how excited I am to train you, Son! I dreamt of one day training you and Timo to be excellent ADF soldiers. Now, I get that chance!"

"Not with Timo," Eron said.

"No, of course not. It's a shame he didn't make it. I thought for sure he had the make up to be one fine soldier. But we can't dwell on what happened. It's not like we can change anything. We must accept it and move on. It's not easy, but that's our way. That's why we fight to preserve our way of life. That's why we need recruits, and who better than my own son?"

"Maybe both of your sons."

"Eron, I will not tolerate you dwelling on what cannot be changed. It is what it is. That's our way."

"But you don't see anything wrong with it?"

"Have you been infected with the poisonous thoughts of the CDL? There's no place for that here.

Just because you're my son doesn't mean I'm going to go any easier on you. I expect the same attention and respect as I would get from any other recruit. Got that?"

"Yeah, sure."

"No. Try again."

"Yes. Sir," he said. Eron stared through him as though he were nothing special. He understood his father's loyalties. It was all too clear.

Then Ahimo lightened up. "So, what about Samantha? Have you seen her lately? What's her husband's name? Maybe I know him."

Eron replied in a monotone voice, "No sir, I have not seen her, sir. I expected her to be in Beta Prime but have yet to make contact, sir. I can try to establish a connection if you prefer. Sir."

"Boy, don't you ever mock me or act like that again. You watch that tone, or I'll have you scrubbing latrines for weeks. My son or not, I will not tolerate your disrespect. Do you understand?"

Eron looked him in the eye. "Yes sir."

"Good. Your bunk is over there, number fifteen. Set up, and I'll have your squad leader come get you. Training won't be easy, but if you can survive the Selection, you'll make it through here." He stood and left, his boots echoing in the cavernous barracks.

My dad is here and he's my instructor? What's wrong with him? Why does he not care about Timo? He didn't even mention Mom! He's more ADF than anything else.

Moments later, a boy of about his age strolled into the barracks. "Eron?" he said as he approached.

Eron wasn't sure if he should say yes, sir or not. He

didn't know the protocol for squad leaders yet, so he opted for the safer course. "Yes, sir?"

"I'm Lieutenant Dragor."

Eron's stare lingered long. This boy, this Lieutenant Dragor. His skin was a deep shade of red. He thought Phelan's blue skin was odd, but this was different. Dragor's hair was bright yellow like his eyes. He stood a few inches taller than Eron, his shirt baggy on his slight frame.

"What are you looking at, Recruit?" Lieutenant Dragor asked. His face was serious but his tone a bit lighter.

"I apologize, sir. In my colony, the colors of our people are not so varied. I meant no disrespect, sir."

Dragor smiled.

"I get that a lot, actually. It's cool. For some reason, few recruits from Cape Rouge survive the Selection. We train hard. We take classes. Maybe it's because we're a bit farther than everyone else?"

His sudden friendly demeanor took Eron by surprise. He wasn't sure how to respond.

"But I thought Victory Point was the same distance away for everyone?" Then he followed up with a quick, "Sir."

Dragor smiled wider.

"That's what they say, but in Cape Rouge, we see it differently. Anyway, I'm here now, and so are you. I have three others besides you under my command. I expect you'll fit in well; just follow commands and you'll be fine. I'm not tough to deal with, but cross me, and I will be. That's why Sergeant Ahimo promoted me. I don't take failure well. I expect my team to be the best. Got it?"

"Yes, sir."

"Good. Let's get to the basics and bring you up to speed."

It took Eron several days to understand the training schedule. Early morning physical training, daily briefing on weapon care, squad formations, and a host of other classes intended to take a rough recruit and mold them into something useful for the ADF.

He'd grown used to the routine, even enjoying much of the training. Learning intrigued him.

"Great job with that weapon," Sergeant Ahimo said to Eron during a late afternoon session. Fifty boys, all close in age, sat on the floor of the barracks with their weapons in front of them in various stages of separation. Eron's lay in front of him in perfect order, all the pieces cleaned and prepared for inspection.

Sergeant Ahimo leaned closer, running a hand along the barrel.

"Now that, boys, is how you clean your weapon." Eron beamed with pride, hearing his father praise him in front of everyone else.

"Now, the rest of you," Sergeant Ahimo said, "assemble your weapons and try it all over again. I want each one of you to come over here and look at this weapon." He pointed to Eron's neatly placed weapon parts. "This is how yours needs to look. If you can't do that, you'll do it again...and again until it's right."

Later that evening after lights out, three boys snuck over to Eron's bunk. One of them covered Eron's mouth with his hand, whispering. "Quiet, or you're dead. Understand?" Eron nodded. "If I take my hand away and you make a sound, I will kill you." He brandished a blade, turning it so it glinted in the faint light of the barracks. Again, Eron nodded.

His heart raced. He thought his days of dealing with someone trying to kill him were over, but they weren't.

The boy removed his hand. Eron noticed the other two boys standing beside the first one.

"Don't you ever make us do that again."

"Do what?" Eron whispered. The boy punched him in the stomach.

"I said no noise!" He leaned close to Eron's ear. "Don't ever make us look bad again, or you'll wish you died in the Selection. Got it?"

Eron nodded.

"Good. I expect you'll fall in line with the rest of us, now."

The next day, Eron learned the boy, Asher, had been in trouble before. His goons, Whent and Vitty, were new to the barracks and had fallen in with the bully.

Twenty-Eight

Balla lay on the muddy bank of the river, Gwenny and Gunther at her sides. The three of them were soaked, tired, and sore, but alive.

"We made it across," Balla said. Gunther grunted. Gwenny remained quiet.

"We need to find shelter for the night. I don't like being out in the open. Who knows what other dangers lurk out here," Balla said.

Gunther perked up. "Craates. Vulbores. Veenams. And worse," he said.

"What?" Gwenny chimed in. She raised herself on her elbows, looking at her brother with her brows furrowed.

"Those are the dangers out here. Mother asked. I was only trying to help."

Gwenny rolled her eyes and flopped her head back down on the riverbank.

"Thank you, Gunther, but I didn't mean I wanted a list of the dangers. It was an expression, that's all. Anyway, let's go. It'll be dark soon."

It took a while, but eventually the children were up and moving, following Balla into the forest. About an hour later, they discovered a small cave that appeared to be empty.

"This ought to work," Balla said. "Stay here while I check it out." She pulled the pistol from her belt and climbed inside, exploring the depths of the cave. After a few minutes, she returned to the entrance.

"Good news! This leads to one of our Traveling Tunnels. We can try going back underground and make our way to Novus."

"Sounds cool," Gunther said. Gwenny nodded.

"Great, let's go then. I saw a glow not too far in; maybe there's a rest station."

The children followed Balla down the dark tunnel, the faint glow of dirt grubber blood calling them forward.

"These don't look like they've been used at all," Gwenny said. "It's like no one comes here anymore."

Balla noticed the same thing. "I agree, Gwenny. These tunnels don't appear to be well travelled like the ones near Freedom. I wonder when the last visitor was here. Someone had to be here, though; how else would dirt grubber blood be on the walls?"

Gwenny nodded, though it was difficult for Balla to see her.

"You two, stay close. These are our tunnels, but there might be something dangerous down here."

Gunther clung to Balla, barely giving her enough room to walk. Gwenny stayed close, but unlike Gunther, she refused to hold onto her mother's side. Balla forged ahead toward the glowing light at the end of the tunnel.

They moved slowly. Skittering sounds made Gwenny jump.

"What are you afraid of? Those are only dirt grubbers," Gunther said. "We use 'em all the time! They won't hurt you."

"Whatever. The sound startled me, that's all," she said.

"Come on, keep moving," Balla chimed. She'd prefer the children not bicker. Her senses were on high alert. Preserving her children and finding Nagi pushed her forward when the sounds grew louder.

As they approached the glowing wall, the rest station appeared out of the cavern walls.

"There we are, one of our very own rest stations," Balla said. She was relieved, yet apprehensive. When Gunther started toward it, she pulled him back. "Not yet," she said, "let me go first. Everything appears to be in order, but we can't be too careful."

"But, Mother..." Gunther began.

"Don't argue, Son. We're in this together. All of us. I intend on keeping us together, too."

"Fine," he huffed. Gwenny remained quiet, almost contemplative. Though not the most active company, Balla preferred the silence to the constant bickering and chatter. She listened for any sign of danger.

Behind them, she heard the same skittering sounds as before. Gunther was right; it did sound like dirt grubbers. They were harmless enough. Their saliva could sting, but their phosphorescent blood was too valuable to ignore. It's what had allowed the Truth to build their elaborate tunnels over the centuries and stay away from the Topsiders.

"Stay out here; let me inspect the place," Balla said to the children. "Gwenny, you're in charge."

"But, Mother..." Gunther said.

"But nothing, Son. Your sister is in charge. I'll be right back."

Balla slipped into the rest station, blood rushing in

her ears. The station was quiet. She couldn't hear the dirt grubbers outside anymore, as the thick walls muffled most anything. Inside the main room where all visitors checked in, she found a torch barely glowing with waning dirt grubber blood. Someone had to have been there recently to leave such a trail. She grabbed the torch and passed through the reception room, stepping carefully inside the first bedroom on the left. It was empty. She waved the torch around, but nothing appeared to be out of the ordinary. The bedroom on the right was the same. Finally, she entered the last bedroom on the far right.

Lying on the bed was a large, dark lump. It looked human, as if a Topsider had fallen asleep on the bed. Balla backed away from the figure on the bed. It didn't move. Is it dead? She hesitated, then moved closer to find out what it was.

She brought the torch lower to investigate. The soft glow made it difficult to see, but when she passed the torch over its face, she almost ran.

It was a man's face; definitely a Topsider. He wore ADF grays from head to toe.

"An ADF soldier? Down here? How can that be?" she said aloud.

She stepped closer, wanting to get a better look at this interloper, and when the torch passed his face, a bright orange milliburg crawled from his nose, curling around his head, and entered his ear. Balla covered her mouth to stifle a scream. She hadn't seen milliburgs since she was a little girl. They preferred isolation and only came out when the promise of a meal presented itself.

Slowly, she backed out of the room, her eyes fixed on the head of the soldier. Milliburgs were fast and efficient eaters.

She stepped back and bumped into something solid. Balla let out a small scream and spun, almost knocking Gwenny in the face with the torch.

"Hey, watch it!" Gwenny said. Gunther was at her side and they stared at their mother, their eyes large and white.

"What are you doing here? I said to stay at the entrance."

"Gunther heard a sound in the tunnel. It wasn't a Truth."

Balla clutched her chest, holding the torch high. "What do you mean?"

"It sounded like voices, but I don't think they were Truth. They said something about the Forgotten," Gunther said.

Balla's heart raced. "Are you sure? How many voices did you hear?"

"I don't know. Maybe two? It was hard to tell. Then we heard you make a noise and we couldn't stay out there any longer."

"It's alright, Son, you did the right thing. We need to stay away from this room, though."

"Why? What's in there?" Gwenny asked.

"Milliburgs. We need to avoid them if we can."

"Yuck!" Gunther said. For all his fascination with nature, Balla was surprised to hear him say that.

"Yeah; yuck is right. How close were the voices?"

"I'm not sure. They came from that way," Gunther said, pointing.

"Shhhh," Gwenny said. "I hear something."

Balla cocked her head to the side. She heard it, too. Milliburgs scurried behind them. Balla turned, and in the faint torch glow, she saw several long milliburgs crawling out of the soldier and scuttle toward them.

"We need to leave! The milliburgs!" she said.

They ran out of the station and smacked into two ADF soldiers with rifles strapped to their backs carrying flashlights.

"Well, what do we have here? Some dirty Forgotten. Kill 'em!" the taller soldier said. Balla pushed him, knocking him into the other soldier.

"Run!" she yelled.

Twenty-Nine

When the shock of meeting Samantha had worn off, Mina relaxed a bit. The inside of the office building was as dark and rotten as the exterior, but they were safe from prying ears and eyes. Samantha motioned for her to sit on a torn chair at the far side of the room near a small glowing lamp.

"Annabelle tells me you want to join our cause. Can we trust you?" Samantha asked. Mina was taken aback by the blunt question.

"Yes. I think. I guess I want to help. Why would I betray you?"

"You cannot guess or be timid. If you are with us, you'll be expected to do many things you might not do otherwise. You probably won't ever see that boy...Sar...again."

Mina fidgeted in her seat. The mention of the name brought back thoughts of Sar's arrogance and ignorance. He didn't care for her at all. Eron did. He survived the Selection to be with her, and was crushed by the outcome. She wanted so badly to tell him the truth, but she couldn't. Not then.

"I really don't care if I ever see him again, to be honest. He creeps me out. I know what the ADF is doing. I believe what the queen is doing is wrong."

Samantha paced the room with her arms crossed, muttering to herself.

"I can bring you along; let you meet the others, but if you give the slightest hint of betrayal, I can't promise things will go well for you. Our cause cannot stand on flimsy legs. We need everyone to buy in."

Mina nodded. She'd made up her mind when she'd met with Annabelle, but only now realized it.

"Good," Samantha said, "'cause I'd hate for Eron to know something bad happened to you!" Samantha smiled, and so did Mina; the mention of Eron breaking the tension.

"Do you know where he is?" Mina asked. She straightened up in the chair. It creaked as she moved.

"Actually, yes. He enlisted in the ADF."

A long, awkward silence filled the dusty room.

"The...ADF?" Mina asked.

"Yep. He's at the barracks in basic training as we speak. Most likely, he's met our father, too."

Mina leaned back, the chair expressing its displeasure with her movement.

"Your father? He's here in Beta Prime? Eron talked about him, but he didn't know anything about him. He hadn't heard from him in a really long time."

"He's full-fledged ADF. He's in charge of training new recruits. Seems to enjoy poisoning their minds with the queen's demands. His loyalty is to her and the ADF."

She looked to a hallway, her focus on something beyond Samantha.

"I fear one day we'll meet up with him and it won't be the reunion I've always wanted," Samantha said.

Mina crossed her legs, tapping her knee before she spoke. "So, why did Eron join the ADF? Does that mean he's part of them now? Does he believe in their cause? Does he agree with all the atrocities they inflict on the colonies?"

"The colonies? Their evil goes far beyond that. Didn't you see what they did to that Truth settlement?"

"Truth settlement? I saw them crush the Forgotten. It broke my heart to see those animals killed."

"Animals? You've got a lot to learn, Mina. The Truth, or as the ADF has called them, the Forgotten, are humans. They're us. They are what happens to us when we live too long in the Anastasian wilderness. They're exactly like us, but with a coat of thick fur. It's how our human bodies adapt to this world. The colonies are former mines, sitting right above the remaining deposits of the most valuable resource on this planet, and the source of the queen's power.

"That settlement you saw? That was one of the transport ships from Earth. The Truth live underground in the wreckage. The ships are still functional. They're more advanced than the colonies! The royal line, with the ADF, has kept the colonies in the dark for as long as anyone can remember. They created the population imbalance on purpose. They created the Selection with the intent of weakening the colonies and strengthening their own military."

Mina closed her eyes, digesting Samantha's words. It was too much. The conspiracies were too far-fetched. Had she thrown herself in with crazy fanatics? How could the Forgotten live underground in huge ships without everyone knowing about it? Did the queen and her military really have that much control? How could the Forgotten be human? What resources was she talking about?

"I don't understand," Mina said. "How can all of that be true? How could the queen keep all this silent for so long? She's close to my age!"

"It's not just the reigning queen. Dating back to when the humans first stepped foot on this planet, the royal line has protected their claim with brutal efficiency. They grasped power early on, and no one's ever taken it from them. That's going to change. It has to. They're wrong."

Mina's mind reeled from the revelations. Her simple life back in the colony seemed so long ago. Now, everything was much more complicated. She didn't regret being here with Samantha, but the overwhelming cause that Samantha represented was daunting.

"How does Eron fit into all this? Has he given himself over to the ADF?" Mina hoped not. Her entire reason to seek out Samantha was to reunite with him. But even if he succumbed to the ADF, she was sure what Samantha told her was worth fighting for. She'd seen the queen's policies, and matched with what Samantha shared, it was enough. With or without Eron, she was joining their cause.

"I met with him and Sarai."

"Sarai?" Mina asked.

"Yeah, the female he was paired with at Victory Point. She's a nice girl; doesn't seem to subscribe to the queen's policies, either. Though, to be honest, we haven't vetted her yet."

Mina's heart sunk. A nice girl? Does Eron actually like her? Should that matter anymore?

"Did you know about her?" Samantha asked.

"Well, sort of. I remember her being there under the tent, but to be honest, my mind wasn't in the moment."

"I understand. Maybe she'll join us, too. We need as many as possible."

Mina only wanted to make things right with Eron. Before he left for the Selection, she was positive he'd make it and they'd be together. Once her mother told her what would really happen, she was crushed, but there was nothing she could do about it. Now she had a chance to set things straight. No one should be forced into something they didn't want, no matter what the queen or anyone else said. Tradition didn't mean it was right.

"So, where is he? Can I see him?" Mina asked.

"I doubt it. They keep the barracks on lock-down, but he is with the ADF."

Mina jumped from her seat, shaking. "Is this a set-up? Are you trying to get me in trouble?" She looked around the room, expecting ADF soldiers to drag her away to prison...or worse.

Samantha raised her hands in a calm down gesture. "No, no nothing like that. Please, Mina, it's okay. Eron is with us."

Mina sat back down, her face betraying her confusion. "What do you mean?"

"He's agreed to help. He knows the queen is wrong. He's agreed to infiltrate the ADF and gather intel for us."

"But, your father? What about him?"

Samantha looked away. Her voice dropped to a whisper. "He's ADF to the core. He's the enemy."

"Oh, I'm so sorry, Samantha."

Samantha closed her eyes. When she finally could speak, her voice was harsh. "It doesn't matter anymore. He's too far gone to bring back. He's one of them now; has been for a while."

When she opened her eyes, they glistened.

"Well," Samantha said, "we need to get going. We've got a lot to do and not much time left. You're with us, right?" She held out her hand and Mina inspected it before grasping it, shaking on their deal.

"Yeah, I'm in, Samantha."

Thirty

Gar led Nagi and their new-found responsibilities—the young male Truth named Trober and his younger sister, Callia—through the barely-lit tunnels until they were on Anastasia's surface. Red and yellow trees surrounded them, a bright alternative to their underground dwellings.

Once outside, Gar and Nagi searched for suitable cover from the elements. In the distance, thunder boomed, and green lightning lit the sky.

"We better find a place to hide soon," Nagi said.

"Why? I thought we were safe from those things in the tunnel," Callia said.

"We are, but there are many more dangers up here. The rain is one of them."

"The rain?" she said.

"Yeah, Callia; it'll burn you. But once it soaks into the ground, it's fine," her brother said.

"He's right. That's why we need a place to hide from the rain. We can't go back in our tunnels. Don't worry; we'll find something," Nagi said.

"I'll go this way; scout ahead and see if we've got any possibilities," Gar said. "You kids stay with Nagi and watch out for animals. There are all kinds of dangerous things up here."

Gar sprinted off into the forest, leaving behind Nagi and the children. Just looking at them made Nagi think of his own children and how he hoped they were safe with Balla.

"I'm sorry about what happened in the tunnels. Did you have any other family?"

"Our mom died a couple years ago," Trober said, "and our dad...our dad left to join the Truth army. We were supposed to go with our grandma to Novus before she..." Trober said. Nagi put a hand on his shoulder.

"It's okay, Trober, we'll get you there. Do you have family waiting on you?"

"We've got an aunt and uncle willing to keep us until our father returns. They are a bit older and not able to fight a war."

"Well then, I suppose we ought to get you there. I'm sure that's where my family is, too," Nagi said.

"You have kids?" Callia asked.

"I sure do. A boy and girl. My daughter is older than my son. We got separated in Freedom, and I haven't seen them since. That's why I was at Inventa. I hoped they were there, but we couldn't find them."

Lightning illuminated the sky, followed by a loud boom of thunder.

"Let's get moving. Follow Gar's path. I'm sure he's found something for us."

Nagi gestured for them to move. He followed, making sure nothing was behind them.

Thunder boomed louder, shaking nearby trees.

Callia shrieked.

"It's okay, Callia; we're fine for now. We gotta find Gar, though." The girl clung to his leg, much like his children did. It felt comforting, yet different.

A loud crash in the forest ahead startled Nagi, and he ran in front of Trober, preparing to fight. Gar emerged from the thick brush.

"Come on! This way!" he said. He pointed forward, breathing heavy.

He led the way through heavy ground cover. Red bushes clung to their fur, pulling and tugging on them. "Hey, hold on a minute," Nagi called to Gar. Callia was caught in a sticky orange shrub with yellow spots. Its leaves were tangled in her fur, her tunic caught on a branch. She'd been trying to free her leg.

As Nagi fought with the shrub, an ADF soldier emerged on their right.

"Halt! Stop, or I'll shoot, by order of the queen!"

Nagi whipped his head toward the sudden intrusion. Callia cried out. Trober went silent.

"There's no need for that," Nagi said. He slowly raised his hands to show compliance.

"Stop moving! You filthy animals need to be put down. You shouldn't be out here. You don't belong!"

A second ADF soldier emerged to his left, his weapon trained on them.

Nagi's heart raced. How would he get them out of this? The children didn't deserve this. None of them did. *Where's Gar?* he thought. When they were ambushed, the older scout had disappeared.

"Stupid animals," the second soldier said. He fired at Trober, felling the boy. Callia screamed and ran to him. Nagi's instincts took over.

He rushed the soldier, shouting incoherent words. Gar slammed into the first soldier's side, sending him stumbling into the second. Nagi's attack was too quick for him. He landed on top of the soldier, knocking his gun away and pummeling his face. Gar subdued the other soldier as Nagi continued to beat the one beneath him.

A raging fury took hold of Nagi. He envisioned his own son shot by the ADF just for being part of the Truth. Nagi himself would have killed the Forgotten before he joined them. But now, belonging to the Truth, he saw things differently. He knew what really happened. The bloody face beneath him represented all that had gone wrong since his arrival in Freedom. He wanted to wipe it out; to eliminate the source of his pain. He punched and punched, the soldier screaming through bloody lips and broken teeth. The screams echoed those of Callia, who attended to her brother.

Nagi didn't care. The soldier deserved much worse for shooting the innocent boy. Large black, furry fists matted with blood continued to rain down on the soldier as Nagi relentlessly punished him. The soldiers who attacked their underground city and killed all those innocent families. The image burned in Nagi's mind and pushed him harder. "Where is my family?" he screamed as he continued his onslaught. The soldier couldn't reply. Nagi's beating was brutal. "I want my family back!" he growled.

Soon, he grew weak. Blood matted his fur all the way up his arm. When he finally stopped, he was horrified at the mess. The soldier's face was no longer there, turned instead into a sickening mound of bones and gore. Nagi looked at his hands, realizing for the first time what he'd done. He closed his eyes and breathed heavy, trying to hold back the tears. "I'm so sorry," he whispered.

Behind him, Callia was screaming. He turned and saw huge tears stream down her face. "He killed Trober! He killed my brother!" She cradled her older brother's now lifeless body in her arms, his head flopping backwards and an enormous bullet hole in his chest.

"No!" Nagi said, "No! Not the boy! No!"

Callia clung to Trober, laying her head against his body, the boy's blood matting her fur. Nagi closed his eyes, blaming himself for being too slow to stop the soldiers. When he opened them, he saw Gar holding the other soldier tight, a calm expression washing over his face.

"What about this one?" Gar said.

"What about me?" the soldier replied. "You gonna kill me like you did him? Wouldn't put it past you animals to do something like that."

Gar kicked the soldier. "Shut up before something happens to you."

"Are you animals even capable of thinking past your stupid instincts?" the soldier replied, earning another kick from Gar.

"I want to take him out, Nagi. This ignorance shouldn't be allowed to live."

Nagi looked at the bloody mess beneath him and back to Gar. "I've got a better idea. He needs to know. He needs to understand. He can become one of us...the thing he hates."

"Are you insane? He's a murderer!"

"Not that we know of. This one was," Nagi said nodding to the mess beneath him, "but we don't know about him. We could use his insight. He might know more about what's going on. If nothing else, we can use him for information and then kill him. But I think he'll come around. We all do."

The soldier struggled and Gar kicked him again. "Damn lucky my friend here wants to see you re-formed. I'd enjoy taking my frustrations out on you." Gar kicked him again.

Nagi stood and went to Callia, hoping to soothe her pain and help her move on. They all had to. It was all they had left.

Thirty-One

Two weeks passed without incident.

Eron spent much of his free time in the library on base. Unlike the colony, this one had access to limitless books and journals; many of them not available to the public.

They had finished with their daily drills, and with an hour before dinner, Eron went to the library. As usual, it was quiet; only one other recruit was there studying. Eron nodded to him and went to a terminal at the far end of the main research room. Lately, he'd been researching the Forgotten and found a few references to stones and the colonies that intrigued him. He searched through countless journal entries logged by early transport captains. After nearly forty minutes of searching, he ran across an entry that made him gasp.

Captain Gray, 195 days after crash

Today we re-established contact with surface colony and were astonished at the most bizarre situation. While we have attained a certain thickness of muscle and darkened body hair, our colonists have retained their normal human form. Upon inquiry, it was noted the colony was situated on a settlement of a peculiar stone, which according to them, counters the planetary effect we've witnessed since our landing. They've established a second colony along the outer edges of the massive forest on the far side of the planet, and it is also situated on a bed of this particular stone. We will determine in the future whether it is truly the reversal of our bodily changes. Until then, we remain jovial in Freedom, our well-built ship that provides spectacular living quarters for our people.

"What the..." Eron said to the room. The other recruit looked his way and Eron waved. He turned back to the screen and reread the passage, almost falling out of his chair. Here it was! The link between the Forgotten and the Anastasians! It couldn't be any clearer than this. How did they ignore it for so long? If the queen knew the Forgotten are humans, then she's killing her own people! But, why? Who else knows about this?

Eron spent the rest of his time researching, but found no other passages detailing the revelation he'd uncovered. If what he found was true, then Samantha was right to oppose the ADF. Timo's declaration that Eron could stop all of this felt like a massive weight upon him. He had knowledge of something so profound that it threatened to overturn the queen's power. Fear mixed with elation stirred within. He had to get to Samantha somehow. She needed to know.

"Eron!" a loud voice called in the still of the library, breaking Eron's thoughts. It was Dragor. "Come on, let's go," he said. Eron wiped his face, trying to remove the shock of his discovery, and followed Dragor.

Eron and Dragor had grown close, the officer acting more like a friend than a superior. Often when not researching, or "reading," as Eron called it, they'd often hike to the far reaches of the enclosed base.

"So, what's it like in Rippon?" Dragor asked. The

boys hiked to a fence at the southern tip of the base where no one else was in sight.

"Not bad, really. I honestly didn't know about Beta Prime when I lived there. I'd heard of the other colonies, but we had little contact with them. We had a couple schools, a greenhouse, and not much else, really. It was an easy life...then."

"Yeah, I can understand that. The Selection changed everything, didn't it?"

Eron nodded, his thoughts drifting back to what he'd read earlier.

"You think we'll see action soon? The full-scale assault on the Forgotten is gonna take all our re-sources and then some."

Eron's eyes widened. "Full-scale assault? What do you mean?"

"The queen's orders. She wants them eliminated. She says those mongrels need to be put down. They're abominations."

Eron held his tongue, considering his next words. "How do you know they're abominations? Ever meet one?"

Dragor smiled. "Sure did! Killed one in the Selection. Stupid thing actually tried to speak to me. Something about the truth. I sliced its stomach open and watched it die. Coolest thing ever."

The thought of someone doing that to Timo angered Eron. They were people just like them, only...different. They deserved to live.

"Have you ever met one?" Dragor asked.

"Yeah, a couple of them."

"Nice! Did you kill any of 'em?"

Eron shook his head. "No, I wasn't able to."

"Shame. We coulda swapped stories. I heard we've already wiped out one Forgotten city and are on the verge of destroying another. I don't remember how many there are; maybe three or four. If it keeps up, we'll be in the fight soon. I hope so, too!"

Eron went quiet. He thought of Timo and hoped he'd made it free of the destruction. His sister was right. The ADF were killers. They were bent on eliminating their fellow humans to preserve themselves. The Forgotten weren't killers and murderers. They were just like them with slight physical differences, and if the passage he'd found was correct, the transformation was completely reversible.

"You ever hear of the Combatant De Liberty?" Eron asked.

Dragor spun on him. "The CDL? The traitors? Yeah, I've heard of them! They're worse than the grubby Forgotten! I'd slice out all their hearts and feed them to the Forgotten if I could. Hate 'em."

The Forgotten are humans like us! They don't feed on humans! How ignorant are you?

"Yeah, that's them," Eron said. His voice was weak, and he stared off in the distance. "I heard about them in Beta Prime."

"Did they try to recruit you? Wow; if they did and you kept that door open, we might be able to infiltrate their ranks! We've been wanting to do that for years!"

"We? Years? Dragor, you haven't been here much longer than me. You were from the previous Selection, right? What do you mean 'we' and 'years?' I'm confused."

Dragor rolled his eyes. "Of course, not me personally. The ADF! It's been their goal for some time now to wipe out the traitorous CDL. I've never met anyone that was recruited by them. That could be helpful!"

"I never said they recruited me," Eron said. "Only that I'd heard about them in Beta Prime. I heard rumors and stuff. I didn't get many answers when I tried to find them. Seems like they're pretty secretive."

"Heck yeah, they are! I'm telling you, Eron, not many people who ask about them live long. They either join them and are lost to the rest of us, or they end up getting killed by them. Something about protecting their secrecy, I guess."

Eron fought back the urge to punch him. It was like every thought in Dragor's thick head was planted by the ADF, and he believed every word. The Forgotten were not animals and the CDL were not traitors. Technically, they could be labeled as such, but they were on the side of right. The queen and her military were brutally wrong. Everything they stood for was oppressive and evil. His sister was right. The ADF needed to be brought down. There had to be more of them like Dragor.

"We gotta tell Sergeant Ahimo when we get back. He'll want to know all about this. I bet we can connect with the CDL through you."

"You sound pretty sure of yourself. I told you I wasn't recruited. I only heard about them and asked around."

"That's enough, though. They're ruthless. No one just 'asks around' about them and lives. In a way, I kinda admire that about them."

Eron closed his eyes and breathed in deep. He didn't realize asking a simple question would put him in this situation.

He was startled when a loud siren blared across the base.

"That's it! We're gonna kill us some Forgotten! Come on, Eron! That's the call; it has to be!"

Eron jumped to his feet and scanned the area outside the base, searching for an incoming attack.

"Eron, let's go. Now!" Dragor said, tugging on the boy's arm. Eron let him lead them back to the base. They ran most of the way, joining the chaos unfolding in front of them.

Within the perimeter of the main cluster of buildings, recruits were running everywhere. Drill sergeants barked orders, and shouts of joy rose up from the soldiers. It seemed like everyone was excited to kill the Forgotten except Eron. Had they all lost touch with reality? Did they all actually believe the queen's words about the Forgotten being animals? Couldn't they think for themselves? He doubted any of them had ever spoken with a Forgotten or met one that they weren't trying to kill. They had to know the Forgotten were humans like themselves.

Dragor led them back to their barracks where Sergeant Ahimo waited their arrival.

"About time you two returned! We've got serious business ahead of us, and you idiots are nowhere to be found! I expected better of you, Dragor."

Eron's father barely looked at him through his tirade. It was as if Eron was nothing special at all; just another recruit from the far-off colonies that had no clue about reality. Eron wanted so badly to reconnect with him ever since he'd met him. There was never any time to talk privately. His father was always busy. The longing Eron had for his father's attention waned as each day passed. He was under the impression that his father was so wrapped up in the ADF that blood ties meant nothing. It was a stark reality that Eron didn't want to believe, though the truth was right there in front of him.

"You two, grab your gear and meet me with the rest of the recruits in ten minutes. We've got a lot to cover. The queen demanded an all-out assault on the enemy. You boys are gonna face combat much sooner than expected. I don't think you're ready yet; in fact I know you aren't, but my opinion ain't worth a damn. Get moving. Ten minutes!"

The boys scurried to their bunks and grabbed their combat uniforms before securing the rest of their gear. Eron's hands trembled as he packed his bag.

I can't kill the Forgotten. It's not right. I've got to do something!

Thirty-Two

Balla pulled Gunther along, almost dragging him across the dirt floor. Gwenny stuck close, nudging her way past her mother. That's good, Balla thought. If they shoot, she'll be safe on the other side of me. She glanced back to see the ADF soldiers scrambling to their feet and removing their rifles from their shoulder holsters.

The tunnel grew darker. Balla tossed the torch aside, not wanting the soldiers to be able to track them by the faint glow. Shots rang in the tunnel. Small puffs of dirt obscured the torch.

"Come on, keep going," Balla said.

"But I can't see anything," Gunther said.

"I know, but we have to keep moving. They'll be on us soon if we don't."

Gwenny couldn't see and slammed into a wall. Balla and Gunther, also blind in the darkness, ran into her, hitting her in the back.

"Ouch!" she screamed.

Gunther grunted. Balla tried to steady herself.

"Over there!" a soldier shouted. Lights bounced off the dark walls as the soldiers ran toward them.

"We need to hide," Gunther said.

"Where?" Gwenny asked.

Balla pulled the ADF gun from her waistband. "I have this, but only a couple shots left. They won't expect it. I don't want to kill them, but it will slow them down."

Balla crouched in front of her children. "Stay behind me and cover your ears. This is gonna be loud."

Flashlights came into view, looking like head-lights on a Topsider transport. Balla fired the gun twice, aiming low. The lights flew into the air as screams echoed.

"My leg!" a voice shouted.

"Where is it?" another said. Balla saw a light rise from the ground and shine in her direction. She'd missed him.

"How'd you get a weapon, you dirty animal?" The soldier still hadn't seen her.

I hope I can get another. Balla squeezed the trigger and a shot fired, downing the soldier.

"Stay here," she said to her children.

Balla crept closer to the soldier, his flashlight beam pointing away from her. She saw movement, though it looked more like spasms. In the glow of the flashlight, she saw a dark liquid pooling around the soldier. His rifle lay by his side.

When she approached him, she kicked the rifle away and grabbed the light, shining it on him. There was a dark circle spreading on his chest where her bullet ripped. "Oh no," she said. He opened and closed his eyes, his breathing growing weak. When he saw her standing above him, his eyes grew wide. He looked afraid.

"I'm not going to hurt you again. I didn't mean to hit you there," Balla said, pointing to his chest. "I just wanted to scare you away from my family. We aren't animals. We're just as human as you."

He shook his head back and forth, still denying in his last breath who they were.

"I'm sorry that you don't understand. Your queen has warped you. She has lied to you about us for a long time. None of the stories are true. We are not the Forgotten. We are the Truth."

He convulsed, bloody foam leaking from his mouth. With a great inhale, he stopped moving, and slowly, his final breath escaped him.

Balla closed her eyes, holding a hand over her face. What kind of person am I to kill another? One that protects her family! You did what you had to. It's not your fault they were coming for you. It was you or them. There was nothing else you could do.

She rose, looking back to where her children were, and approached the other downed soldier. He was moaning and calling for his partner.

"Grant? You there, man? I need help. I'm in a bad way over here. Grant. Grant?"

Balla blinded him with the flashlight beam as she walked closer.

"Grant, I need help, man. That thing shot my leg. I didn't know they could do that! Where'd it get a gun, anyway?"

"I'm not a thing, I'm a human," Balla said in the darkness. Behind the bright light, the soldier couldn't see her.

"Who are you? You're not Grant," the soldier said.

"No, I'm not. I'm that thing that shot you. I'm the Truth. We aren't animals."

"The truth? I don't understand. Please don't shoot me. I don't know what you did to Grant, but don't kill me. Please. I have a family."

"So do I, and you were trying to kill us. Why shouldn't I end you right now?" Balla had no intention of killing him, but fear had a way of motivating people to do what was necessary to survive. She'd seen that ever since Freedom's destruction.

"We're under orders. The queen's command is to wipe out the Forgotten. Wipe out you animals...I mean...to take you out." In the cone of light, Balla saw real fear in the soldier's face. He expected to die. She wasn't about to let him have the satisfaction.

"How many are down here with you?" Balla asked.

"None. We had another, but he got lost. Haven't seen him in days." The soldier shifted on the ground. "We've been scouring the tunnels looking for your kind—"

"The Truth! We are the Truth! We aren't a 'kind,' or 'animals.' We're humans. We have every right to live, just like you."

Balla felt something inside her snap. She'd been holding onto the thought of preserving life. The horrible Selection showed how brutal Topsiders really were. Now, down in these dark tunnels, facing hunters bent on killing her people, Balla's compassion waned. She fought the urge to end the soldier's life.

"Can you stand?"

"I don't think so. You shot my leg!"

"Better your leg than your head. You're still alive. Unlike Grant."

"You killed him? How could you!"

"Don't even start," Balla said. The pull to shoot him again grew more intense.

"You stupid animal. How could you even shoot a

gun!" The soldier's voice grew intense, dripping with hatred.

Balla closed her eyes. She didn't want to do this. Murder was wrong.

"Shut up! We're not animals! Our ancestors are the same. We all trace our heritage to Earth. You have to know this."

"How would we know? How are we to know that you filthy animals are supposed to be the same species as us? You may talk like you've got intelligence, but for all we know, you're no different than a craate or an oversized gracer."

Balla shook. She couldn't take his ignorance any longer.

"Be quiet!"

"Why? You gonna shoot me, too? I bet with enough time, any animal can learn to mimic us humans. Maybe we didn't give you enough credit, but you aren't the same as us. I mean, look at you!"

"Give me a reason not to shoot you," Balla said. She clenched her jaw and breathed heavy. Her finger twitched, poised on the trigger.

"Because you can't, that's why. You lack the ability to do it. Not in some coherent manner. You got lucky catching my leg, but I bet you weren't aiming for that. I assume your finger fluttered and that's how you caught Grant. You don't have the ability to coherently think it through."

Balla's voice lowered. "Enough," she said, and pulled the trigger.

Thirty-Three

Mina never returned to her apartment. If Sar returned, he'd find it empty. Maybe he'd worry; maybe not. She honestly didn't care. Sar was a jerk. He got what he deserved. As far as she could tell, he committed to the ADF. That meant he was the enemy.

After their meeting, Samantha took Mina to another building on the far side of Anastasia. In the basement was a secret tunnel that led out of the city deep into the southern forest. Most humans didn't venture out that way for fear of the Forgotten, but to the CDL, it was a safe haven. The Truth didn't mess with them because the CDL respected their ways.

They gave Mina a place to stay, and she soon began classes in martial combat and the true history of Anastasia. Within a week, she'd learned so much that her head hurt.

Samantha spotted her in the large tent in the middle of the compound that served as the cafeteria for all the recruits and officers of the CDL to enjoy their daily rations.

"Mind if I sit down?" she asked. Mina waved to the seat across from her, her mouth full of a grantham berry bar.

"I hear you're performing exceptionally in the combat drills. You're a natural, they say."

Mina swallowed her food and smiled. "I pretend it's

Sar or the queen, and my opponent doesn't stand a chance."

Samantha grinned. "Well, that would do it for sure! How about the rest of the lessons? Are they going well?"

"Well enough, I guess. I feel so ignorant. I should've known all this before. How can they keep us so blinded?"

"Don't worry, Mina; all new recruits feel like you do. We've been fed lies for a couple of centuries, and it's hard to adjust."

Mina opened her mouth to speak when a siren blared through the compound.

"An attack?" Mina asked.

"Come on, follow me!" Samantha said.

The two of them rushed from the table, knocking over plates and cups.

"Where are we going?" Mina yelled. The sirens were deafening. If the ADF were near, they'd know where they were for sure.

"Staging grounds. I fear we're in for a fight."

Samantha and Mina entered the staging grounds, along with the entire CDL force. There were close to five hundred men and woman, most young like Mina, but several older people. They stood out in the sea of youth, but their expressions were just as fierce.

Everyone gathered in front of the wooden stage with a red frond canopy in the center of the grounds, wondering the reason for the sirens. Finally, the deafening alarm stopped wailing, and Mina heard a rumbling in the crowd. The tension felt electric. Either something bad had happened, or was about to. The hairs on the back of her neck rose as a chill ran through her.

"Brief in two minutes," a voice called out. Loudspeakers were placed throughout the compound for quick alerts, and the voice echoed. The crowd noise rose higher. Samantha scanned the scene.

"What is it?" Mina asked.

"I don't know, Mina. The last ADF presence I heard about was spotted in Freedom, a Truth home north of here."

A small man in a black uniform took the stage. His blue skin and green hair reminded Mina of Sar. For a moment, she thought it was him, but he was far too small and moved a bit slower than Sar.

"Director Bowen," Samantha said. Mina shook her head, confused.

"Oh, the head of the CDL? I didn't know he was here."

Bowen took the center of the stage, raised his hands, and stepped to the microphone.

"Ladies and gentlemen: the ADF, under the queen's command—" A chorus of boos erupted from the crowd. "The ADF," he began again, "has attacked and destroyed another Truth stronghold. That's two cities completely wiped out." The crowd shouted their disapproval.

Bowen held up his hands again to silence the crowd.

"The Truth are on the run. The queen has demanded their slaughter. We cannot stand by idly while our brethren are hunted like animals. We must act on their behalf. The time to strike has finally come. We must stand with the Truth. We must fight the evils brought upon our lands by the queen. We must resist."

The crowd erupted in applause. Shouts of triumph and excitement filled the grounds. The electricity of the moment flooded through Mina. More than ever before, she believed. Convicted in her mind of the validity of their actions, she cheered with the crowd. Samantha raised her hand in solidarity, and they applauded Director Bowen's speech.

From the left of the stage, a feeble female Truth lumbered toward Director Bowen. He smiled and waved her closer. As she approached the microphone, Bowen leaned forward, arms raised to quiet the crowd, and said, "My fellow Libertarians: I present to you Council Chair for Inventa and acting leader of the Truth, Chair Deelia!" The crowd burst into applause, Mina and Samantha cheering loudly.

"This is exciting!" Mina said to Samantha. Samantha's face was radiant.

"Mina, you have no idea! It's happening! We're joining forces! This is what we've been waiting for!"

Chair Deelia brought the microphone lower, as she was much shorter than Bowen. The crowd quieted.

"My fellow fighters for freedom and the Truth: I am Chair Deelia. I come to you, requesting your aid against a common threat. You, more than anyone else, know the dangers and destruction the ADF has caused on our planet under the direction of the royal line for as long as anyone remembers. We Truth have lived peaceful lives, and seek to share our reality with any who will listen." She paused to cough, two larger Truth rushing to her side. She waved them off and they stood at a distance as she grasped the microphone for balance.

"The queen has ordered the destruction of my people." Boos and shouts echoed her words. Director Bowen raised his hands to calm the crowd.

"Our people have suffered a great loss. The ADF, under the queen's orders, have destroyed two of our cities, killing thousands of our men, women, and children." Deelia closed her eyes, holding tight to the microphone stand with both hands. "We have lost many, many Truth to their brutality. This tragedy touches all of us. Not only have we suffered greatly, but so have you, along with all who live under the queen's dominion. Our people have been in constant contact with Earth since the moment humanity landed on this planet. The queen would like them to be forgotten, but we have not, and we have tried unsuccessfully to bring an end to the tyranny on Anastasia."

Mina grabbed Samantha's arm, facing her. "What does she mean? Earth abandoned us long ago. We were a colony that was left to fend for ourselves."

"There's more, Mina...so much more."

Chair Deelia continued. "With the destruction of our cities, our ability to communicate with Earth has been disrupted. Our remaining cities are trying to get back online with them, but if the ADF continues its onslaught, we will soon face annihilation. The time to resist is now. Can we count on your assistance to thwart the menace to our people? To your people?" The crowd erupted in thunderous applause. Director Bowen raised his fist in the air, leading the assembled in a chant of "Fight! Fight! Fight!"

Mina and Samantha thrust their fists high in the air,

chanting with the others, eager to push back the evil of the ADF.

Deelia raised her arms and spread her hands wide, the crowd slowly quieting. "The Truth accept your aid, and we will fight together to bring harmony and peace to our world. We no longer must accept the tyranny of a few."

With those words, Deelia was escorted off the stage by her two Truth assistants.

Samantha scanned the crowd, then turned to Mina. "It's war, Mina. The time has come for us to fight."

Thirty-Four

Five days after their encounter with the soldiers, Nagi, Gar, and Callia travelled deep in the forest, nearing Novus. Their captive was at first combative and abusive, struggling with Gar and hurling obscenities at the small group of Truth as if he still had the upper hand.

"You know, it would be a whole lot easier if you would shut up and listen," Nagi said. Callia hadn't left his side since her brother's murder. She had been quiet for most of the journey. Nagi felt sorry for her, and hoped his own family hadn't had to deal with such tragedy. He longed to be with them and protect them...if they were still alive.

"Listen to your nonsense about all of us being the same! You're ignorant. I don't care if you can talk and make informed decisions; you're nothing but a dirty animal. All of you! You exist as you are because you're weak. Your species couldn't handle being part of our world," the soldier said. His face was bruised, as Gar occasionally punched him to get him to shut up.

"We're the ignorant ones? Really?" Nagi said. "You do know we're exactly the same, right? Other than this thick fur, of course." He held out his arm, the blood which matted it days ago now cleaned away.

"Come on; you expect me to believe that? You're animals! We're taught that as part of our basic training."

"I was once one of you," Nagi said.

"Me, too," added Gar, kicking the soldier.

"Stop it! I doubt it. That's not how it works," the soldier replied.

"Yes, it does," Nagi replied. "I grew up in Rippon. I was forced into the Selection like all the boys my age, and I was shot. I couldn't leave, or they'd kill me. I hid in the forest, hoping to die a quick death, when a Truth found me. Like you, I called them the Forgotten, but that's not right. They—we—call ourselves the Truth because we know who we are. You don't. Not yet, but you will. It doesn't take long to transform. It's nature. The craziest things happen when you're free from the settlements and get out into the natural elements of Anastasia. Ever notice the short white walls around the colonies? There's an element unknown on Earth that exists here. It interacts with our bodies and en-hances excessive hair growth and enlarged muscles. We still don't understand it, but we do know that after some time away from the surface settlements, every-one starts to turn. Why do you think the Selection only takes thirty days? Have you noticed your arms? I did."

The soldier held out one of his arms. "No! It's im-possible! You've infected me with your animal genes. This can't be happening!" He struggled to free himself, but Gar held him tight.

"Not impossible, but inevitable. It's natural. We're the same as you, only wiser since we know who we are. We've been in constant contact with Earth. Every few years, we receive a message to let us know it still exists. They know we're here, but they can't do anything. War has ravaged the planet for centuries. Maybe one day, we'll reconnect with them through more than a few static messages, but for now, we're on our own, as we have been since we landed," Gar said.

The soldier ceased his struggles. "How can this happen? How can you animals know any of that? It's not true!"

Callia threw a large red rock at him, striking him in the chest.

"Ouch! What was that for, you little beast?"

Gar smacked him on the back of his head. "Don't talk to her that way. We ought to kill you right now for what you did to her brother."

"Why'd you shoot him? He didn't do anything to you!" Callia shouted. Nagi held her back. She struggled against his grip.

"Please try and stay calm, Callia. He's ignorant. He didn't know better," Nagi said.

"But what about your family? If they were killed, wouldn't you be upset?" She looked up at him with large eyes, tears running down her cheek. "Wouldn't you want to hurt them?" she said in a quiet voice.

Nagi paused. He'd been wanting to destroy the entire ADF, the queen, and anyone else who stood in his way. His family was innocent. All the Truth were innocent. None of them deserved what the ADF had done.

"Callia, I understand. I also know that wanting to hurt anyone associated with the bad guys might make you feel better, but it doesn't change what happened."

"But you killed the other one! You beat him to death! Why do I have to hold back? Why can't Gar just kill him now? We don't need him."

"Callia, dear," Gar said, "Nagi is right. I don't care much for this one," he kicked the soldier, "but killing him won't do us much good. We might be able to use him for information. Right now, that's what is valuable to us."

The soldier looked from Callia to Nagi. "You think I'm telling you animals anything? Forget it!"

Gar smacked him on the back of the head again. "You'll eventually give us what we need. Heck, you might even join us if we keep you out here long enough."

"I'll never be an animal like you! There's something wrong with you...something wrong with your genes. No way humans turn into hairy creatures like you. You're abominations. You shouldn't be here!"

"Gar, I can't keep trying to explain it to him. Can you shut him up or something?" Nagi said.

Gar ripped the soldier's uniform, shoved a fist-sized wad of the material in his mouth and tied a strip around his head, placing the other end in his mouth. "That ought to do it. He's either gonna see the truth, or die in denial. Either way, he's quiet for now."

They marched through the forest, Anastasia's red sun dropping near the horizon. It was quiet, except for the occasional muffled outburst from the soldier and Callia screaming at him to shut up. Nagi kept her apart from their captive, afraid she'd do something rash. Not that he didn't deserve every bad thing her imagination could inflict on him; they needed to see if he had any useful information. After that...maybe he'd live. Maybe they could convert him. He was more stubborn than most, but given enough time, most Topsiders eventually listened to reason and gave in.

"Nagi, we need to find shelter," Gar said.

"I was thinking the same thing, Gar. Maybe we can find a grantham tree to take cover under. I think I saw some up ahead."

They followed Nagi's lead to a small clearing with several grantham trees. "This'll do," Gar said. He lifted the lower leaves to get underneath and a craate rushed him, knocking him over.

"Gar!" Nagi yelled. Soon, five more craates had darted out from the grantham tree, circling them. Snarling and growling red, purple, and blue craates closed in on them, tightening their circle.

"Nagi, what are those?" Callia said. She gripped his leg tight, trying to burrow into him. Their captive screamed, but the gag muffled his voice. His eyes were giant white orbs, straining to keep track of the craates.

"Stay close to me, Callia! Don't get near them!"

Gar regained his composure and grasped the craate by its throat. It struggled in his grip, paws pumping furiously, trying to push itself away from him. The muscles on Gar's arms bulged as he squeezed tighter until the craate stopped fighting. A loud, sickening crunch as he squeezed one last time indicated the thing was dead.

The rest of the craates closed in on the group, nipping at Callia's legs. Nagi swatted them back, but they continued to move closer, drawing the circle smaller. One of them bit into the soldier's leg and ripped off a chunk of uniform and flesh. He screamed through the gag, his face turning bright red. Nagi crouched, waiting for a craate to rush him.

One of them crept closer, its large yellow fangs

dripping saliva. The one beside it moved to flank Nagi. He pushed Callia behind him. Gar slowly stood as the other two craates fanned out in his direction, trying to keep him in the center of their circle.

"Use the gun, Nagi!"

Nagi had forgotten about the soldier's gun he'd slung around his shoulders. He swung it around and began shooting at the craates. He got one in the head, dropping it. He clipped another on the leg. It howled in pain and writhed on the ground. He missed the other two, but at the crack of the rifle, they backed away and fled. He fired in their direction, unsure if he'd hit either one, but at least they were gone. He fired again at the one rolling in pain on the ground, punching a hole through its chest, and it went still.

"What is happening?" Callia said. She fell to the ground, sobbing. The soldier moaned in pain, a large bloody wound on his leg. Gar was breathing heavy, but looked to be unscathed. Nagi held the rifle in his hands, his arms shaking.

"It's our world now, Callia. It's not going to be easy out here, but we'll make it. I promise."

Nagi hoped he wasn't lying.

Thirty-Five

After the rally, Mina and the others were separated into combat groups. They divided into groups of intermingled CDL members and Truth fighters. Although there were more CDL than Truth in each group, clearly, the Truth were better prepared to fight.

During knife training, Mina sparred with a small male Truth named Panna. He was from Cape Rouge and new to the Truth. He was maybe two years older than Mina, yet his thick brown fur made him appear larger than he actually was.

"Come on, you can do better than that," Panna said. They circled each other in the sparring arena.

Mina grunted.

"Don't worry, Panna; underestimating me will only lead to your downfall."

Panna laughed, then lunged at her with his training knife. Once in combat, they'd be issued long metal knives, but for practice, they used wooden ones. Panna's blade knocked Mina on the arm. "Come on! Fight, Mina! The ADF won't go easy on you." She retaliated. He spun, swiping down on her arm and forced her to let go of the blade. It thudded on the packed red dirt.

"Ouch," she said, rubbing her arm. "You didn't have to hit me so hard."

"Sorry, but you need to be better prepared. Maybe

you need to go back to that Sar guy. He'll watch over you."

She grabbed her knife off the ground and took her stance. Panna lunged, and Mina shifted slightly to the left, then charged at him, knocking him down. She smacked his hand, flinging his knife to the next circle. She held the point of her blade just above his eye. "Give me a reason not to," she said.

Panna raised his hands to his face. "Hey, hey, I'm on your side. I was just trying to get you off guard."

They took a break from their training.

Soon, another pair sparred in the circle. All around the camp, others were training as hard as they could, knowing the time for attack was closing in on them.

"You think we'll be able to do anything? I mean, are we strong enough to force the ADF back? Can we stop them?" Mina asked Panna. The two of them sat on the dirt under a tree, sipping water and watching the others practice.

Panna scanned the white-walled camp. "Yeah, I think we can. We have something to fight for. They're fighting out of orders. There's a difference."

Mina considered his words for a few moments. "Maybe. I guess. I've known others who joined the ADF, and they seemed pretty intense about it. They weren't forced, but they were strongly guided to their decision." She thought about Sar's eagerness to join the ADF, as if his entire life revolved around being a soldier. Then she thought about Eron and what he must be going through. She wondered if she'd ever see him again. She hoped so. She missed him. Maybe one day, they could at least talk again. If Samantha was right and Eron had joined the ADF to infiltrate their ranks and pass on intel, he could be in serious danger.

A week after Panna and Mina had discussed the ability of their combined forces to thwart the ADF, an alarm sounded in the camp. As before, the CDL and now Truth soldiers streamed into the grounds, surrounding the stage to await the latest news.

Mina and Samantha ran to the grounds together, nervous and wary of what was to come.

The sirens died down and a nervous energy flowed through the crowd. Director Bowen and Chair Deelia approached the center stage together, Bowen taking the lead. He grasped the microphone. A loud squeal forced Mina to cover her ears. He cleared his throat and began.

"My fellow fighters and assembled Truth: the time has come. The ADF has dispatched a convoy to the Truth city of Novus. Their path is not far from here. We must halt this advance at all costs. If they reach the city before we can stop them, it means an irreparable blow to our cause. This is what we've been preparing for. This is the moment we begin to reclaim our home in the name of peace and harmony. The queen's insistence on genocide must be dealt with. We are the only ones capable of such a feat. Are you ready to face this challenge?"

The crowd erupted in applause, shouts of "Victory!" and "For the Truth!" loud in the air.

"Some of us will not make it back from this battle, but our lives will not be lost in vain. Our cause is just. We fight for freedom. We fight for each other. We fight for all. We fight...for Truth!"

Mina raised her fist high in the air, screaming,

"Victory!" Samantha did the same, also caught up in the frenzy sweeping the crowd.

"Your orders are clear: repel the ADF, begin the end of their tyranny, and return this planet to all," Bowen said. Cheers rose from the crowd.

"Return to your barracks for your assignments. May the great goddess Anastasia light your way." Bowen waved to the crowd, Chair Deelia nodding as they left the stage.

"Come on, let's find out where we're going," Samantha said. She grabbed Mina's arm and they ran back to the barracks.

"Can you believe it? You're in my squad!" Samantha said after they were given their assignments. She was giddy from the outset, excited at her chance to finally do something to fight the ADF.

Mina was more reserved. "Wow. Second in command of our squad? Me?"

Panna walked up behind her and clapped her on the back. "Congrats, Mina! You deserve it. And guess who gets to join you?" He grinned, his white teeth in stark contrast to his dark fur.

"You? I get to fight in a squad with you?" she said. He nodded.

"Sure do. And I couldn't think of more fierce leaders than you and Samantha. We'll be in good hands for sure."

Mina grinned. "Yeah, just don't provoke me to turn on ya." He returned the smile and walked away.

Samantha nudged her arm as they watched Panna make his way through the camp. "I think he kinda likes you, Mina."

"Him? No. I don't think so."

"Ummm, yeah, I'm pretty sure I've seen that look before. Guys aren't good at hiding their feelings on their faces."

Mina looked at Samantha. "Well, he can like me all he wants. He's nice enough, I guess, but now's not the time." She pictured Eron and wondered where he was and what he was feeling. Did he think about her like she thought about him? She hoped so. She wanted to make it right with him. Even if they weren't together, at least she could explain why things had happened like they did. Maybe that other girl, Sarai, explained it. Even so, Mina needed to talk to him at least once to clear the air. If they were meant to be together, they would be.

Her cause was now aligned with the CDL. She'd seen too much abuse perpetrated at the whim of the queen. Her policies and those of her predecessors were wrong. Samantha showed her. Annabelle showed her. She'd seen it with her own eyes. Training alongside the Truth brought it all home to her.

Thirty-Six

The ride from the base to the suspected Forgotten home was bumpy. More than once, Eron's head smacked against the inside of the transport. In the darkened hull of the gray vehicle, Eron scanned the faces around him. There were at least twenty other boys around his age, most looking like they'd seen combat up front and personal.

Near the large back door of the transport, Dragor smiled as he admired the long dagger in his hands. He held it up, trying to catch the fleeting light inside, making it glint off the pristine blade. He noticed Eron watching him. "This is what killed that Forgotten back in the Selection. It has tasted blood once; now it can again. I can feel it calling for another chance."

Eron turned and closed his eyes. Dragor's bravado and ignorance had set new lows. How am I going to stop this? I have no power. I have no control over this. Somehow, I must do something. Eron's mind drifted as the transport trundled along an unknown road. There were no windows inside for the soldiers to watch the surroundings shift and change. Wherever they stopped, they were expected to engage anything in their path.

The transport leered to the right then slammed into something hard, forcing all the boys to the front of the vehicle. Eron landed in the lap of a boy he didn't know, and the boy pushed him off. The transport stopped.

"What was that?" one of the boys called out.

"Stay calm. We probably hit a rut or something," Dragor said.

Grumbling and whispers surrounded Eron as the boys tried to reclaim their composure.

A loud explosion rocked the transport, making it sway side to side. Several of the boys fell off their bench and landed on the floor, their arms and legs tangling together. Another explosion, smaller this time, blew off the door at the back of the transport. When the smoke cleared, five masked and hooded figures stood at the opening with guns drawn on the boys.

"All of you, get out now!" a female voice called. The boys inside hesitated. "I said now!" she said, raising her gun and firing into the sky. Eron winced and followed the boys in front of him out the transport.

"Down on your knees," a masked gunman said once the boys were outside. This one was a male, and Eron thought the voice sounded like he was young.

"Look, what do you want from us?" Dragor said, "We're not much of a threat. We don't want you. We've got other plans. Our directive is to—" one of the shooters smacked Dragor in the mouth with the butt of his rifle.

"Shut up! Don't speak unless spoken to. You aren't in control here; we are," the gunman said. Dragor opened his mouth, and the shooter feigned another blow, making Dragor shut it immediately.

The female who stood at the opening turned toward them. "Now, this is gonna be a quick and easy situation for all of you. We don't wanna kill you, but give us a reason, and we won't hesitate to put a bullet in your skulls. Got it?" The boys nodded. Eron closed his eyes, hoping death was not soon at hand.

"Good. Hand over your weapons. All of them. Then you can go. Simple as that. We aren't in the game of killing our fellow humans, no matter what line your superiors are feeding you, but we can't have you roaming the wilderness, intent on murder. We must be free. All of us. Any of you decide to get brave, and you will be put down. Don't force our hand like your drivers did. Those were unfortunate casualties of the madness of your queen. You have a choice now. Leave and be free, or fight and die. I'd rather be free if I were you."

A couple of boys handed over their weapons without hesitation.

"Good boys. Now, get out of here," she said.

"But where do we go?" one of the boys said.

"I don't care. You can't stay here. Live free, like we were meant to."

Both boys stared at her, shifting from one foot to the other.

"Go!" she said, firing in the air. The boys ran toward the forest on the far side of the road.

"Anyone else? Don't try anything stupid."

Dragor rose and walked slowly toward the girl.

"Stop there," she said when he was about five feet away from her. "Hand over your weapon."

Dragor shifted the rifle's strap from his shoulder and handed it over. As she reached to take it, he reached inside his shirt for his dagger.

"No!" one of the masked female shooters called out. She dove to knock the leader out of the way, but in doing so, chose her fate.

Dragor plunged the blade into the woman's side. She screamed in agony. The other masked shooters opened fire, riddling Dragor's body with bullets. Blood sprayed over the girl, staining her gray cloak with crimson. Dragor fell to the ground, his body twitching once before all motion ceased.

The lead gunman ran to the girl, while the others trained their weapons on the boys.

"Don't anyone move!" a gunman yelled.

The girl lay on the ground, a dark crimson pool growing beneath her on the packed red soil. Their leader ran to her and dropped to her knees, removing her own mask and that of the girl bleeding on the ground.

"Are you ok?" she said. She moaned. When Eron tried to get a better look at the two of them, the shooter nearest to him threatened him.

"Look the other way, boy, or we do to you what we did to this one," he nodded toward Dragor.

Eron resisted the urge to see who the girl was. He hoped neither one was Samantha. Losing her like this would be too much.

The girl moaned in pain, louder than before.

"We need to get you out of here, now!" their leader said to her. She cried out when the leader tried to lift her from the ground.

"Stop touching me! I can take care of it myself!" she called out.

A lump grew in Eron's throat. A deep pit in his stomach twisted and pulled on him. He knew that voice. Both of them. He'd heard them so many times before. They called to him in the darkest moments. He didn't recognize them with the masks on.

"Stop. Let me help you up," the leader said.

"Whatever, just don't touch the blade," she replied. She grunted when the leader lifted her off the ground.

Despite the threat of injury, Eron chanced a glance at the girls. It was them!

Samantha! He'd found his sister again!

Then, he peered at the other girl. Long red hair had been cut short, but it was definitely her. How could he not have recognized her before?

The nearest shooter smacked Eron in the back of the head. "I said, turn the other way! What's wrong with you, ADF? They turn off your ability to listen?" Eron recoiled from the blow, but wouldn't turn his head.

"I said, look the other way!" the gunman screamed. Eron was about to say something when the leader spoke.

"Eron? Is that you?"

Eron smiled as best he could. "Yeah, it's me. Hello, Samantha; hello, Mina."

Thirty-Seven

When Balla squeezed the trigger, nothing happened. Her mind prepared for murder, but was shockingly torn from its trajectory by the misfiring weapon.

"Ha! You stupid animal! Don't you know when you're out of bullets?"

Balla's mind raced. What could she do? Should she kill him with her bare hands? Maybe use the rifle from the dead soldier? Yes! That was it; get his rifle! Shut the mouthy one up. But should she? Doesn't he deserve to live? Isn't that what you preached?

Balla turned to the dead soldier, intent on finding his weapon. She was unsure if she was going to shoot the other soldier yet, but she needed protection for her family even if she didn't.

The body lay on the tunnel floor. The gray uniform was now tinted pink from the pouring blood. His rifle lay a few feet away from him. Balla carefully maneuvered around the body to secure the rifle. The moment she grasped it, a shot rang out in the tunnel, deafening her.

A bright, sharp pain radiated upwards from her leg. Blood sprayed the wall in front of her. The ringing in her ears disoriented her. For a moment, she wasn't sure if she was dead as she looked at her surroundings in a misty haze, unable to hear her children shouting or the soldier screaming at her from behind. Everything moved in slow motion, as if she was watching the crawling playback of a show on a video screen in Freedom. Her leg alternated from numbness to extreme pain. She took a step on the injured leg and staggered backwards, winded.

Balla turned her head to the side and watched as Gwenny and Gunther screamed silently in the tunnel, gesturing behind her. She slowly turned her head, catching a glimpse of the soldier stumbling toward her, grinning. He'd raised his rifle with one hand and held it pointed at her. His mouth moved in silent anger, his eyes betraying the words she couldn't hear.

Then, like a vanishing dream, her ears were filled with the sound of screaming. Her children were frantically trying to get her attention, to get her to move away from the soldier.

"Don't kill my mother!" Gunther cried. "She's all we have left! Don't kill her, please!"

Gwenny added to the confusion. "Mother, get up! Move, Mother! He's coming for you!"

The soldier's voice dripped hatred. "You ignorant animals. I'll kill all of you! I'll enjoy ridding our world of three more filthy beasts. Maybe I'll mount your heads on my wall." He dragged his injured leg behind him as he moved closer.

"I'll kill you all for what you did to Grant. His wife and two kids will now have to live in the colonies because of you. Stupid animals."

Balla could see he was unstable on his injured leg. She had one chance to stop him. Her leg throbbed, but she was determined, no matter how painful it was. One opportunity to catch him by surprise. She could at least muster that much strength.

"We shoulda killed all of you when we had the chance. Bombed you back to nothing, but no...the queen wants every one of you to face your executioner. She's got it bad for you...things. I don't care. I enjoy the hunt."

Balla pushed herself off the ground, spun on her injured leg, and hoisted the rifle into position. "No more," she said, pulling the trigger several times.

Each bullet found its mark. The soldier's body was soon riddled with red puncture wounds as the bullets ripped through him. The rifle flew in the air as he fell backwards. When he landed, he convulsed for a few moments before his body gave up the fight.

Balla felt the agony in her leg and collapsed on the ground. Her children ran to her.

"Mother, are you okay?" Gwenny asked. Gunther could barely talk through his sobs. He clutched Balla, burying his face in her thick fur.

Balla moaned. Her leg screamed at her.

Gwenny grabbed the flashlight and inspected her mother's leg. "Mother!"

Balla raised herself up to view her leg. Blood flowed from the wound, matting her fur.

"Mother, can you stand on it?" Gwenny asked.

Balla tried to speak, but she couldn't form the words. It was as if she was mute. Her vision turned black. *Gwenny, the light! Turn the light back on!* Then it faded away.

She woke sometime later, still on the ground in the tunnel. Gwenny and Gunther sat beside her, flanking her. Gwenny held a rifle across her knees and Gunther scanned the flashlight both ways in the tunnel.

"What if more of them come?" Gunther asked.

"Then I shoot them; that's what happens. We can't risk it."

"But Mom didn't want to kill them. She said we all deserve to live."

Gwenny looked to the side. "Yeah, but she did that." She nodded to the dead soldier sprawled on the ground behind them. "And that one," she said pointing toward the other.

"But, Gwenny, they were trying to hurt her. She didn't mean it. She wanted them to live."

Balla moaned and they turned her way.

"Mother? Are you awake?" Gwenny asked.

"Mother!" Gunther said. He bent near her face. His eyes were red. Balla wanted to comfort him, to tell him she was going to take care of them, but could she? She could barely move; how could she protect them?

"I'm awake," Balla said. Her voice was weak. "I'm okay."

"No, you aren't," Gwenny said. "Your leg is bleeding bad. I don't think it's broke or anything, but you've got a bad wound. We gotta get you out of here."

Balla felt feeble. "Help me up," she said in a low voice. Gunther grasped her arm, tugging on her. Gwenny dropped the rifle and pulled on her other arm. They raised her to a sitting position.

"Okay, hold on," Balla said. She blinked a few times and looked at her leg. "Gunther, shine the light there," she said. He pointed the light at her leg and she cringed.

She could see the pink muscle underneath her fur, blood oozing. "Well, that might be bad." She chuckled, trying to ease the tension.

Gunther looked at her, his face twisted as if he wasn't sure he heard her right.

"It's okay, Son; my leg will be fine. Just a little pain, that's all." She smiled, though her leg felt like it was on fire. She didn't want them to lose what little physical strength they had left.

"We need to move. We can't stay here. Let's try and find one of the exits...maybe go back the way we came. It's too dangerous down here. I'd rather take our chances up top instead of being stuck down here." She paused, closed her eyes, and bit her lip as a fresh wave of pain shot up from her leg. "We'll make it to Novus, I promise."

Balla pushed herself off the ground, Gunther and Gwenny aiding her on both sides. It was a struggle, but eventually they were able to stabilize her. She stood for a moment, wobbly, then leaned on Gwenny. "I'll need a little bit of help, but I'll be fine."

She took a few steps, then stopped. Death was all around her. The ADF meant to exterminate the Truth. It wasn't right. They couldn't be allowed to continue their destruction.

Thirty-Eight

Nagi, Gar, Callia, and the soldier pushed their way to Novus. Twice they escaped possible craate attacks when Gar spotted packs in the distance. The group now found themselves staring at an open field with no trees in sight.

"Gar, do you know where we are?" Nagi asked. The older scout held a hand above his eyes to shield them from the red sun. He looked out over the waving orange grass and shook his head.

"I don't know for sure. Is this Fenix Plain?" Gar asked.

"Kinda looks like it, doesn't it? If this is Fenix, that means we're close to Beta Prime."

The soldier shifted on his feet, wincing when he stepped on his sore leg. The craate wound looked infected; yellow pus oozed from the center. Nagi smelled the foul stench when he neared the man. If they didn't find him medical help soon, he'd be dead...which wasn't the worst thing that could happen, if Gar had his way.

"You think we ought to drop him off at the city?" Nagi asked.

"Are you kidding? The moment we set foot near that place, those idiot ADF troops will be gunnin' for us. I'm not about to let them shoot me or Callia, here."

"But we need to do something about him. His leg is

getting worse."

"So what? He's a bad guy. Bad guys don't get good things," Callia said. Nagi wanted to scold her, but in a way, she was right. He was the bad guy. But then again, so was Nagi. And Gar, for that matter. They were both bad guys at one time, but they were redeemed. They knew the truth. They were the Truth. How could he let the man die or continue to suffer when they had the opportunity to convince him of his ignorance? They couldn't act like the ADF. They were better than that. They had to be.

"Callia, I'm so sorry about your brother. I've lost a lot of loved ones, too. As the Truth, we have to rise above the ADF. They're misguided. They don't know any better."

Gar harrumphed, but otherwise remained quiet. Nagi saw the anger in the older Truth's eyes. Nagi understood what Gar was feeling, but killing just because they were different was no way to handle the ADF or any of the Topsiders. There had to be a better way.

The soldier didn't say much when they removed his gag to eat, but his arms were becoming increasingly hairy. The muscles in his arms were also growing. The once short hair on top of his head was now thicker and longer. His transformation had begun. It wouldn't be too much longer; maybe a few weeks before he would physically be no different than Nagi and Gar. Mentally was another thing. It took Topsiders a while to come to terms with what their new reality of being a Truth was. However, once they did, it was as if an alternate life had opened up for them.

"How long you been out here?" Gar asked the soldier.

"Long enough to know you animals are poisoning me with your sickness."

Gar smacked him on the arm. "Come on, quit being stupid. You know better by now, right?"

The soldier closed his mouth and turned away.

"I'm gonna ask ya again. How long you been out here?"

"Too long," the soldier said. "I've been on patrol for five weeks now. I haven't been to base in six."

Gar and Nagi exchanged a curious glance. Gar spoke up. "Six weeks since you been on base? That's too long for most ADF. They keep ya on short assignments. Always have."

"Yeah, so what? The sooner I get back to Beta Prime and get this wound looked at, the sooner I'm done with you."

"You? Done with us?" Gar asked. "I think ya got it wrong, kid. We're the ones that decide when we're done with you. And far as I can tell, it ain't gonna be anytime soon."

Nagi shrugged. "Then what, Gar? What do we do with him? Bring him with us? He's hurt, and we don't have the meds to treat him. He's going to die out here with us. You know as well as I that our priority is to always save lives. Always."

Callia tugged on his tunic. "But Nagi, he's a bad guy," she whispered. Nagi ran a hand through the fur on her head. She reminded him so much of his own children.

"I know, but it's the way of the Truth."

"Where were you headed when we got you, anyway?" Gar asked the soldier. When the soldier refused to speak, Gar kicked him in the shin. The soldier yelped and hobbled on his bad leg.

"I swear, when I get free, you'll pay for that, old man."

"Wait. Did you just call him old man? As in, he's a person and not an animal?" Nagi asked.

"It was a mistake. He's every bit an animal as the rest of you. Maybe more so."

Nagi looked at his group of Truth and smiled. He adjusted his tunic and extended his large hand. "My name is Nagi. This is Gar and Callia."

"I heard your name already. What kind of stupid animal are you?"

Nagi held his thick furry hand out, waiting.

"What?" the soldier said.

"I'm waiting for you to shake it. Like a man. Like a human."

Gar raised a hand as if to strike the soldier. He shook his head and grasped Nagi's hand. "Jon," he said. "My name is Jon."

"Well, isn't that nice," Gar said. "He has a name. Nagi, we need to get rid of him."

"Jon, what my friend here means is we need to look after you and make sure you get the help you need. Even if it means putting ourselves in danger. We humans must stick together."

"Whatever," Jon said.

"Perfect! Gar, Callia, we leave for Beta Prime in the morning, or close enough to it. Jon needs help before it's too late."

"Already is," Gar said.

"Still, we gotta do what we can. If he chooses not to

join us, it's not a problem. Our homes are already in ruins, so what else can he do?" Nagi said.

They travelled until the bright pink sky turned a darker shade and the moon rose above them, casting a pink glow over everything.

"We camp here for the night," Nagi said. "It's better than traveling in the dark."

"Jon, you okay with that, or do ya need some convincing?" Gar asked. Jon said nothing.

"Once day breaks, we should be able to get close enough to the city to let you get back to your people. I do hope you don't forget what you've learned out here. We're not animals. We're like you, only enlightened. And a bit furrier," Nagi said.

"Yeah, whatever," Jon said. "Just get me out of here before your sickness gets to me. I don't wanna end up like you. It's not right. It's got to be the worst thing that can happen to a person."

"I doubt that, but I'll let ya think so," Gar said. "You go to sleep. I'll get the first watch," he said to Nagi. "Don't want him escaping us, do we? Not yet, anyway. We gotta get him help, right?"

Nagi nodded and he and Callia found small indents in the land to lie down in. Nagi waited until she drifted off before closing his eyes and giving in to his own restless sleep.

Thirty-Nine

After the ambush, the young ADF soldiers scattered, choosing freedom over death. The only soldier that didn't leave was Eron. It took several harsh commands from Samantha before the CDL squad allowed him to approach Mina, as weak as she was from Dragor's blade.

"Mina!" he said as he knelt beside her. "I'm sorry about Dragor. He's been trained to kill. He was following orders."

She winced and turned to him. "So, what about you? Are you just following orders?" She coughed and held her hand to her wound.

"What? No! I was doing what Samantha wanted. She asked me to join the ADF. They aren't all bad, you know."

Mina closed her eyes, Eron watching as the pain ran through her.

Samantha sighed. "He's right, Mina. I asked him to. We needed the intel. He gave us locations we wouldn't otherwise know about."

"Locations? What are you talking about?" Eron asked.

Samantha shook her head. "Your tooth."

"Huh?"

"Never mind, I'll tell you later."

"Look, Eron, I have no sympathy for the ADF. The

queen has you brainwashed. The ADF is evil. Everything it stands for is wrong," Mina said.

Eron looked down, unable to meet her gaze. "I know. I've seen enough in my short time with them. The queen ordered attacks on the Forgotten."

"The Truth," she interrupted.

He nodded. "Yeah, the Truth. We were on our way to support the larger mission. I think we were on our way to Novus."

"I know. That's why we're here," she said, coughing again.

"Mina, you need help. Is there a first aid kit or something? If not, we should have some supplies in the transport, or what's left of it."

"I'll check," Samantha said. She left and inspected the transport, coming back empty-handed.

"Looks like whatever was in there was destroyed."

"You guys gotta have something, right?" He looked at Samantha and the rest of the shooters, now all with their hoods removed. There were two human males, both about his age; another human girl; and a male Truth. They were resting, yet keeping a watchful eye on him.

"We aren't a regular military, bud," the human female said. She was about his height with short blonde hair. Her skin was pale green.

"That doesn't mean you can't have medical supplies," he replied. She shrugged and turned away, focusing on something far off.

"Mina," he said looking down at her, "we need to get you out of here. Fast. How close is your base?"

"We aren't gonna tell you that, soldier," one of the

boys said to him. "How do we know you won't lead them to us?"

"Come on. Really? I'm one of you. Sort of. My sister knows. Right, Samantha?"

Mina coughed.

Samantha turned to her squad. "He's telling you the truth. He infiltrated the enemy to help us."

"I don't buy it. None of those ADF scum ever did us any good. All you do is kill," the male Truth said. His eyes narrowed and Eron felt uneasy.

It took a few moments, but Mina pushed herself up to a sitting position, steadying herself on one hand as she scanned her fellow rebels. "He's a good guy. He's not been converted to their ways yet. He hasn't been with them long. Even so, I say he's okay. Leave it," she stopped to cough and hold her side, grimacing. "He's on our side. End of story."

The male Truth shrugged. "Whatever. He does one thing out of line, I'm gonna take him out. I know we want them all to live, but I've seen enough. I don't trust him."

"Same here," said the boy that mocked him earlier.

"Fair enough. If that's what it takes to convince you, then whatever. You'll see," Mina said.

"No one is gonna hurt my brother. He's one of us now," Samantha said. She narrowed her eyes, looking at each rebel in turn.

The others grumbled but said nothing. Samantha's words were enough, and if not, the threats from the others sealed it. They looted as much of the ADF weaponry and supplies as they could, though not much was left. Eron tried to help Mina to her feet. She struggled to stand upright, but wouldn't ask for help.

"Hurry up. Soon the ADF will know something's wrong. They'll probably send reinforcements. We aren't in the best shape to handle that right now," Samantha said.

They finished grabbing whatever they could and headed down a path cut through thick vegetation. Large orange leaves curved in on the path, creating a canopy from the larger red and yellow-leafed trees above. It was the perfect place for an ambush by soldiers or predatory animals like craates.

As they walked along the path, the three CDL attackers pushed farther ahead of Samantha, Mina, and Eron. Eron stayed back with Mina, her wounds preventing her from moving quickly. The male Truth turned back and waited. "You three gonna hurry it up? The ADF will be on our tails soon."

Samantha replied, "Go ahead, Panna, we'll catch up. We know our way back." The Truth waved them off and joined his partners.

"Seems like a fun bunch," Eron said.

Mina giggled and held her side. "Yeah, you could say that. Excellent fighters. Motivated, too. Panna is tough. He came from Freedom. He knows your brother."

"Timo?" he replied. "He knows him? Where is he? Is he safe?"

Mina stopped walking and closed her eyes. Eron noticed her hold her breath, then let it out slowly. When she opened her eyes, they betrayed the pain inside her. "Sorry, that was a tough one. Yeah, I think so. He escaped Freedom. So did his family. His wife and son and—"

"Family? What? He never told me about that! I'm an uncle?"

Mina nodded. "Seems so. He's got a boy and a girl, though technically they aren't his. He's their stepfather, but they're his now."

Eron couldn't believe it. He was an uncle...again! He knew Samantha had a son, but not Timo. He imagined the cute little furry Truth running around playing and teasing each other, much like he and Timo when they were kids.

"So, you both have children?" he said to Samantha.

She grinned. "Yeah, you're an uncle on both sides."

A loud explosion sounded in the distance.

They froze.

"What was that?" Eron asked. "Did your team do that?"

Mina shook her head. "I don't think so. Our next closest squad was too far away for that."

A sudden crush of animals overwhelmed them. A huge pack of gracers flew overheard, the large number of small bodies almost blotting out the midday sun. Larger animals crunched through the brush. On either side of them, it sounded like herds of animals were scared by the explosion. Chattering and annoyed animals sounded their alarms. A v pattern of snims glided behind the pack of gracers. They were cousins to vulbores, minus the poisonous touch. What they lacked in passive killing efficiency, they made up for in brutal shredding with their claws. Once they latched onto their prey, they did not let go, even it if meant their own death. They weren't the smartest animals, but their lethality was well known.

"Snims," Eron said, almost to himself. Samantha and

Mina looked up.

"Oh no, they've spotted us!" Mina said.

The v formation turned downward, spiraling out of the sky like a giant corkscrew. Usually that was the last thing their prey ever saw.

"Come on, we gotta hide! Hurry!"

He grabbed Mina's arm, and she screamed as he scraped against her wound. He ignored her and pulled her forward, looking for somewhere; anywhere to go.

The first snim slammed into Mina, knocking her to the ground.

Forty

Nagi awoke from a dream about his children. They were still in Freedom, dancing and playing and aggravating each other. When he opened his eyes and looked up at the pink sky above, he was reminded of how far they really were from him and how deeply he missed them and Balla. For now, he had Gar, Callia, and Jon to care for. They weren't his family, but he'd look after them just the same.

Then, a thought struck him. Shouldn't Gar have awakened him so he could take watch? He bolted upright and scanned the makeshift camp. The only other person there was Callia.

"Gar? Gar! Where are you? Jon? Where are you two?" Nagi called out. Callia stirred and opened her eyes. "Hey, did you see Gar last night? Or Jon?"

Callia rubbed her eyes. "No, why?" she said in a sleepy voice.

"They're gone. They aren't here."

Callia turned on her side, looking around. "Where are they?"

"I don't know. I should've been up long ago. Gar should've woke me to relieve him so he could sleep. Gar..." he said and covered his mouth. Did Gar take Jon away to kill him? He was adamant about not getting near Beta Prime.

"I'm scared. What happened to them? Where'd

they go?"

"I don't know, Callia. Come on, we need to get up and search for them." It's not like we have the extra time to spend looking for them. My family needs me. We must get to Novus.

Nagi and Callia set off on the plain, calling for both men with no response.

"Gar! Jon! Where are you?" Nagi called. He cupped his massive hands around his mouth to shout louder. "Gar! Don't do it Gar! It's not worth it!" The breeze picked up, the long orange and yellow grass swaying back and forth. Still, no sign of either one.

By midday, they were both exhausted and hungry. "Is there anything to eat?" Callia asked. "I'm so hungry. My stomach's been hurting for a long time. I need something to eat."

Nagi didn't reply. He knew looking for the two men was wasteful. He knew it was cutting into their plans. He had to find them. Gar might be doing something terrible, if he hadn't already.

They marched through the plain when Callia spotted a large shape off to their right. "Look, something's there!" They headed toward it and as they neared, Nagi recognized what he saw.

"I can't believe it," he said.

"What is it?"

"That, my dear, is a Traveling Tunnel entrance! We can go down there, and it will take us wherever we need to go without interference from the Topsiders. We might even find something to eat!"

Callia ran for the large rock, which was almost twice her size, screaming and calling Nagi to follow her.

When they reached the rock, Nagi saw the cover over the entrance had clearly been moved recently. "That's where they went! Gar must be down there with Jon," Nagi said.

"Let's go! I wanna go there, too! I don't like it up here," Callia said.

Nagi shifted the cover to allow them to climb down the steps built into the red dirt wall. He slid the cover back in place, obscuring all the light from Anastasia's sun. The pit grew dark, though the dirt grubber blood smeared on the wall near the lower tunnel emitted enough light for them to see the steps as they climbed down.

"This feel more like home," Callia said. Nagi ruffled the fur on her head.

"Yeah, it sure does. Come on, this way. We can follow their path. Looks like Gar found a dirt grubber to light their way."

Without hesitation, they followed the lit path ahead of them, caution thrown aside. Soon they'd catch up to the two men, and hopefully, Jon was all right.

Nagi couldn't explain to Gar earlier or to himself now why keeping the ADF soldier alive was so important to him. Maybe it was because of Eron, who was part of the ADF now, but also committed to the Truth cause. What if more of the Truth decided to murder ADF soldiers at will? Would Eron be safe?

They turned a corner and Callia screamed.

Jon lay dead, his body twisted into an odd shape on the packed-earth floor.

"Gar, why?" Nagi cried. The older scout was nowhere to be found. Nagi pulled Callia close, shielding her eyes from the dead body. "Don't look, Callia."

She clutched his leg and sobbed, her face pushed into his fur. Nagi slowly patted her head. "Shhhh, it's okay, dear. Maybe something happened, and Gar had no choice. Maybe Jon attacked him. I don't know. We need to find him."

Callia pulled back from Nagi and stared up at him. It was hard to see her eyes in the dark tunnel, but her tears glistened in the dirt grubber glow.

"I don't care that he's dead! I wanted to kill him! Why'd Gar have to go do it without us?" Callia asked. Nagi was taken aback.

"Callia! What are you saying?"

"I wanted to kill that bad guy for what he did to my brother. I hate them!" She tore from his leg and began kicking Jon's leg as though it would hurt him.

Nagi pulled her back. "Callia! Come on, now; stop that. This is wrong. I don't know what Gar was up to, but this is all wrong. Nothing seems right about—"

He paused, staring off in the distance. "What?" Callia said, her voice shaky.

"Callia, I don't think Gar did this."

He pulled her to the far wall where he spotted several holes in the surface. "These are new. Look at how the dirt is different than the rest of the wall. And look here," he said, running his hand across one of the holes. "There's still a bullet in here." He worked on the bullet until he freed it from the wall. "Gar didn't have a weapon. Neither did Jon. Someone else was here. Someone else did this. But why would the ADF kill one of their own? I don't like this at all. Something's very, very wrong."

"If they took Gar, where'd they go? We haven't seen anyone down here."

Nagi squinted as he inspected the ground for more clues as to who was there and where they went. Finally, he stopped and stared at the floor.

"Look," he said pointing at the ground. "Footprints. And they aren't from one of the Truth. These look like the patterns on the soles of ADF boots. They go that way," he said, nodding to the tunnel leading to Novus.

"So, what's that mean?"

"It means we need to hurry and warn the Truth. If the ADF finds Novus, more innocents will die. We must stop them before it happens. If they've captured Gar, they might be trying to get him to talk; to tell them where the city is. He's tough, and I expect he'll hold out, but eventually the ADF will dispose of him whether he tells them anything or not. We've got to save him."

Balla. Gunther. Gwenny. And now, Gar. Nagi's list of people he'd lost and desperately wanted back kept growing. Soon, if the ADF had their way, they'd all be dead, and nothing would oppose the queen.

Forty-One

Eron fell on top of Mina, shielding her from the snims. Samantha lay next to him, covering her face. The snims ripped at his back, long streaks of blood seeping through the shredded gray uniform. The snims screeched, sounding louder in the confines of the forest. There were at least ten of them, all dark green with full-feathered wings and elongated heads. Eron felt a gust of air when they snapped their jaws at him, trying to tear into his flesh.

Eron twisted, pulling Mina with him, and they rolled under a thick bush. Eron winced, scraping his wounds. Samantha crawled to the other side of the path, burrowing under thick cover. Mina screamed when he landed on top of her. He knew her wound hurt bad, but there was nothing he could do about it. She'd have to get mad at him later; now wasn't the time.

Snims crashed through the brush, caught in the heavy foliage. Those behind the trapped ones didn't seem to care that they were pushing their fellow snims into the bush, or that they were tearing into it rather than into Eron and Mina. The creatures' screams grew louder and more intense. Eron covered Mina with his body.

A talon broke through the bush. It struck the ground near Mina's head. Eron smashed it with his fist.

"Get out of here!" he yelled. The claws blindly lashed out, but Eron forced them away from Mina. When they caught his arm or back, he said nothing. His focus was on protecting Mina. They kept coming, relentless and terrifying.

Samantha screamed. A couple snims broke from the pack and repeatedly dove at her, though it didn't appear they had broken through the protection offered by the foliage.

Eron fought them off as best he could. Their talons were a blur of death and blood. He felt them on his back as the long, sharp nails tore at him. He couldn't see Mina through the commotion, but he only hoped she was shielded enough from the attacks to survive.

A booming explosion sounded again. The snims scattered like leaves in the wind, their terrifying dives toward Eron and Mina over as the sound scared them off.

Eron collapsed on the ground next to Mina. His back, shredded by the sharp talons, burned as he lay there. He closed his eyes and willed the pain away as best he could. The snims screeched in the distance.

"Are you all right?" Samantha called.

ADF? Eron thought. Whatever had frightened the snims was something more terrible than those vicious killers. They'd need to get moving. He wasn't in any shape to fend off something worse than the snims.

"Mina," he said in a weak voice, "we gotta get moving. Something's coming, and I don't know what it is." He coughed, his back on fire from the attack.

She didn't respond.

"Mina, come on, we gotta get moving," he said. Another loud explosion, this one closer, forced him off the ground. He turned to Mina and froze.

"Mina? Mina! Come on, get up!" He grabbed her shoulders and shook. Her eyes were wide and staring up at the sky.

"No, Mina, get up! Come on, get up!"

Samantha joined him, her hand resting on his shoulder.

A small gash on Mina's neck leaked a strong, steady stream of blood. "No!" he screamed.

"Oh, no! Not Mina," Samantha said. "Oh Eron, I'm so sorry."

Another explosion, this one even closer than the last, shook the trees around him. The ground vibrated. Something large was on its way. It had to be ADF. He knew they were on the move, closing in on Novus and ready to destroy the Forgotten—the Truth, he reminded himself—city. They must be near it, or the Truth were close by and the ADF was on the offensive.

Mina's beautiful red hair was matted with blood and dirt. Her golden eyes, once so full of life and love, were empty. He wanted nothing more than to be with her when he finished the Selection. The hope of joining her once again was all the catalyst he needed to survive. The crushing disappointment at Victory Point burned a hole inside him. It was then he decided to fight against the evils of the queen. The Selection and everything the ADF stood for was exposed as an evil force ruthlessly ruling Anastasia.

Watching Mina leave with that other boy had crushed him.

Mina. His crush from as early as he could remember. She meant so much to him. When he saw her face unveiled in the forest, his feelings overwhelmed him. The desire he once had for her erupted anew. He wanted to mend her wounds; to protect her; to care for her. He realized how much he had truly loved her.

He heard the snap of tree branches and the metal on metal crunching sound of a small ADF attack vehicle approaching. A whistle was followed by another explosion, this one straight ahead of him. The ground shook. Trees swayed. The vehicle rumbled ever closer.

"Oh, Mina," he whispered. He clutched her body, sobbing as he held her. "I should have done so much more. I'm so sorry, Mina."

"We need to move, Eron," Samantha said.

Eron clung to her, not wanting to lose her yet again, though inside he knew better.

She was gone. He'd lost her for the final time, never to return. His love, his reason for surviving, now lay dead in his arms.

The vehicle was in sight and headed directly for them.

"Now, Eron, let's go!" Samantha said.

Panicked, Eron pulled on Mina's body, realizing she was in the vehicle's path. He lifted her as the vehicle shot off another round, the sound so loud it startled Eron, and he dropped Mina to the ground.

"No, Mina, I'm so sorry," he said. He bent to lift her, but the vehicle was too close. Samantha grabbed him and pulled on his arm. Trees smashed to the left and right as the vehicle forced its way through the forest.

Branches snapped as they dashed out of the way moments before the vehicle drove right where they'd been standing.

"Mina!" he screamed. Samantha held him tight. The horrific possibility that she had been crushed under the vehicle filled Eron with anger. "Mina, no!"

"We can't do anything now," Samantha said. She held him close to her.

He turned away as the vehicle ran over the ground where Mina lay. He couldn't bear to see her body defiled in such a way. The vehicle continued on its route.

When the sound of the vehicle grew distant, Eron risked a glance in Mina's direction. Her body lay unharmed between two deep tracks.

Despite the pain radiating on his back, Eron broke Samantha's grasp and ran to Mina. He fell to his knees, holding her body to him, sobbing. He clung to her lifeless body for an eternity, blood staining his gray uniform.

Panna emerged from the brush.

"What did you do? I thought she said we could trust you."

Samantha held up a hand.

Eron turned to him, his dirty faced streaked with tears. "I tried to save her. The snims overwhelmed us. The ADF—"

"The ADF what? You expect me to believe your story?" Panna's eyes narrowed.

"I swear, it wasn't me. I, I...loved her. And now, she's gone."

Samantha stood. "He's telling the truth. Help us bury her before the animals consume her body."

Eron stood, exposing his bloody back to Panna, who grunted. "So, you saved her, huh? From snims, you say?"

"I tried. I failed."

Panna didn't say another word. The two boys carried Mina to a small clearing not far off. The three of them gathered enough rocks to cover her, protecting her body from the forest scavengers. Eron didn't sleep at all that night as he lay next to her tomb, one hand resting on the rocks.

Forty-Two

Nagi ran through the tunnel, Callia having a difficult time keeping up.

"Nagi, please don't leave me," she called from behind him. He stopped and turned around, and his eyes went huge.

"Callia, run!" he yelled.

"Huh, what are you—" she said, and then she heard the deep, menacing growl behind her. She slowly turned her head, and five feet away loomed the largest animal she'd ever seen. It stood on four legs with a head the size of her body. Its long tail swished back and forth as it eyed her. Long sharp fangs protruded from its mouth, two on each side. Its body was covered in thick gray fur with black spots. Its yellow eyes reflected in the dim dirt grubber glow.

Callia screamed and the beast hissed, spewing saliva all over her.

Nagi froze, unsure what to do. He'd never seen a bastien before. He'd read about them; heard they existed, but they were rare. They were becoming extinct. However, looking at one now, he wasn't sure how that was even possible.

"Callia, back away slowly. Don't take your eyes off it. Move to me, but go slow. Got it?"

She cried louder, stumbling as she stepped back.

"That's it, come my way," Nagi said, his calm voice

masking the terror he felt inside.

The bastien growled, the sound echoing off the tunnel walls.

"I'm scared, Nagi. It's going to get me!"

"Back away slowly, Callia, that's it. Come to me."

The bastien raised its head and sniffed, its large nose flaring with each inhale. It lowered its head and bared long teeth. Rows of razor-sharp fangs looked poised to strike.

"Callia, a few more steps, and then I want you to run to me. Not yet!" he said as she turned his way. "Face the bastien for now. You need to move away just a little farther."

"Nagi, I can't! It's going to get me!"

The bastien scratched the ground with its immense paw, sending up a puff of dust.

"Okay, now Callia! Run!"

She turned and ran to Nagi, the bastien slow to react. She rushed into Nagi's waiting arms and the bastien tore off after them.

"Come on, let's go!" Nagi yelled. He carried Callia and ran away from the bastien. It was almost as tall as the tunnel and though it was fast, the tight squeeze made it difficult for the bastien to gain much speed. It swiped at them. Nagi felt a quick whoosh of air as the claws missed their mark on his back. He ran harder, his legs burning.

Up ahead, the tunnel split into two sections.

"Hurry, Nagi! It's getting closer!"

Nagi stumbled, almost falling and losing his grip on Callia, then ran into the left tunnel. The glow from the dirt grubbers was weak here. The tunnel seemed to be less travelled than the others, but it was their only hope. The tunnel narrowed as they ran further in.

Behind them, the bastien growled and hissed. It swiped at them, but they were too far ahead, and the tunnel had narrowed enough that the beast couldn't follow them. It spit and hissed, its anger growing fierce. Nagi ran. He'd not let that thing get ahold of Callia. Soon, the hissing grew weak and Nagi finally paused to turn around. The bastien blocked the tunnel, but they were too far away for it to harm them. His hunch about the smaller tunnel was right. The bastien was too large to chase them. How it survived down in the tunnels, he didn't know, but he did know they were almost its next meal.

Callia cried into Nagi's chest. "Why is everything after us? What did we do?"

Nagi held her tight, breathing heavy. "We didn't do anything, Callia. Sometimes bad things happen. There's no reason; no logic. They just are."

"I hate it!" she shouted. She pulled her head back from him and in the faint glow, he noticed her eyes were bloodshot and her face was soaked with tears. She beat on his chest with her fists. "Why, Nagi? Why is everything so bad? Why does everything hate us?"

"Shh, shh," he said. He held her tight, closing his eyes. She sobbed into his chest, soaking his tunic. He'd wanted to sob like that for a long time, but it wouldn't help. Searching for his family required him to be strong, and crying wasn't the way. Not for him. Not where anyone would see him.

Several minutes or an hour later—Nagi couldn't tell—Callia composed herself and wiggled free of his grasp.

"I'm so tired, Nagi," she said in a weak voice. "Can we just go to Novus now? I want to be safe again."

He nodded. "Yeah, we can go. I don't think the bastien can make it down here. Hold my hand. I don't want you getting separated from me. Maybe Gar is ahead. Now I'm not so sure he's the one that got Jon. It could've been that bastien. But if it got Jon, then, where's Gar? What about those footprints and the bullets?"

Callia shrugged.

They travelled further into the tunnel, listening carefully, hoping to avoid danger and find Gar or the way to Novus.

Nearly two hours later, the tunnel grew brighter, as if someone had added fresh dirt grubber blood to the walls. As they approached the lit section of tunnel, they found themselves at a travel station.

"Be careful, Callia, I don't want us getting caught in a trap."

They moved slow, Nagi holding Callia back behind him. He took a few steps and stopped, listening for surprises. When he was satisfied nothing was there, he slowly approached the entrance.

He bent and whispered in Callia's ear. "Stay here. Let me check it out before we go in." She nodded as he slung the rifle from his shoulder and held it in front of him, ready for the ambush he fully expected.

He stepped inside the entrance. In the far corner of the reception room, a small lamp glowed. Someone had been there recently. There were two chairs, one at either end of the room, yet both were untouched, covered by a thick layer of dust. Travel stations were always manned by the Truth. At least, that's what Nagi knew. Every one of them he'd been to had two, sometimes three guards. Other than the glowing lamp, this one looked deserted. There was a single set of footprints in the dust on the floor. Nagi followed them to one of the two resting rooms in the back of the station.

He pulled the rifle higher, hoping he wouldn't have to use it. In such close quarters, it wasn't the smartest thing to do, but it was all he had. Two lamps on either side of the bed lit the room. The bed looked untouched. He crouched to see if there was anything underneath, and found nothing. He backed up and scanned the other room. It was dark inside. His pulse quickened. He stepped out of the small hallway into the reception room, grabbed the lamp, and headed back into the dark room.

Light radiated from the lamp, illuminating a small halo around it. Nagi crouched, trying to get a better look under the bed. It still seemed clear, but he wasn't sure. "Is anyone there?" he called out. He waited, listening. "I will fire on you if you are. Gar? Are you there?" A long silence followed. He walked farther into the room, relieved not to find anyone.

When he was finished inspecting the station, he deemed it safe enough for them. "Callia," he called out, "you can come in." She ran to him.

"Why'd it take you so long? I was scared out there!"

"Sorry. I had to make sure it was safe."

"Did you find anything?"

"Other than a few lit lamps, no."

"Who did that?" she asked.

"Well, I'm not sure. Maybe it was Gar. Maybe he's scouting ahead to make sure we're safe." I hope he is. I hope he didn't kill Jon and leave us to die. He's better than that, right?

Callia blew on one of the chairs, scattering dust everywhere, then sat down. "So, what now?" She swung her legs back and forth, the chair too tall for her to rest her feet on the floor.

"We take a break and rest here for a while. You can sleep in the bed. I'll guard the door. Nothing's here and nothing will get in. I promise."

Callia stopped swinging her legs, looking up at the ceiling. "Okay, but you have to stay near me. Don't leave me."

Nagi smiled. "I promise I won't leave you. We'll stick together. You know what? I bet my daughter would love to play with you. You'll meet her soon." *I hope. I want nothing more than to find them.*

Callia jumped down from the chair and went into the room, crawling onto the bed. Nagi waited outside the room. "I'll be right here, watching."

"No! Come in here."

"But, Callia," he said. "Okay, how about I stay over here and guard the door?" He pointed to the end of the bed.

"Fine, but don't leave me."

He sat on the floor at the foot of the bed, leaning back. He held the rifle across his legs and waited.

Forty-Three

When day broke the morning after burying Mina, Eron was exhausted. He'd been up most of the night crying and blaming himself for her death. He'd barely been able to reconnect with her after the Selection, and now she was gone forever. The unfair nature of the Selection and the queen's rule weighed heavy on him. By the time the sun poked through the leaves above, he was determined to continue the mission to honor his feelings for Mina and help bring down the ADF, no matter what.

"You gonna get up?" Panna asked. Eron forgot he was even there.

"Yeah, whatever," Eron replied. His body ached, and lack of sleep made him irritable. His back felt like a fire had smoldered on it all night long. Anger grew inside, threatening to overwhelm him.

"Then, let's go. We aren't done yet. Your ignorant soldiers are bound to tell on us. We should've never let them go."

"It's what we do, Panna. Do you have a problem with my orders?" Samantha said. She'd been sitting against a tree, watching Eron.

Eron mumbled something about "queen" and "pay," then stood. He took one long last look at the burial mound next to him, closed his eyes, and listened for Mina's voice in his head. After a few moments, he opened his eyes, and in a soft voice said, "Goodbye, Mina, I'll never forget you."

He joined Panna and Samantha, and the three of them pushed their way through the forest, Panna taking the lead. He pushed them hard, traversing through the brush with almost reckless abandon. It was difficult to keep up. The scratches on Eron's back screamed at him with every movement.

When the hot Anastasian sun reached its peak at midday, Panna relented on his torrid pace.

"Panna, see if you can find someplace to rest. I know we need to hurry, but I think we can afford a break," Samantha said. Panna nodded and took off. A few moments later he returned, motioning them to follow.

"We can rest here," he said. "I'm hungry. I'm sure you are, too. Here, have some of these." He handed Eron and Samantha each a handful of thinkleberries, their soft orange husks bruised. Eron hesitated.

"It's all right; they're fine," Samantha said.

He accepted the offering, mashing the entire handful into his mouth at once.

"You better slow down; that's all I've got for now. I hadn't planned on being out here long."

Eron nodded, the sweet, delicious taste of the berries lingering on his tongue. He understood what it was like to go hungry. He lasted through the Selection, and he was sure he'd make it through the forest now. He had to. He needed to avenge Mina's death.

They rested for about an hour. Though he wanted desperately to talk with Samantha, the time didn't feel right. He'd reconnect with her when Panna wasn't around.

"I think it's time we go. Panna," Samantha said, "lead the way please."

Panna leapt up, held out a hand for Samantha and then Eron, and started their trek again.

"Where are we going?" Eron asked.

Samantha turned to him. "Novus. The ADF plans on destroying the city. We've concentrated all our efforts on preserving it. Once that goes, we have little hope of stopping the ADF. We must make our stand. We must defend the city."

"My home is all I have left," Panna said. "I want to save it."

Eron said nothing. Novus wasn't his home, but he understood. If the queen was allowed to run over anyone and everything in her path for the sake of her own power, she had to be stopped. Her madness had to be put in check.

"I've never been to a Truth city," Eron said.

Panna called back over his shoulder. "Most of you Topsiders never have. We stay hidden, for the most part. We've got more tech than you do in the colonies. You've been duped into believing you don't have the resources for technological advancement. You're wrong."

"He's right, Eron; they're so far advanced. Our colonies were nothing more than controlled outposts for the queen," Samantha said.

Eron thought back to his time in the colony, and a brief memory of Mina flashed before him. He closed his eyes to force it away.

In the colony, their tech was restricted. They had no communications system, other than what the ADF soldiers had access to in the guard post at the edge of the colony. Even in the library where he could use the reading tablets, the information was limited and restricted. They were forced to use scrapped ship parts for buildings. At the time, it felt natural. He'd grown up with it, but after coming to Beta Prime, his eyes were opened to a greater world outside the colony.

They travelled further, Eron silently thinking about how his entire life was a lie. He'd grown up in a dirty, backwards colony while an entire city teeming with people and tech existed. It felt wrong. It fueled his anger, as if Mina's death wasn't enough. He paused, Samantha stopping with him. It took Panna a bit before he realized they had stopped. He called back to them, "What's wrong? Why'd you stop?"

Eron looked from Samantha to Panna. He grasped the ADF patch sewn on the shoulder of his uniform and ripped it off, tearing the fabric as he did. He grimaced, the pain from the wounds on his back duller, yet still there. He flung the patch into the forest, watching as it spun in the air until it was lost in the brush.

"Nothing's wrong." Samantha put her arm around him and they hurried to rejoin Panna.

"In another day, we ought to be close enough to Novus to rejoin our people. This is going to be the end of it, Eron. We either stop the ADF, or we end up dead. We've directed all our efforts into this. Every Truth that can be there should be there. Every able-bodied member of the CDL is ordered to be there. It's our last stand. We live and die by what happens there," Samantha said.

Samantha's words hung in the thick forest air. The enormity of their task weighed on Eron. He only wished Mina could be there to see it, too. She seemed to be a leader of some sort with the CDL, though he didn't have enough time with her to find out.

"My squad was on its way to Novus, as was every other squad from the base. We were to meet up with other ADF companies for an all-out assault on Novus. We had five transports on the way that I know of from our base."

"Five? Are you sure?" Samantha asked.

"Yeah, why?"

"We only intercepted two. That means three squads escaped. That's not good at all."

Eron winced as a branch caught his uniform and tugged on his wounds.

"No," he said, " that's not good."

A craate howled in the distance. "Oh great; that's what we need right now," Panna said. "Come on, let's find shelter and steer clear of those things. We'll get to Novus tomorrow."

Panna led them through the brush, looking for something. He cleared a patch of thick trees and found it.

"Here, we'll go in the Traveling Tunnel. It's the fastest and safest route back."

He pushed aside the cover and a pit appeared, like the one Eron had fallen into and hurt his ankle during the Selection. They climbed down the dirt steps, Eron and Samantha first, so Panna could close the cover. When they reached the dirt floor, Eron was blind in the dark.

"Stay here a moment," Panna said and walked away.

Eron listened for his movements, worried about the dirt grubbers he'd experienced the last time he was in one of these.

"These are Traveling Tunnels?" he called to the dark.

"Yeah, it'll take us straight to Novus and other Truth cities," Panna said.

"You should've seen me the first time I found these. I was so scared, I almost peed my pants!" Samantha said, nudging Eron's arm.

Suddenly, a glow appeared in the distance, growing larger as Panna approached. He carried a stick wrapped in glowing cloth. "Dirt grubber blood," he said, nodding to the glow. "Come on, we gotta hurry." He turned and led them deeper into the dark as the sounds of explosions resumed, muffled by the dirt above them.

Forty-Four

Gunther found the exit well before Balla saw the speck of light at the end of the tunnel.

"Over here! I think this is the way out!" he said, the beam from his flashlight bouncing off the dirt walls.

Balla struggled to walk, leaning on Gwenny for stability. When she shuffled toward the ever-growing point of light, she heard crunching leaves and what sounded like explosions in the distance.

"Gunther," she said, "I'm not sure we should go out there. Don't you hear that sound?" she said.

"But, Mother, you need help! We can find something out there, right? Maybe we can find a doctor."

She shook her head, but didn't argue. Her leg throbbed with each step; her strength threatening to fail her.

"It's okay, Mother; we'll make it," Gwenny said. Balla smiled as best she could through the pain. Gwenny was so much like Nagi at times. Mother and daughter had their differences, but that didn't diminish the pride and love Balla had for Gwenny.

The explosions grew louder as they neared the exit. They weren't too close, but close enough to make Balla cringe with each one.

"What is that?" Gunther asked. "Is it thunder? We should stay here if it is." His earlier joy at finding the exit soured with each loud explosion.

"I don't think so," Gwenny said. "It sounds like something's blowing up. That might be more soldiers."

"The Truth?" Gunther asked. His eyes went wide, and he fidgeted, shifting his feet back and forth. "Maybe Father is out there!"

Balla closed her eyes. She wished more than anything to be in his arms, Nagi holding her and comforting her. She wanted them to be together as a family again; the four of them removed from the horrors of the ADF.

"We can't be too careful, Gunther. I'm not sure who's making that noise. If it's the ADF, we might be in trouble. If it's the Truth, we can get help." And maybe find Nagi.

Gwenny escorted her mother to the exit, all three of them peeking out, careful to avoid being spotted.

"Doesn't seem to be anyone out here," Gwenny said. Another explosion sounded far to their right. "But those keep going off. What is that?"

"I'm not sure, but be careful. It's not like we can outrun anything out here," Balla said.

Slowly, they crept out of the exit tunnel, scanning the forest around them. The explosions kept on as they made their way out of the comforts of the dark underground into the brightness of the forest. Animals scurried away from the explosions. Gracers flew across the trees. Other unseen animals rushed through the underbrush, making Gunther jump several times.

"Whatever it is, it's scaring the animals, too. Must be the ADF," Balla said. She stopped, wincing.

"Mother, are you all right?" Gwenny said. Balla nodded.

"Gwenny, I think if I had something to help me walk, we'd go faster."

Gwenny looked around. "Gunther, see if you can find a straight stick. Something about this tall," she said, holding her hand several feet off the ground. Gunther poked around until he came back a few minutes later with a stick about as tall as he was.

"How about this?" he said, handing it to Gwenny.

"Here, Mother; maybe this will help," Gwenny said to Balla. It was tall enough and fairly straight. She let go of Gwenny's shoulder and took a few steps.

"Ouch," she said, then took another step. She closed her eyes, breathing heavy, but continued. "Come on, let's go," she said.

Balla led them away from the constant explosions. They were louder, too, as if whoever was setting them off turned their way.

The forest teemed with scared animals. Balla felt a nervous energy, as if danger was everywhere.

It was so different from their home in Freedom. There, they were safe. They lived in peace. They cared for one another. But it was gone, as was Inventa. The ADF had turned their full force against the Truth. By the nature of being a Truth, she and her children were now the enemy of the ADF, if for no other reason than being different. Because they had fur instead of hair like the Topsiders. Because they were more "human" than the "humans" were; though in truth, they were exactly the same.

After a few hours of traveling, stopping every so often so Balla could rest her leg, they made it to a small creek that ran across the forest. Red water shimmered in the afternoon sun. When the explosions sounded, the water rippled. The stream was small enough and shallow enough for them to cross in a few steps. Once on the other side, Balla stopped. "We can rest here. For a little while, anyway," she said. The children flopped to the ground, laying on their backs. Balla found a large rock nearby and carefully sat, propping herself up with the walking stick.

There was a crash in the brush about fifty feet from them. Balla's head whipped toward the sound. Gunther and Gwenny leapt to their feet, Gwenny holding the rifle in front of her.

A male voice called out, "Come on, get up! You're hurt, but you can make it. I knew we should've stayed in those tunnels!"

"Yeah, I'm trying. It's a little hard with all this brush in the way. Ouch!" a male voice replied.

Balla whispered, "Children, come here. Stay close. It could be the ADF."

"I think I hear water over here; maybe we can get a drink," a female voice said. They were closer now. Small trees were pushed aside as they forced their way through the thick brush, right toward Balla and the children.

"Gwenny," Balla said in a quiet voice, "be ready with the rifle. If it's ADF..." she paused. Should she have her shoot them or scare them? Was taking more lives worth it? How far would they go to save their own lives? "If it's ADF, shoot them. Maybe not to kill, but to slow them down."

Gwenny nodded.

"Ouch!" the second male voice called out. "Panna, slow down. I can't move as fast. My back—" he said when they stepped out from the brush, face to face with Balla and the children.

Gwenny held the rifle steady, trained on the ADF soldier that appeared from the forest. A Truth stood next to him with a female in some sort of uniform.

"Don't move," Gwenny said.

"Panna, I think we might need your expertise, here," the female said.

"I got this," Panna said. "Follow my lead."

Panna raised his arms high. Eron and Samantha did the same.

"Please don't shoot. He's not an ADF soldier, I promise. He's with us, he's part of the CDL. We fight against the ADF," Panna said.

Gwenny looked to her mother and then back to them.

"How do we know that?" Balla asked.

"Because Truth don't work with the ADF. You know I'm not lying. Look," he said, pointing to the ripped sleeve of Eron's uniform, "no patch. He's not one of them. He's with us."

"You keep saying us. What do you mean by that?" Balla asked.

"We're the resistance. We've joined with Topsiders to stop the queen and her madness."

"He's one of my squad," Samantha said. "We've been commanded by the joint leaders of the CDL and the Truth to fight the ADF."

Eron spoke up. "Our brother is a Truth." He waved a hand at himself and Samantha. "His name is Timo."

Balla gasped. She hadn't heard that name in a long time.

"You're Eron? And Samantha?" she asked, and the

soldier nodded.

Forty-Five

At some point in the night, Nagi nodded off. Lucky for him, no one entered the rest stations. He and Callia were both able to get much needed rest. When he woke, Callia was already stirring. He stretched, feeling every ache in his body. "Come on, Callia, we better get going." Nagi stood, extending his legs, and held out a hand for Callia. She rubbed her eyes, then took hold, allowing him to pull her up to a sitting position.

They left the station after a fruitless search for food. Nagi hoped they'd find something, but they came up empty.

The tunnel was dark; the only source of light a lamp they carried with them from the station. Its faint glow cast misshapen shadows on the walls. Callia stuck close to Nagi. "Make sure no one follows us," he said.

She looked back every so often.

They travelled along the tunnel for several hours without a person or animal in sight.

"We've got to be close, Callia."

"I hope so. I'm hungry."

"Me too. Once we get there, we'll be able to eat and get something cold to drink."

"I can't wait. Nagi, do you think they'll let us in? What if they don't want more people in Novus?"

"Don't worry. We Truth stick together. There's no way they'll turn us away. It's the last city we have left.

If Novus falls, we're in serious trouble."

Callia didn't say anything. Nagi assumed she was contemplating the fall of Novus or the big meal she'd enjoy once they made it. His thoughts turned to his family. He consoled himself with the thought of Balla and the children escaping with other refugees. He feared for her if they were alone above ground. She didn't have the experience that he did. Not that she wasn't capable, but she had limited exposure to the world above. He pictured his children's smiling faces and his heart broke. He wanted to see them so badly; to play with them; to hold them once again.

He thought of Eron. It had been so long since he'd seen him. A lot had changed since then, and he wondered where he was and if he was strong enough to resist the temptation of the ADF. He thought so, but without knowing for sure, the fear lingered. His brother had a kind heart; surely, he saw the devious path of the queen. If Eron knew about the colonies...knew about the mines and the source of the queen's power...

"Nagi, look!" Callia said, startling him from his thoughts. Ahead of them, a soft glow appeared like a pinpoint at the end of the tunnel. It blinked as if something had crossed in front of it.

"What do you think it is?" Callia asked.

"If I had to guess, it's either a warning to others like us. Or..."

"Or what?"

"It could possibly be a crossing. We may have found our way to Novus."

Callia grabbed his hand and pulled forward. "Come on, let's go! We're almost there!"

Nagi resisted. "We can't be too careful here, Callia. We've experienced enough problems to know not everything is as it seems."

"But, Nagi!"

"I just want to urge caution, that's all. Let's be careful."

They approached the flickering light and Nagi became convinced it was a crossing. Movement flowed right to left. Soon enough, they were able to see Truth walking across the light.

"Nagi, it is a crossing!" Callia said. She clutched his hand tightly, a surge of energy flowing through her. Nagi felt the same.

"It is, Callia! Come on, hurry!"

He threw caution to the wind as the sight of scores of other Truth urged him forward. When they closed in on the crossing, Nagi looked toward the Truth and stepped back.

"What's wrong?" Callia asked him. Her voice was hard to hear over the commotion.

"It feels...wrong. Something isn't right." He looked at Callia, and then to the flood of Truth.

"Hey, where is everyone going?" he asked an older female Truth. Her dingy tunic was shredded at the bottom. Her eyes were wild.

"Novus. We must hurry. They'll be shutting it up soon. ADF is on the way. They're shelling the forest, trying to kill us all!" She brushed past him and rushed along the tunnel.

"Shelling? Shut us off?" Nagi asked.

"What?" Callia said. The noise in the tunnel grew intense. Scared and worried Truth, some with crying children and babies, forced their way through the tunnel.

"This way. Don't let go of my hand!" Nagi said. Pulling Callia behind him, they entered the flood of refugees seeking the safety of Novus.

They marched along the tunnel for half an hour before it turned to the right, opening to a large, brightly-lit cavern.

Nagi stood transfixed by the site. Novus was twice as large as Freedom or Inventa. It had been the largest colonial ship when humans set off for this new world. It was also the home of the first queen of Anastasia, the crowning an event so covered in controversy that Truth scholars had been debating it for centuries. Staring at the massive ship, Nagi felt a touch of hope.

"My family," he said quietly. "They could be in there."

"What?" Callia said, tugging on his hand.

"Nothing, let's go," he said over the noise.

They proceeded down the slope to the city entrance. Scores of Truth filled the path like a long line of insects. The cavern was enormous. A band of artificial lights along the top showed the walls were coated with intricate patterns of dirt grubber blood. Swirls, figures, and odd shaped geometric patterns glowed bright, adding to the intense, growing light.

Novus rose higher as they descended lower in the cavern. Two long lines of Truth merged together about fifty meters before the entrance to the city. Guards guided the mass of people, encouraging them forward and waving their arms toward the entrance.

"Come on, we've got plenty of room. One at a time, please. We will accept you all," a guard called out. Despite the massive numbers of Truth, the line moved quickly. Much like at Inventa, they were assigning rooms for all the refugees.

"This way, please; you will be given rest. We have room for all," another guard called out.

When Nagi and Callia made their way to the guard assigning rooms, Nagi asked the guard about his family.

"Huh? No. I don't think so. Really don't know. Please, hurry in. The line is long. Yours is 253." He waved them on, assigning the next room.

"253?" Callia asked.

"Yeah, this way," Nagi replied. He assumed they'd be cramped in small rooms like at Inventa when he met Gar. The old scout confused Nagi. Was he still alive? Did he kill that soldier? Where'd he go?

Before he could answer himself, they were standing at the door to 253. Nagi knocked, some Truth behind him bumping him against the door. "My apologies," a voice called. Nagi couldn't make out who was speaking in the mass of thick-furred Truth. When no one answered, he opened the door and they stepped inside to find an empty room.

"Do we get this all to ourselves?" Callia asked.

"Maybe, but I think it best to assume we'll have more joining us."

Callia ran around the room, jumping up and down. "There are beds! And running water! And heat, and blankets, and..." She rattled off a long list of amenities they'd lacked while in the wilderness. Nagi understood her joy. Inside, he felt the same giddiness, but without his family, it was meaningless.

Forty-Six

Balla almost fell over when the Topsider said his name.

Timo.

Was this really his brother and sister? Or was this a Topsider trick?

"Mother, are you all right?" Gwenny asked. She alternated between training the rifle on the intruders and checking on her mother. The moment the Topsider said Timo, Balla felt a chill run through her. No one called him that anymore; that was his Topsider name. Now that he was part of the Truth, he'd changed his name like all the rest.

"You say you're his brother, and she's his sister?" Balla asked.

Eron shifted his feet, his eyes darting from the rifle to Balla.

"Umm...can she put the rifle down? We aren't a threat. I promise," Eron said.

"Gwenny, it's okay. I believe him...for now. Just be ready, in case he tries anything stupid."

"I'm right here, you know. Why would a Truth help Topsiders against their own?" Panna said.

"I can't be too careful. It's been a long journey from our home," Balla said. Panna grunted, but said nothing.

"Yeah," Eron said, "he's our brother. Our older brother. I thought he was dead until..." he hesitated, closing his eyes, "until the Selection. He found me. He helped me finish so I could be with Mina, but that's not how it played out. The queen...had other plans." He clenched his fists at his sides.

Balla held a hand to her heart. What this boy was telling her was exactly how Nagi described his time in the last Selection. According to Nagi, Eron was determined to help fight the system that created the horrific Selection. But here he stood, in front of her wearing an ADF uniform, the symbol of their grief and pain.

"So, why are you in ADF gear? Why are you fighting for them?"

"I asked him to. We needed intel, and I knew we could trust him," Samantha said.

"I'm not fighting for them, I swear. I joined so I'd have a chance to make a difference. I joined to gain information for my sister and her group."

"The Combatant de Libertie, or CDL for short," Samantha said.

"My squad was heading to Novus when Samantha and her team ambushed us. I was lucky enough to escape severe injury, but not everyone survived."

"Novus? Is that where the ADF is attacking next?" Balla asked. "We were traveling there ourselves. After what happened to our home and Inventa, we had nowhere else to go. Our hope was to find Nagi—I mean, Timo—when we got there."

Eron scrunched up his face. "Nagi?"

Panna turned to him. "It's a long story, Eron, but in short when Topsiders renounce their allegiance to the queen and join the Truth, they also change their names."

"So, you don't know where our brother is?" Samantha asked.

"No, I don't. We were separated a long time ago. I've been with our children since the attacks."

"I'm an uncle!" Eron said, as the thought occurred to him from nowhere.

Balla laughed, holding steady to her stick. "Yeah, I guess you are. This is Gwenny and Gunther," she said, gesturing at each child respectively.

"So, out of all the creeks in all the forests, we meet at this one," Panna said.

"Huh?" Eron asked.

"Nothing; something I remembered seeing once."

"I guess that also means I'm an aunt." Samantha grinned.

They made themselves comfortable along the creek bank. Eron washed his wounds as best he could. Balla's injured leg throbbed. Balla, Eron, and Samantha couldn't stop talking about Timo, whom Eron finally began to refer to as Nagi, as they exchanged stories. Balla explained that the children weren't Nagi's by birth, but by choice. She told them about Mabuz and his death while serving in the scouts, a concern she had for their brother.

"So, wait; you're telling me the Truth seek us out during the Selection to recruit us into the fold? Why didn't Nagi do that with me?" Eron asked.

"He told me our cause was better served if you followed your heart to that girl. Mina, was it?"

Eron looked down, brushing his cheek. "Yeah, that was her name."

"Was? Oh, I'm so sorry. I didn't mean to bring up something painful."

"It's okay. We found each other again before she

passed. It's not fair, but what about any of this is?"

Balla nodded. "You have my sympathies, Eron. Losing a loved one is not easy."

"Yeah, thanks," Eron said.

The explosions began again; this time, much closer.

Gunther ran to Balla. "Mother! They're back!"

Gwenny slung the rifle from her shoulder and pointed it into the forest. Panna jumped up, readying himself for intruders. Eron and Samantha stood, looking in the direction of the explosions.

"ADF," Samantha said. "They're annihilating everything in their path on the way to Novus."

"So, we're close?" Balla asked.

Explosions rocked the forest to their left. A large pack of gracers flew overhead, chattering as they fled.

"About a kilometer that way," Panna said, pointing to the south.

"Then Nagi might be there?" Balla asked.

"Maybe; I don't know. I do know that the ADF was under strict orders to kill any Truth they found. The queen was adamant that we take no prisoners this time," Eron said.

"Why is she so mean?" Gwenny asked.

"I don't know, dear, but we can't do anything about her right now. She's not the immediate problem," Balla said.

Explosions again shook the forest.

"They are," Balla said, holding her hand out toward the destruction. "We must get to Novus before the ADF. If we can find Nagi, maybe we can find safety."

"Pfff, safety. We won't be safe until we bring down the ADF," Panna said.

"No matter; we need to get to Novus. The ADF is on a destructive path and we have to get there first," Eron said.

"I agree," Balla said. "Children, it's time to go." She raised herself on the walking stick. Explosions rocked the forest again, the ground trembling.

"It's getting closer," Samantha said.

"I've got the lead," Panna said. He picked a narrow path among the red and orange undergrowth, hacking away at rogue branches with his hands.

Balla had a difficult time keeping up. Her injured leg wouldn't allow for much weight and keeping up with the fast pace Panna set.

"Go on, I need a break," Balla said to Panna. She leaned against a tree, breathing heavy.

"No. I'm done with leaving people behind. We all go. Together," Eron said.

"We won't leave you," Samantha said.

The explosions blasted again, though it was muted as they were some distance from the shelling.

Eron lifted Balla's arm and placed it around his shoulder. "Just watch the back; it's still a bit raw. I've got you."

Balla nodded.

He was very much like Nagi. His gentle nature and concern reminded her of him.

"He'd be proud of you, you know. You're so like him. Your parents raised you well."

"It was our mother. Our father...wasn't there."

"I'm sorry. Seems as though I have a knack for uncovering sore spots."

Samantha snorted. "No, he's not dead. He's ADF and brainwashed to their cause. He's not a good man."

Balla had nothing to say. The look on Eron's face was enough to convince her.

The explosions grew more frequent, though now they sounded farther off. Whatever the ADF was up to, they were turned away from it.

"Come on, we're getting close. We gotta get away from those shells," Panna said.

Balla followed as best she could, Eron propping her up on his shoulders, and her children ahead talking with Samantha.

Forty-Seven

Nagi left Callia to the comforts of the room and set off in search of his family. He scoured the hallways for Balla's beautiful face. When he finished searching his floor, he decided to go to the control room in hopes of convincing the local leaders to use Novus' systems to search for her.

The crowded elevator to the control room moved slow. It stopped at each floor, as Truth were escorted to their new living quarters. As Nagi watched the doors open on each floor, he saw the scene was the same. Hallways filled with Truth of assorted colors and sizes, jostling with each other to try to find their apartments. It was chaos on floor after floor. When they'd gone ten floors, the doors opened to a young female Truth who was crying and having a tantrum. Her cries reminded him of Gwenny. His heart broke and he hung his head. If only he'd been more careful, maybe none of this would've happened. The moment he thought it, he chastised himself. The guilt wasn't his. The burden of the Truth was not on him.

When the door opened on the twenty-first floor, he saw Gar in the crowd. Nagi's eyes widened.

"Gar!" he yelled out. "Gar, it's me! Nagi!" The old scout didn't react to the cry.

"Can you please not yell in my ear?" a small female Truth scolded him.

"Sorry, but I know him. Please, can I get out?" Nagi said and tried to force his way out of the elevator. After a few moans from Truth who expressed their displeasure at being jostled by Nagi, he stood outside the elevator doors, trying to see where the old scout had gone.

"Excuse me," he said as he bumped into a large male Truth. He must've been a foot taller than Nagi and built just as thick. The Truth grunted, shoving his way forward.

The halls were cramped with so many Truth jostling to get through; their tired and scared eyes looking for places to rest. This many Truth would've overwhelmed Freedom and Inventa. The size of Novus was impressive. It also meant more headaches. Nagi wondered about the security forces in the city and how many resources must've been devoted to it. Controlling a city this size would take several.

He looked down the hall and lost sight of Gar.

"No...no," he said and pushed his way forward. Crying children and their mothers made him think about his family. He paused, almost trampled by a family close behind. He clung to the wall, allowing them to pass, and looked back toward the elevator. He knew Gar was alive, but wasn't sure about his family. He'd find Gar later. Whatever his reason for leaving them, it must've been a good one. What he did to that soldier...

Nagi turned back to the elevator when a female Truth slammed into him, almost knocking him to the floor. When he regained his footing, he held her tight. "Balla? Balla is that you?"

She tilted her head and squinted. "Who? I'm sorry,

I don't know who you're talking about. My name is Elida. Who's Balla?"

He let go, her face morphing back to an unrecognizable smile.

"I'm sorry. I thought you were my wife. You looked...never mind. I apologize." She herded her three children forward, blending with the flow of Truth.

Nagi fought the oncoming crowd until he returned to the elevator. He waited for what seemed like an eternity for the doors to open. Inside, the car was packed, but he pushed his way forward anyway, grunts and aggravation in response from the passengers already inside. He hung his head low, ignoring their moans.

The constant running and the endless worry about his family felt like an immense burden he hadn't known before. As the elevator rose higher, he felt a crushing weight bear down on him. All this time, he'd been able to keep it under control, but the higher he went, the heavier the burden. It was as if someone had unleashed the pain he'd kept under wraps and poured it thick and heavy over him. For the first time since the loss of Freedom, he let it fester. He felt it consume him; conquer him. He let the grief smother him. He had no energy to fight back. That's all he'd been doing since that day. He'd used all he had to get to this point, this moment of reflection.

The elevator moved slow, extending his agonizing pain. He accepted it, all of it. Losing his family stung worse now than ever. Freedom's destruction was his burden once more, no matter what the council or Chair Deelia said. Gar tried talking him out of this guilt, but now, he was too weak to stop it. In the elevator, his body convulsed as he sobbed. The others tried to move away from him, but there was no room. Those closest to him turned their heads, trying not to stare at the crazed Truth ruining their ride.

When the elevator reached the top floor, through the darkness now clouding his vision, Nagi recognized the familiar sight of a control room. The three other Truth in the car pushed past him on their way to anywhere other than with him. He didn't blame them. He'd hate to be stuck in a cramped space with someone like him, too.

The elevator doors started to close. Nagi thrust out a thick, black-furred arm and the doors froze, then opened wide. He stumbled through to the landing, the doors closing behind him with a chime, then a swoosh sound as it dropped to gather more Truth.

In the control room, Truth attended screens filled with shots of various parts of the city. One screen showed a side view of the city, rooms turning from green to red as occupants claimed their new homes. The first five floors were entirely red, while those above were both red and green. Those at the top were all green, but as Nagi watched the screen, he knew it wouldn't be long before the city was full.

Monitors showed every hall in the city. There were so many Truth. Watching the flow of them, Nagi realized how difficult it would be to try and pick out his family from among the masses, if not impossible.

He stood observing the monitors, the heavy weight of his situation bearing down on him still. Off to his right, the council room door opened. He snapped his head toward it when he recognized the voice.

Chair Deelia.

She'd saved him earlier from the accusations of the council. Maybe she'd help again.

Deelia walked carefully with the aid of a cane and a smaller male Truth. Directly behind her was a human male.

Nagi almost ran to her aid. He wore a uniform, though it clearly wasn't ADF. Nagi scrunched his eyes, trying to make sense of it. Topsiders never visited the Truth cities unless they were trying to destroy them.

Deelia and the man headed straight for Nagi, talking as they walked. The Truth helping Deelia tried to move Nagi out of the way, but he stood his ground. This was his chance to seek her help.

"Chair Deelia," he said, eyeing the man with her carefully.

She looked up from her conversation. "Do I know you?" she asked. "Wait. You're that scout...Nagi, right? From Freedom?"

Nagi hung his head. "Yes ma'am, I am. I wondered if you might be able to help me find my family. I was separated from them at Freedom and—"

She waived her hand in the air. "Scout, I sympathize with your plight, but at the moment, I have a tremendous burden to attend to. Director Bowen and I have a war to plan. And win. The ADF is at our doorstep."

Nagi stood, his body shaking slightly. Chair Deelia ran a hand across her face and huffed.

"Ensign," she said, motioning to a Truth seated at a monitor, "please help Scout Nagi here with his request."

"Yes, ma'am," the ensign said.

"Thank you, Chair Deelia," Nagi said.

"I will need you," she said, pointing a long finger at him. "We will need all our forces if we're to win this war with the wretched queen and her ADF. Find your family, but know you will be called upon."

She dismissed him with a wave and walked on with Director Bowen, discussing troop numbers and strategy. At one point, he thought he heard something about a ship.

Forty-Eight

By the time they reached the clearing above Novus, the red sun had slipped past the horizon, giving way to pink twilight. Balla breathed heavy; the pace Panna pushed them being too much for her injured leg. For some reason, the closer they came to Novus, the farther away the shelling became. It was as if the ADF were in the wrong place.

"There it is. Novus," Panna declared.

Eron looked around. "Where?"

"Right there," he said, pointing at the barren field ahead of them. It was surrounded by forest except for a narrow strip opposite them.

"Okay, so I've never been to a Truth city, but come on, it's a field!" Eron said. Balla giggled. She imagined Nagi had said the same thing when he'd first encountered Freedom.

"I'm with you, Eron; I don't see it," Samantha said.

Balla spoke. "It's there, trust us. I've never been to Novus, but it's clear to me where it is."

"Well, I must be missing something, then. All I see is tall orange grass waving in the wind," Samantha said.

"Come on; hurry!" Panna said. "With the fading light, we should be able to find the entrance before it gets too dark."

He led them out into the field, the expanse growing more vast the farther they were from the forest.

Balla hobbled, but Eron held her. She closed her eyes, letting him guide her along the field. If someone would've asked her if she thought she'd ever be above ground with her children and her husband's brother and sister and a Truth resistance fighter, she'd have said they were crazy. But here she was. Her new reality was something she'd never planned.

Either the shelling ceased, or they were too far away from it now to be able to hear it. Balla was convinced the ADF had no clue where Novus was. Fortunately, for them, too. She and Eron both needed medical attention. Her children needed rest. And Panna. Well, he needed a fight. Hopefully he wouldn't find one anytime soon.

The sun hid behind the planet, bringing darkness over the field, broken by the rising moon.

"Come on, we're close," Panna said.

Off in the distance, craates howled.

"Oh no!" Eron said.

Balla's heart thumped in her chest. They weren't in any shape to fend off an attack.

"Panna, how far away is the entrance?" Samantha asked. Gunther and Gwenny closed in on Balla as Panna continued to search.

"It's close. I just have to find it."

"Well, hurry! I don't intend on dying at the hands of those craates," Samantha said.

The craates howled again, this time on the opposite side of the field. Balla's head swung to that side. They were surrounded.

"Keep your eyes open! They can be anywhere. In this tall grass in the dark, it's gonna be hard to spot them," Eron said. Balla felt his body tense beneath her arm.

Eron pushed faster, pulling Balla with him. "Come on, Balla, I won't let them get you."

The sound of paws trampling grass seemed to come from every direction. The howls grew closer.

Several craates had snuck up behind them and were growling. Balla spun, almost losing her balance. About thirty feet away stood seven of the beasts. Eron was aghast.

"No!" he shouted.

Panna yelled out, "Found it!"

The sound of footsteps grew closer all around them. The craates behind them bared their enormous fangs, growling and inching closer. Gunther started crying. Gwenny held the rifle in shaky hands.

"Children, get behind me. Follow Panna," Balla said.

"No, Mother, we won't leave you," Gunther said.

"Please, Son, go now."

"It's okay, kids. Follow Panna, and he'll get you to safety," Samantha said. She turned to face the danger around them.

The craates drew closer. There was a sound behind them like leaves rustling. Balla stole a glance and saw Panna uncovering a Traveling Tunnel in the middle of the field.

"Come on, down here!" he yelled.

"Children, go!" Balla said. Eron waved at them to go.

The craates closed in. Balla stumbled back a step, Eron almost losing his balance when she did.

"Come on, now!" Panna yelled. Balla looked back and the Truth waved his hand, trying to get them in the tunnel.

Snarling craates crept closer.

Panna ran to Balla and Eron, brandishing Sam's rifle. "Get her in there now. I'll hold them back," he said to Eron.

"No! You can't do this by yourself," Balla cried.

"I'll help," Samantha said. "Eron, take her out of here, now!"

Eron nodded and tugged on Balla's arm for her to follow.

"Come on, you filthy beasts, come at me!" Panna yelled. Balla watched as the confident Truth fired at the craates, forcing some of them back. They were surrounded, and if he didn't hurry, Panna would be caught. Samantha pulled a pistol from inside her jacket, helping Panna keep the craates back.

"Come on, don't get stuck out there," Eron called to Panna and Samantha.

They didn't seem to notice. Panna was transfixed on the craates, picking them off when he could, keeping most of them at a distance. Samantha fired at the craates, pushing them back.

Eron turned Balla around to face the entrance to the tunnel. "Come on, in here," he said, pointing down the pit at the footholds in the side. Balla looked back at Panna and Samantha as she descended the dirt stairs, the two of them now surrounded by craates. Panna yelled and screamed as he shot at the craates. One of them lunged at him from behind, Samantha narrowly missing her target.

"Samantha!" Balla screamed, but Eron nudged her to continue.

"Come on, we can't wait. If we don't get down there now, we'll meet the same fate."

Balla held to the edge of the pit, wanting to help, but Eron's words were true. If the craates overwhelmed Panna and Samantha, the only ones with weapons, they were next. Balla hesitated, then let Eron guide her down the steps.

She heard a scream and watched as Eron spun his head back to the fight, a look of disgust and horror flashed across his face.

"Samantha! Come on! Get out of there!"

"What is it? We must help them!" Balla said. Eron paused, caught up in the scene that played out above.

"Samantha!" he screamed, "No!"

Balla pushed him upwards, "We have to help!"

Eron paused, a tear running down his cheek. "No," he said quietly, "we can't."

He stepped on the first dirt foothold, then panicked.

"Oh no! Hurry, now! We gotta move!" He almost fell the rest of the way down, knocking into Balla.

On the pit floor, he and Balla looked up. All along the edge, circling the perimeter of the pit were snarling craates. They howled and snapped their jaws shut, as if trying to bite their scent.

Gunther stood at the wall of the pit, sobbing. Gwenny held him tight as he continued to cry.

"Do you think they can come down here?" Balla asked.

"I don't see how they could, unless they jumped in, but it's too far. I think we're safe," Eron said.

With her ears attuned to the craates above, Balla turned to Gunther. "Son, it's okay. We're safe now.

We're close to Novus." She embraced him and Gwenny, trying to calm their nerves.

Gunshots sounded above them. A craate howled, falling into the pit where it convulsed and died. The children screamed at the sight. Another gunshot sounded and the craates scattered. Then, Samantha peered down into the pit. "Go on, get them to Novus. I'll rejoin the CDL up here. Take care, Eron. Balla, it was a pleasure. Now go!"

"Samantha! No, don't leave," Eron called.

"Sorry, I have to go." She nodded to Balla and ran off.

"She didn't have to leave," Eron said quietly. Balla said nothing, leaving Eron to process what had happened.

"Gunther, do you still have that flashlight from before?' Balla asked. He nodded. "Good. Lead us to safety, then." She ruffled the fur on his head.

"Is Panna dead, Mother?" he asked. She nodded.

"I'm afraid so, Son. He was brave. He and Samantha saved us from those craates. We cannot let his death be in vain. Come, let's get out of here."

Eron extended his hand to help her to her feet.

"Thank you. Come on, we need to move," Balla said.

Gunther and Gwenny led the way through the dark tunnel, the only light the beam from Gunther's hand. Balla expected the walls to glow, especially since the remaining Truth were most likely flooding the city. After traveling through the tunnels for ·close to an hour, they turned a sharp corner and in the distance, the tunnel glowed like daylight. A stream of Truth flowed into the tunnel from a bisecting tunnel, heading away from them.

"We're here," Balla said. "Stay close, Eron; I know you aren't ADF, but I don't want you caught up in a mistake."

They joined the refugees, heading down the sloped path to the cavern and Novus.

Forty-Nine

The enormous ship sat inside an even larger cavern. The walls were illuminated by the blood of dirt grubbers, smeared along the upper edges of the cavern. Eron had never seen anything like it. The Truth entered the ship like thousands of insects headed toward their hive. His mind reeled as he tried to take it all in. He only wished Samantha and Mina were with him to see it.

"Balla, how long has this been here?" he asked.

"What?" she said, turning to him. Thousands of talking and crying Truth flooded into the cavern, surrounding them.

"How long has the ship been here?" he asked.

"Since humans arrived. The Truth have lived underground since."

"But how'd it get underground? Do you live in one of these?"

"I used to. The ADF destroyed our city and Inventa. This is the last one. This is all the Truth have left to hold onto."

His eyes were huge as he tried to take in the entire ship. "How'd the ADF not know about these cities? How many Truth live here?"

"Honestly, I don't know. I assumed the ADF simply forgot their history. As far as how many live here, I don't know. I've never been here before. It does look much larger than the other cities."

They joined the line heading toward the city. Guards at checkpoints near the entrance referenced small electronic pads as the refugees entered the city. When they approached the nearest guard, he paused and narrowed his eyes at Eron.

"What's he doing here?" he growled. "Topsiders don't come here. You know this," he said to Balla, not taking his eyes off Eron. A couple other guards joined him, their large, paw-like hands resting on their weapons.

"He's not the enemy," Balla said, "he's on our side. His brother Nagi is a scout from Freedom. He's also my husband."

"Freedom's gone," one of the other guards said.

"I know. That was my home. I was there," Balla replied.

Eron noticed more guards approaching. "I don't want to be a bother. I'm not the enemy. I never was."

"So, why the ADF uniform?" the guard who stopped them asked.

Eron closed his eyes. When he looked up, five Truth guards surrounded him.

"I joined the ADF at the request of my sister and my brother Timo—I mean, Nagi—to help change our world. He had big plans for me, I guess, but here I am."

"He's not a danger to us. He's here to help and find my husband. Maybe you can assist us. He may have come here earlier—" Balla was cut off by the raised hand from the guard who'd stopped them.

"I don't need to hear excuses. This Topsider will be held in detention until we can sort this out. War looms, and I'm not about to be the one to let the enemy just walk into our city without examining him first. Guards!" he commanded, and the surrounding guards took Eron into custody.

"No! You can't do this!" Gwenny said. "He's not a bad guy. I promise!"

"We will determine that. Now, move; we have too many behind you to carry this out any longer. Your room will be 576. This Topsider will be in detention block C on the third deck. Now, move it!" He waved his hand forward. The guards shoved Eron to the ship.

"It's ok, Balla; I'll be fine," he called over his shoulder. "Find Nagi. He'll clear this up." One of the guards shoved Eron's head forward.

"Shut up and move," he said.

Behind him, Eron heard Gwenny and Gunther crying for his release through the chaos. Balla tried shushing them, but their cries carried through the cavern.

Eron complied with the guards. He understood their apprehension. He'd be careful with someone like him, too.

"I'm really not the enemy," he said to the guards around him. "I'm not part of the ADF. Well, technically, yes, I was in training, but I was doing it to help the CDL infiltrate their ranks. My sister Samantha—"

One of the guards shoved him in the back.

"Shut up and move. Can't you see we're kinda busy around here?"

"Yeah, whatever. Do you keep a log of all your refugees?" None of the guards responded. "I'm sure you do. I saw the data pads the guards at the lines were using. Can you do me a favor and at least look to see if you have a scout by the name of Nagi onboard? If so, can you relay a message—" another smack to his back.

"Ouch! Come on, stop it. I've not done anything other than ask if you'll verify what I'm saying is true. If it is, my innocence will be proven. If not, I'll be your prisoner until you can see I'm being honest."

One of the guards paused, looking at another, who nodded in return.

"Yeah, fine. We'll check. You'd better be right."

They forced him onto an elevator a distance away from the refugees and took him to the third floor. The long, gray corridor ended at a locked door. A guard waved them in, and Eron was directed to holding cell C near the far end.

"You enjoy your stay. We'll check on this Nagi of yours."

They tossed Eron inside and closed the heavy metal door. It closed with a deep thunk, muffling the sound outside.

The cell was a small rectangle without a bed. It was bare, except for a light overhead that was out of reach.

"Great. I'm in a prison underground, and no one knows I'm here."

Hours passed without any contact. Eron sat in the corner with his head between his knees.

Since the Selection, his life had changed in ways he could've never imagined. The Selection was brutal enough. Then, when he'd found his brother, the joy of knowing he was alive was tempered by Timo's words to not follow him. Watching as Mina chose another boy tightened the pain inside him. Realizing the massive, sprawling city of Beta Prime existed, when all he knew was the harsh life of a colony overwhelmed him. Then, reuniting with his sister who encouraged him to infiltrate the ADF for the greater good.

Sarai. Poor Sarai, who actually seemed to care for him. He had no clue where she was. He didn't want to hurt her. He had no choice but to leave. Maybe she'd forgive him.

Losing Mina hurt the worst of all. When he recognized her lovely face, it was the greatest thing he'd ever seen. His heart leapt in his chest at the prospect of finally uniting with her. The overwhelming love he'd felt for her was powerful. Watching as she died was the most difficult thing he'd ever done. It created a dark, deep hole inside him.

And now, secured in a room inside a giant ship that had been hidden underground for centuries, populated by what he once thought were savage creatures overwhelmed his frail mind.

The world was different. What used to be so innocent was more complicated than a chess match with Connor. Long gone were the days of carefree living in the colony, though he wasn't that far removed from them.

Eron heard a commotion in the hallway outside his door. Raised voices shouted orders. Suddenly, the door swung open and a guard stood with his hands on his hips.

"Seems like you were telling the truth. Come on."

"Huh?" Eron asked.

"He said you can go." A large black-furred Truth stepped behind the guard, smiling.

"Eron! It's so good to see you!" he said.

"Timo? Timo!" Eron cried, rushing past the guard,

hugging his older brother.

Fifty

Nagi led eron out of the holding cells into the chaos of the halls where Truth scrambled to find their new rooms. The brothers received strange looks, but Eron didn't mind. He was reunited with his brother at last.

"Timo...I mean, Nagi, I found Samantha! And your wife! And your children!" Eron said.

Nagi turned to him, tears streaming down his black-furred face. He grabbed Eron's arms.

"Please tell me they're safe!"

"Your family is. I don't know about Samantha. I hope she is. She helped us get here. There were craates—"

Nagi leaned against the wall, sobbing uncontrollably.

"None of this should've happened. I wish I could change it all. Samantha," Nagi said, wiping his cheek. "Oh Samantha, I hope you're ok." Nagi closed his eyes and spoke in a soft voice. "Dear Balla, I miss you so much! Gwenny and Gunther...how I've missed your smiles." He stood straight.

"Where are they, Eron? How did you find them?"

"I'm not sure where they are, to be honest. I was detained in the lines outside. Balla thought I'd be safe going with the guards, since I knew you. How'd you know where I was, anyway?"

"You told the guards my name! I was scanning the

city video feeds for my family when I learned you were here. I came down as fast as I could."

"Then maybe you can ask them about your family. I'm sure they'd know," Eron said.

"I'm still surprised to see you. I'd almost given up hope of ever seeing you, Samantha, or my family again. Things are bad, Eron."

"I know. I've seen what the ADF is up to. They're coming for the Truth. The queen wants all of you dead."

After they walked along the crowded corridor for a few moments in silence, Eron spun and grabbed Nagi's arm.

"I found Dad! He's alive!" Eron said.

"I know. Dad is ADF. There's no hope for him. He believes the queen. He views the Truth as animals," Nagi said. Eron nodded his head slightly.

"Yeah, I got that impression from him. Samantha doesn't. She fights against the ADF."

"Now that, I didn't know. It's been so long since I've seen her. How's her family?"

Eron took a deep breath. "Her husband is like Dad. And he took their son away with him. She's angry, but holding it together well enough."

Nagi didn't reply. They entered the elevator, shoving themselves into the crowded car. Nagi pushed the top button.

By the time they reached the top floor, the car was nearly empty.

"Come on, Eron. We can find Balla and the children here," Nagi said, leading Eron to a wall of monitors.

"What is this place?" Eron asked. His eyes were

wide. He'd never seen anything like this.

Nagi smiled. "I was like you when I first saw all this. It's amazing what the queen hid from the colonies in order to preserve the stones."

"The what?" Eron said.

"Here, look," Nagi said pointing to the monitors, ignoring the question. "You can see every floor at this console. This entire floor used to be the command deck of the ship as it flew across the cosmos, ferrying a load of human colonists to escape the destruction of Earth." Eron closed his eyes, recalling lessons learned in his history class about the first colonists.

"Nagi, how many Truth cities are there? Four, right?"

"No, just the three. Freedom and Inventa were destroyed by the ADF. Novus, where we are now, is the last one."

"That can't be right. We learned about four Earth colonial missions. The first one that landed was never heard from, right? Don't you remember that? Freedom, Inventa, and Novus were all ships that followed. What was its name again? Newthon, Shorebound..."

"You mean Newton. Yeah, I do remember that," Nagi said, "but as far as I know, this is the last Truth city."

"That means there is still one last hope. If the ADF gets here..."

"We gotta find that last ship!" Nagi said. "Eron, I knew you could help!" He beamed at his younger brother. Eron shrugged.

"I'm sure I'm not the first one to realize this," Eron said. "And, I found something in the ADF archives when I was in training. Something about—"

Nagi tore his focus from Eron, something on the monitors catching his eye. "Balla!" he yelled, pointing at a screen on the far right.

Eron squinted, and there on the screen was Balla and the two children. "Where is she?" he asked.

Nagi raced to the Truth sitting at a desk in front of the monitors and bent down. Eron couldn't hear him, but Nagi excitedly pointed at the screen.

When he returned, Nagi's eyes were glistening and a huge smile flashed across his face.

"She's on deck five! Callia and I were on deck two!"

"Who's Callia?" Eron asked.

"She was a girl I helped when we fled Inventa. She lost her brother. I had a partner named Gar, but he left with an ADF soldier. I'll tell you later. Come on, let's get to my family!"

Nagi ran to the elevator, Eron trying hard to keep up. "Come on, Nagi! Not so fast."

Eron's body ached. His mind was overwhelmed by the existence of this underground ship, filled with an entire colony of Truth.

Nagi slammed on the elevator call buttons. "Come on, Eron, forget this thing. It'll take too long. We can take the stairs."

"The what? Nagi, that's a long way down."

"It's my family! I need to reach them."

Suddenly, red emergency lights flashed. A wailing alarm deafened them. Eron covered his ears. "What is that?" he cried.

"No! No, no, no!" Nagi yelled. He beat his fists on the wall.

Emergency doors slammed shut, sealing off the

stairwell. Truth scattered, looking for the nearest rooms.

"No! Not now!" Nagi yelled. "Let me get to my family!"

"Nagi, what's going on? Why is everyone running?"

Nagi shook his head. "Come on, this way," he growled. He stormed off to the nearest room, filled with ten other Truth huddled around a small window overlooking the glowing cavern wall.

Eron felt a nervous energy inside the room. The door whooshed shut behind them.

"Chair Deelia?" Nagi said. Eron scanned the room and saw the older female Truth near the window.

She turned to Nagi, a look of resignation in her eyes.

"Scout Nagi? Once again, we meet. It's time. We must begin."

A human male next to her held her arm, guiding her to the window.

"Director Bowen," Nagi said absently.

The floor vibrated. The entire ship shook. Eron watched as rocks fell outside.

"Hold on," Chair Deelia said.

A giant roar echoed in the cavern. A brilliant white light illuminated the darkened space as an enormous explosion above them vibrated the ship. The ship jolted violently, chairs falling and Truth scrambling for stability. How Chair Deelia remained standing was beyond Eron's comprehension.

Eron's arms splayed as he staggered against the now-rocking ship. "What's going on?" he called out.

"War, Eron. We've just begun," Nagi said.

Eron felt the ship elevate. It slammed into the

ground above, a deafening grind of metal on rock. The ship vibrated, sirens blaring. Then with a pause, the ship seeming to brace itself, it punched through the ground above. Red dirt and rocks rained outside the window as the ship rose higher. With a sudden burst, it shot up into the sky, hovering over the planet below.

The alarms ceased, their echoes lingering in Eron's ears.

"All clear," a voice called over the loudspeaker. Deelia bowed her head and exhaled.

Eron's eyes widened as he fought the urge to vomit. His home world sprawled below, the view one he never imagined he'd ever see.

Deelia turned from the window and straightened her tunic and addressed the group.

"The time has come for the Truth to rise. We are Forgotten no more."

The room was silent, the soft hum of the ship the only sound.

War, Eron thought. *What is to come of us?*

The War for Truth

Please enjoy this excerpt from the next book in the trilogy, *The War for Truth*.

———

Novus screamed across the sky, the ship settling into orbit around Anastasia. Scared Truth rushed through the corridors seeking safe places to rest. Chair Deelia watched through the window as the size of the red planet below shrunk.

"Chair, we've achieved orbit. Ready to drop from main power," a Truth engineer called through the room's speaker.

"Make it so," she said without turning from the window.

Eron and Nagi were trapped in the room with Truth and CDL forces as the ship broke free from the ground only moments before. They huddled with the rest of the room's occupants around the bank of windows that once overlooked the underground cavern housing Novus. Now they were high above the planet.

"Nagi, what just happened? How did this—" Eron asked.

"It happened because we needed it to. This ship, the largest Earth vessel ever built, was designed for such a thing. Do not be surprised. Only be scared we had to do it," Deelia said over her shoulder.

"I meant no disrespect, Chair. It's just an amazing sight," Eron replied. The glass felt cold when he leaned against it. The vast emptiness of space unfolded all around them, dominated by a large red sun and their planet below; the moon visible on the far side.

"Chair Deelia, what's to become of us now?" Nagi asked. The quiet awe of their current situation brought his thoughts to his family and the Truth. "Can I reunite with my family now?"

"Scout Nagi, I sympathize with your desire to once again embrace your family, and you will soon, but we must first discuss the predicament of our people. Of all people on Anastasia. Everyone," she said, turning from the window. "Will you please excuse us for the time being? Director Bowen, Scout Nagi, and...Eron, is it? Please remain here with me."

A young male Truth leaned close to Chair Deelia and whispered something Eron couldn't hear.

"No, I'll be fine," she said. The Truth bowed his head and left with the rest.

"It is time we make preparations for what's to come. Indeed, Director Bowen and I have discussed this possibility for quite some time. It seems the ADF has forced our hand. Please, gentleman, have a seat." Deelia gestured to the table and they sat.

"I don't mean to sound ungrateful, but Chair Deelia, I'd really like to find my family. It's been so long, and I fear they might be dead. May I ask leave to find them?" Nagi asked. Eron placed a hand on his brother's large black-furred arm.

"It's ok, Brother, they're safe," Eron said.

"Scout Nagi, you will have ample time to reconnect once we are done here. I know I've cleared you of this calamity, but need I remind you that many still blame you for this mess? You will stay here until we are done discussing our plans."

"But Chair, I'm only a scout! How is my presence here justified? Shouldn't someone who knows better be in my place? I appreciate everything you've done for me, but I don't see how I fit in with all this."

Eron nodded. "I agree, Chair Deelia. Why am I here? I'm nothing more than a boy fortunate enough to have survived the Selection."

Deelia closed her eyes and drew in a deep, raspy breath. When she exhaled, she peered at the brothers.

"I've been following the both of you for some time now. I've observed your actions. I've witnessed your unselfish desire to help others. Eron, you've done so much for us already without even knowing it. It's time I allow you to be yourself and do what you do best— put others first. And you, Scout Nagi. You've been loyal from the moment you first entered the ranks of the Truth. Together, the two of you are the perfect union of Truth and Anastasians.

"True, I have Director Bowen at my side, but you two represent something more, something we must achieve—harmony. We must resist the queen. Her time is over. The Truth must do what we should've done a long time ago. You two are vital to our success. I know it's difficult to understand, but don't discount your value to the cause. Can I count on you?"

Eron looked to Nagi, and together they turned to Deelia.

"Chair Deelia, you have my support. Whatever I

can do—"

"Whatever *we* can do," Nagi interrupted. Eron turned to him.

"Sorry, I didn't want to speak for you. Whatever we can do, we're here for the Truth. We're here for Anastasia. I pledge myself to your cause. We pledge ourselves to your cause."

"We don't have much time. The ADF is quickly marshaling their forces for an all-out ground attack. We must hurry!" Director Bowen said.

"Scout Nagi, I want you to gather what able-bodied men we have on board and bring them to the athletic training facility on deck three. Once there, we'll arrange our forces carefully under the guidance of Director Bowen. The Truth don't have much expertise in military matters, so we will rely on him to prepare us for war. This is not a time for timidity. It is a time for action," Deelia said.

"But my family?" he protested.

Eron thought of his niece and nephew and wanted to see his brother reunite with them.

"Go to them, Nagi. You have until tomorrow afternoon to begin gathering the forces. Take Eron with you now. Make sure he's acquainted with the Truth. And get him something else to wear. I don't want any of our people thinking he's aligned with the enemy!"

Eron stood first. "Thank you, Chair, we will do our best for what must come."

"Thank you for the opportunity to gather my family. I'll be on my way," Nagi said, standing next to his brother.

"Oh, Scout Nagi. One more thing. The other scout

with you...Gar, is it? You must find him. I fear he doesn't appear on any records, and I'd like to speak with him."

"Of course, Chair. I know he's on board. We were separated before coming to Novus. I thought he was in the forest, but I did catch him on the monitors in the control room. He's here somewhere. I'll find him and send him to you."

"Thank you both for your service. What we must do will not be easy and it will test our limits, but it must be done. We have to win at all costs. I fear many of our people might not be willing to pay that price. I need you. Both of you."

Chair Deelia turned from the brothers and spoke to Director Bowen in hushed words.

"Come on, Nagi, let's get your family." The brothers left the room, Eron chancing one long look out the window at the black vastness outside.

To finish the story, please pick up **The War for Truth** today!

ACKNOWLEDGEMENTS

Thanks

I'd like to thank you for spending your time with me and my world. I don't take your time for granted and though you have many other items calling for your attention, to have you spend your time with me is an amazing responsibility. I hope you enjoyed your stay.

I'd like to thank my family for their unending support of my writing endeavors. I know I get lost in the words I write but your kindness and support as I pursue my passion means everything to me.

My Beta readers Lauren Hannick, Chi Robinson, and Ryan Batla were instrumental in cleaning up the finer points of the story. Thank you all for your time and suggestions.

I've grown so much over the years and my fellow authors have been perfect sounding boards and sources of wisdom and inspiration. Thomas Gunther, Pamela Morris, Ryan Batla, Brent Harris, Aaron Hamilton, Ray Wenck, John W. Smith, Shane Bowen, Amy Hale, S.A. Gibson (and the entire On the Horizon authors), and so many more. Your advice and encouragement humbles me. Thank you!

Thanks to my editor Jodi McDermitt for making my

words mean more and sound so much better.

Thanks to my cover artist Dan Brown for bringing my vision to life on the original covers. Thanks to MIBL Art for the sweet updates. You guys rock!

If you enjoyed the story, please consider leaving a review. Thanks!

ABOUT THE AUTHOR

Jason J. Nugent has been a paperboy, pizza maker, dishwasher, restaurant manager, promotional products sales rep, chamber of commerce director, and one time BBQ champion. He has skated with Tony Hawk, had a babysitter with a serial killer brother, and is followed by rapper Chuck D on Twitter. He and his wife share a home in beautiful Southern Illinois with their son, three cats, and two dogs.

He's the author of the thrilling young adult scifi series **The Forgotten Chronicles:** *The Selection, Rise of the Forgotten, The War for Truth* and two collections of horror / dark fiction short stories: *(Almost) Average Anthology* and *Moments of Darkness.*

More information and his blog can be found at jasonjnugent.com.

To stay updated with my current projects, please sign up for my monthly email newsletter on my website. You will get one email on the 15th of every month and whenever I have a new release.

For doing so, you will get a free *Forgotten Chronicles* prequel short story.